If Chloe was the kind of woman who believed in destiny, she would be willing to admit Arizona Smith was the man for her.

But she wasn't, and he wasn't.

"You're very beautiful," Arizona said, drawing her against him.

Chloe supposed she could have resisted, but she didn't want to. She wanted to feel his arms around her again. It was almost like dancing, but they were alone in the shadows and the only music came from inside her head.

His face was so familiar. It was as if she'd known him forever. Had they really made love, or had it just been a dream?

"What are you thinking?" he asked. "Sometimes you look at me and get the strangest expression on your face."

"It's nothing," she said quickly. There was no *way* she could tell him she'd been thinking about that dream. She didn't dare think what he would make of the Bradley family legend....

BRIDES OF BRADLEY HOUSE:
Coming in May, Cassie turns twenty-five—
will she find her very own DREAM GROOM?

Dear Reader,

Hold on to your hats, because this month Special Edition has a lineup of romances that you won't soon forget!

We start off with an extraordinary story by #1 *New York Times* bestselling author Nora Roberts. *The Perfect Neighbor* is the eleventh installment of her popular THE MACGREGORS series and spotlights a brooding loner who becomes captivated by his vivacious neighbor.

And the fun is just beginning! *Dream Bride* by Susan Mallery launches her enchanting duet, BRIDES OF BRADLEY HOUSE, about a family legend which has two sisters dreaming about the men they are destined to marry. The first book in the series is also this month's THAT SPECIAL WOMAN! title. Look for the second story, *Dream Groom,* this May.

Next, Christine Rimmer returns with a tale about a single mom who develops a dangerous attraction to a former heartbreaker in *Husband in Training.*

Also don't miss the continuing saga of Sherryl Woods's popular AND BABY MAKES THREE: THE NEXT GENERATION. The latest book in the series, *The Cowboy and his Wayward Bride,* features a hardheaded rancher who will do just about anything to claim the feisty mother of his infant daughter! And Arlene James has written a stirring love story about a sweet young virgin who has every intention of tempting the ornery, much-older rancher down the wedding aisle in *Marrying an Older Man.*

Finally this month, *A Hero at Heart* by Ann Howard White features an emotional reunion romance between an honorable hero and the gentle beauty he's returned for.

I hope you enjoy this book, and each and every novel to come!

Sincerely,

Karen Taylor Richman
Senior Editor

Please address questions and book requests to:
Silhouette Reader Service
U.S.: 3010 Walden Ave., P.O. Box 1325, Buffalo, NY 14269
Canadian: P.O. Box 609, Fort Erie, Ont. L2A 5X3

SUSAN MALLERY
DREAM BRIDE

Published by Silhouette Books

America's Publisher of Contemporary Romance

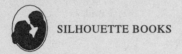 SILHOUETTE BOOKS

ISBN 0-373-24231-X

DREAM BRIDE

Printed in U.S.A.

Books by Susan Mallery

*Hometown Heartbreakers
†Triple Trouble
§Brides of Bradley House
‡Montana Mavericks: Return to Whitehorn

SUSAN MALLERY

lives in sunny Southern California, where the eccentricities of a writer are considered fairly normal. Her books are both reader favorites and bestsellers, with recent titles appearing on the Waldenbooks bestseller list and the *USA Today* bestseller list. Her 1995 Special Edition novel, *Marriage on Demand,* was awarded Best Special Edition by *Romantic Times Magazine.*

Long ago, on a dark night in a darker forest, angry men chased an old woman through the woods. Some said she was a healer, others called her a witch. They whispered she was blessed…and cursed. The old woman knew each was correct.

When the men were upon her, fists poised to strike, the old woman cried out her fear. Only one in the gathering crowd faced them fearlessly. Only Clarinda Bradley ignored the blows and offered a safe haven.

In return, the old woman thanked her with a legacy. A promise of love, faithful enough to last a lifetime.

She gave Clarinda a special nightgown that, if worn on the night of her twenty-fifth birthday, would reveal to her the face of her one true love. If Clarinda followed the prophecy and married the man, she would know great joy all the rest of her days. If her heirs did likewise, they, too, would be blessed.

Two months later, on the night of her twenty-fifth birthday, Clarinda donned the nightgown and dreamed of a handsome stranger. The next morning he rode into the village. Clarinda married him and, as foretold, knew great joy all of her days. So began the legacy of the Bradley women….

Chapter One

"I wish I was going to dream about the man I was going to marry," Cassie said and grinned. "I know how excited you are about it."

Chloe Bradley Wright looked at her sister. "Oh, yeah. Too excited for words." She fingered the soft lace of the nightgown she held. "Do I have to do this?"

"You don't *have* to do anything."

If only that were true, Chloe thought with regret. But she did have to wear the stupid nightgown. It was her twenty-fifth birthday and time for her to participate in the family legend. Not that she believed in magic or happily-ever-after. As far as she was concerned, falling in love or caring about someone was a one-way ticket to heartache.

She opened her mouth to express her opinion, then pressed her lips tightly together. *She* might not be a believer, but her sister, Cassie, had more than enough faith for the both of them.

Chloe stared into the face that was nearly as familiar as her own. Cassie was adopted, but younger by only six months. The two girls had been together since Cassie was two weeks old and they were best friends. Chloe had shared her admittedly cynical opinion on more than one occasion, but Cassie's belief in the legend had never wavered. Who was she to try and change her sister's mind now? It was just for one night. What could it hurt?

"I'll wear it," she said, trying to sound gracious.

Cassie leaned forward and hugged her. "I knew you would," she said and bounced off the bed. Her short, thick brown hair swung around her face. "I'll go tell Aunt Charity. Won't she be surprised?"

"Probably not," Chloe muttered when she was alone. Aunt Charity had a sixth sense about these things. No doubt the older woman figured she already knew whom Chloe was going to dream about.

"I'm not going to dream about anyone," she said aloud as she pulled her T-shirt over her head, then slipped out of her jeans. "It's just a nightgown. It has no mystic powers. It's nearly the twenty-first century, for heaven's sake! No one believes that kind of thing."

She unfastened her bra and tossed the garment onto the floor, then picked up the nightgown. The cotton was cool to her touch and she shivered involuntarily.

"It's nothing," she insisted. But she hesitated before pulling the soft fabric over her head. What if the legend was true? What if she was really going to dream about the man she was destined to love? What if—

"What if people have been abducted by aliens lurking in cornfields?" she asked aloud.

"Oh, I don't think those stories are true," her aunt said as she entered the bedroom. Charity raised dark eyebrows.

"So how much did Cassie have to twist your arm to get you to wear it tonight?"

Chloe shrugged as she smoothed the nightgown in place. "Not too much. I figure it's an inevitable rite of passage for Bradley women, as inescapable as birthdays and taxes. I'm just sorry she's going to be disappointed in the morning."

"Yes," Charity said as she moved to the bed and pulled back the covers. "It will be sad. Cassie is one of those rare types who is a true believer. There aren't many left."

Chloe had turned twenty-five that very day, but suddenly she felt like a ten-year-old with a favorite relative staring at a less than perfect report card, all the while telling her the low grades were fine, as long as she'd tried her best.

"You can't tell me you believe in the legend," Chloe said as she plopped down on the edge of her bed.

Charity settled next to her. The older woman was of average height with the Wright family's dark eyes and hair. She had to be in her mid-fifties, but she could have easily passed for someone a dozen years younger.

"I've traveled all around the world," Charity reminded her. "I've seen many amazing things. As for magic and legends?" She shrugged. "Who's to say what's real and what isn't?"

Chloe snorted indelicately. "Give me a break. So you're saying that this nightgown is several hundred years old and is magical?"

"You never know."

Chloe fingered the soft cotton. "It's in pretty good shape for an antique."

"So am I, dear." Charity patted her hand.

"You're hardly an antique." She drew in a deep breath. "It would be nice if it were all true, but I just can't take that step of faith."

''That's the reporter in you.''

''Agreed. But someone in this family has to be practical. Between you and Cassie, you've always got your heads in the clouds.''

''I'm back,'' Cassie announced as she bounded back in the room. She held something in her hand and before Chloe could figure out what it was, she tossed it in the air. Dozens of red, pink and cream rose petals drifted over Chloe, Aunt Charity and the bed.

''My contribution,'' her sister said with a smile as she settled in the small wing-back chair by the closet door.

Chloe pulled rose petals from her hair. Her irritation faded in the presence of such loving support. Who was she to fight against tradition?

''You win,'' she said as she stood up.

Charity rose as well. ''It's best, dear. You'll see.'' She waited until Chloe climbed into bed, then tucked in the covers. ''Sleep well.''

When she'd left, Cassie moved close and crouched down. ''Dream of someone wonderful,'' she instructed. ''Rich and handsome and very loving.'' Her wide dark eyes softened at the thought. ''Someone who will want to be with you forever.''

''What a romantic,'' Chloe teased. ''I'll do my best.''

Cassie straightened. ''In the morning, I want details. Lots of them.''

''I promise. Oh, and thanks for the party. It was great.''

Her sister smiled. ''My pleasure.'' She walked out of the room and closed the door behind her.

Chloe leaned up on one elbow and clicked off the lamp, then settled onto the bed that had been hers since she'd turned thirteen. The room had been decorated several times, but except for three years in high school, she'd slept here her whole life. Everything about the room, the house and even the town was familiar to her. Yet tonight, it all felt different.

"Atmosphere," she told herself softly. It was all the talk of magic and legends. Even a confirmed cynic like her was bound to be affected.

She pulled the covers up to her chin and closed her eyes. Memories from her twenty-fifth-birthday party drifted through her mind and made her smile. She'd wanted something small, friends and family only. Cassie and Aunt Charity had prepared dinner. The presents had been mostly gag gifts, which she preferred. Nothing sentimental for her.

She had a busy week planned at the magazine. She mentally listed all she had to do in the next few days.

As her mind relaxed and she started to get sleepy, thoughts of the legend intruded. According to family lore, several centuries ago a young woman had saved an old gypsy from certain death. In return the gypsy had given her a magic nightgown. If the women in her family—the Bradley family—wore this nightgown the night of their twenty-fifth birthday, they would dream of the man they were destined to marry. The union would be long and happy.

"Yeah, right," Chloe muttered as she turned on her side. "He'll probably come riding up on a white horse and sweep me away."

She knew exactly what she was going to dream about— what she always dreamed about. Nothing. Her nights were as quiet and uneventful as an empty drawer and that was just how she liked them. The nightgown wasn't magic. The legend wasn't real. And she was suddenly very, very sleepy.

He appeared out of the darkness, not on a white horse, but in a Jeep that roared up the side of the mountain.

"This isn't happening," Chloe told herself even as anticipation filled her. She clung to the side of the rocks as the wind whipped at her hair and made the hem of her nightgown snap like a sail.

"Nightgown?" She stared down at herself. Dear Lord, she was naked except for a thin layer of lacy cotton. What on earth?

"You're dreaming," she told herself. "That's all. Just dreaming. Go with it and you'll be fine."

But the reassurance didn't keep her heart from pounding as the Jeep drew closer. The man inside stopped it a scant two feet from her, then climbed out.

He was tall—substantially taller than her five feet nine inches—and lean. "At least he's really good-looking," Chloe said to herself. "I mean if I have to dream about some strange guy, I don't want him to look like the king of the nerds or something."

The man didn't speak. Instead he walked over to her, ripped off his shirt, then pulled her hard against his gleaming chest.

"I like this," she said, feeling the masculine length of his body pressing into hers.

"Hush, love. I am your destiny."

"Uh-huh. And I'm a direct descendant of Queen Victoria."

She stared into the greenest eyes she'd ever seen. The dream was amazingly real. She could feel the wind, the heat of the man's body, his breath on her cheek. She swallowed. She even felt him pressing up against her. Wow! She had to get out more. Her subconscious was obviously way too bored with her life.

"I want you," the man said.

"Then take me, big boy. I'm yours."

He kissed her. Chloe stifled a shriek of both shock and pleasure. Talk about going for it. His mouth claimed hers

.

in the most perfect, masterful way. She felt small and delicate and incredibly free. This was a dream, after all. She could say or do anything she wanted and no one would ever have to know.

She clutched his face and pulled back. "I have one request," she said.

"Make it. I'll do anything for you."

"Great. Just don't disappear on me until we're finished, okay? I hate those sex dreams where I wake up about thirty seconds from the good part. It does *not* make for a restful night."

Instead of answering, he swept her up in his arms and carried her into the cave. There a fire burned low. Their bed was soft, fresh, sweet-smelling straw. How nice of her brain to supply the details.

The stranger made love to her with a tender thoroughness that left her breathless and trembling. He touched and kissed every part of her. Much to her relief, she didn't wake up before the good part. In fact the good part happened at least twice. He even made her scream once and she'd never been a screamer.

"Who *are* you?" she asked when they at last stretched out together. They were both slick with sweat and breathing hard. She traced his perfect body, her fingers lingering on a scar on his left forearm.

"Your destiny."

"So you said, but do you actually have a name, or should I just call you Mr. D.?"

He raised his head and stared at her. His gaze was so intense, she felt as if she could see down to the bottom of his soul. Whatever lurked there called to her. She wanted to respond, but didn't know how. This was still a dream, right? It wasn't real. But for that second, she desperately wanted it to be.

"You'll know me," he told her as the world around them faded to black.

She tried to grab on to him, but his hand slipped through hers. Before she could even cry out, he was gone and she was alone.

"How was it? Start at the beginning and talk very slowly."

Chloe blinked at the bright light and realized it was morning. She glanced around in confusion, then saw she was back in her own room, in her familiar bed. Cassie bounced on the mattress next to her and grinned.

"So, who is he? Who did you dream about?"

"What?"

Chloe sat up slowly. Her head was spinning and she couldn't quite wake up. Maybe because she didn't feel rested. It was almost as if she'd spent the night running around. *Or making love with a handsome, mysterious stranger.*

She pushed the last thought away. Nothing had happened. She'd had a couple of weird dreams. They were probably the result of too much chocolate cake and ice cream. They didn't mean anything.

Cassie was still in the oversized T-shirt she regularly wore to bed. Her thick hair was mussed, her face flushed from sleep. "Do you mean to tell me you didn't dream about anyone? Not even one guy?"

Chloe sat up and hugged her arms to her chest. Her body ached pleasantly and there was a definite dampness between her legs. Too weird, she told herself silently. But she did *not* believe in family legends. The dream had been a fluke, not a prophecy. She wasn't going to encourage Cassie's flights of fancy.

"I didn't dream of anyone," she said slowly, instantly

picturing the handsome man who had swept her into that cave. It was all too embarrassing. What was she supposed to say? That the sex had been great, thank you very much? She couldn't admit anything to anyone.

Cassie's smile faded. "But I thought it was real." She sounded as if someone had stolen her last hope.

Chloe grimaced. She had done exactly that. But she couldn't tell the truth. She just couldn't!

"I'm sorry," she said and touched her sister's arm. "It's just a nightgown, kid. Like any other."

"Okay, Aunt Charity warned me the legend might just be a story, but I didn't want to believe her. I guess I'm going to have to." Cassie looked as if she was going to say more, then untangled herself from the covers and stood up. "I'll go start the coffee."

When Chloe was alone, she collapsed back on the pillow. She felt strange inside. Off center somehow. Was it the dream?

"There is no legend," she said aloud. "The dream was just my subconscious's way of telling me it's time to start dating. I'll take the hint. Today in the office, I'll look around for a likely candidate."

But as she walked to the bathroom, instead of trying to figure out which eligible men would interest her, she found herself picturing *him*. She shivered…not in fear or irritation, but at the memory of what his touch had done to her.

A hot shower went a long way to restoring her spirits. As she toweled off, she checked her arms and the tops of her breasts. Nothing. Just her regular skin. She'd half expected to see the lingering marks from his lovemaking.

"I must remember to ask Aunt Charity if insanity runs in the family," she said as she chose her clothes for the day.

Fifteen minutes later, her hair was dry and she was

dressed. She headed for the kitchen and that healing first cup of coffee. As she reached for the coffeepot, Cassie flipped on the small television. They usually watched one of the morning shows while they ate breakfast.

Chloe had the pot in one hand and a mug in the other. Then a familiar voice filled the room and she froze.

"The gem exhibit is an exciting find," *he* said. "But I can't take full credit for bringing it to the university. It takes a very large committee to pull this kind of thing together."

Goose bumps puckered up and down her arms. She set the coffeepot back on its burner so she wouldn't drop it, and put the mug on the counter. Then, very slowly, she turned to face the television.

The camera focused on the perky hostess of the local morning show. Then the picture on the screen panned right. A man came into view. A handsome man. A man who, until sometime last night, she'd never seen before. But she knew him. She knew every inch of his body. She'd touched and tasted him, she knew his scent so well, she could have found him in the dark.

"Why do you think you're always the one to make the great discoveries?" the woman asked.

The man smiled. Chloe felt her heart shudder in her chest, and she began to tingle all over. She might not want to remember, but her body wouldn't let her forget.

The man smiled. "Just lucky, I guess."

The hostess practically sighed. "Unfortunately we're out of time. Just to remind our viewers, Arizona Smith will be lecturing at the university on his fabulous gem find. There are still tickets available, but they're going fast. The gems themselves will be on display throughout the month. Mr. Smith, it's been my pleasure having you here this morning."

Chloe's mouth twisted. The woman was practically cooing. So much for professionalism, she thought, refusing to acknowledge the white heat inside of her that some might call jealousy.

So her mystery man had a name. Arizona Smith. Which meant he was real. She thought about the nightgown, the Bradley family legend, the dream. Oh, Lord, it couldn't be true. He was *not* her destiny. He couldn't be. She didn't want a destiny like that. She avoided relationships.

It doesn't matter, she told herself fiercely. The man is in town for maybe a week. It's not as if I'll ever run into him.

"I've got to get to work early," she told Cassie.

"Don't you want your coffee?"

Chloe was already heading out the door. "I'll grab some on the way," she called over her shoulder, and made her escape to freedom.

Arizona Smith was everywhere, Chloe thought with dismay as she sipped her coffee at the small diner across the street from her office. His picture had been plastered on three buses and on four different billboards she'd spotted on her way to work. Even now he was staring at her from the bench directly in front of her building—or at least his *picture* was. She couldn't escape the man.

"Deep breaths," she told herself. The trick was to keep breathing. And moving. If he couldn't catch her, she would be safe.

It was too weird. All of it. Maybe she'd seen his picture over the past couple of days and not really noticed. Somehow it had gotten lodged in her brain and only surfaced last night. A perfectly plausible explanation.

If only the sex hadn't been so good.

"I don't believe in destiny," she reminded herself again as she left the diner and made her way to the foyer of her building. The magazine office was on the second floor. She stopped by reception long enough to pick up her messages.

"Jerry wants to see you," Paula, the receptionist-gofer called. "Something about a special assignment."

"Great." That was what she needed. Something challenging to take her mind off her temporary insanity.

She dropped her things at her desk, then headed for her editor's office.

Bradley Today was a small but prestigious magazine that came out twice a month. Chloe had gotten a job there when she'd graduated from U.C. Berkeley with a degree in journalism. Eventually she planned to make her way to New York, where the big magazines were published, but for now she was gathering experience and building her clippings.

"You wanted to see me, boss?" she asked as she stepped through the open glass door.

"Yeah, sit." Jerry waved to the seat opposite his desk.

It was only eight-thirty in the morning, but his long-sleeved shirt was already rumpled and his tie hung crooked. If the clothes hadn't been different from the ones he'd worn the previous day, Chloe would have sworn he'd slept in them.

"It's like this," he said, then stuck one hand into the pile of folders on his desk. He pulled one out, looked at the label, shoved it back and grabbed another. "Nancy's pregnant."

Chloe nodded. Nancy was one of their most experienced writers. "She's been that way for about seven months."

"Tell me about it. Babies. Who needs 'em? Anyway, she says she's too far along to be running around for me. She wants to write stuff that lets her stay in the office. Can you believe it?"

His outrage made Chloe smile. "Wow. How insensitive of her."

"Exactly. Does she give me any warning? No-o-o. She calls me at home last night and drops the bomb. So now I pass it along to you. Good luck, kid." With that, he tossed her the folder.

When she touched the stiff paper, Chloe felt the same shivery chill she'd experienced the previous night when she'd slipped on the nightgown. The tiny hairs on the back of her neck rose. She knew exactly what she was going to find inside that folder, and there was nothing she could do to change it. It was, she admitted, inevitable.

"He's in town for about three weeks," Jerry said. "Follow him around. Shouldn't be hard. He wants this piece as much as we do. Decent publicity and all that garbage. Get to know the real man. Write me something brilliant and it just might be your ticket out." Jerry looked at her. "A bigger publisher or maybe even a book deal. Do it right, kid. Breaks like this don't come along very often. Now get out of here. I'm busy."

With that Jerry picked up his ringing phone and probably forgot she'd ever been in the room.

Chloe gingerly took the folder and returned to her cubicle. She didn't want to open it. Maybe if she waited long enough, it would go away. Wishful thinking, she thought, and drew in a deep breath. She flipped back the top cover and saw him. He was standing on the edge of a mountain, leaning against an outcropping of rock. She recognized the clothes, the place and the man. She knew that just around the corner was a cave and in the cave was a fire and a bed of straw.

"I don't like this," Chloe whispered. "It's too strange."

"I brought it," Paula said as she walked into the tiny space and dumped a stack of folders onto the spare chair pressed up by Chloe's desk.

"What is it?"

"Research. All the stuff Nancy had gathered on that Smith guy. She said to call her at home if you want any tips." Paula's gaze drifted to the photograph. "Wow, he's good-looking. Just like that guy in the movies. You know—Indiana Jones. Although he doesn't really look like Harrison Ford. He's taller. Still, I wouldn't shoo him away if he turned up in my bed." She waved her fingers and left.

"Apparently I wouldn't either," Chloe said glumly. So much for escaping her destiny. In the space of twelve hours a strange man had invaded her subconscious and now her work. What was she supposed to do?

But Chloe already knew the answer to that. An assignment like the one Jerry had just handed her was one any junior writer would kill for. Talk about a stroke of luck.

Or destiny, a little voice whispered.

"I don't believe in little voices either," Chloe muttered, "So I'm going to get to work now."

She spent the rest of the day reading through Nancy's notes, clippings from other articles and some information she'd pulled from the Internet. By four-thirty her eyes hurt and she had a major headache. She still didn't have a strategy for dealing with everything that had happened, but she needed to get one and fast. Her first meeting with Mr. Smith was in the morning at the university. Nancy had already set it up. He was taking her on a private tour of the gem exhibit.

She gathered up all the papers and stuffed them into her briefcase. Maybe she could work better at home.

Forty minutes later she pulled into the driveway of the Victorian mansion that had been in her family for generations. Safe at last, she thought as she climbed out. She walked up the steps and into the foyer.

"It's me," she called. Cassie's car hadn't been in the garage, but Aunt Charity's had.

''We're in the kitchen.''

Chloe made a face. Aunt Charity had spent much of her life traveling the world. She seemed to know someone from every possible corner of the globe, and at one time or another they all liked to visit. Who was it this time? A tribal elder from Africa or some obscure prince from the Middle East? She felt that familiar wave of resentment toward her aunt Charity for not being around when she'd needed her the most. But she filed those unpleasant thoughts away. She just wasn't up to dwelling on that tonight. And she wasn't in the mood to play hostess, either.

Still, she straightened her shoulders and forced herself to smile as she crossed the hallway and entered the kitchen. She already had her arm extended so she could shake hands with Charity's mystery guest.

She came to a complete stop just inside the oversize room. Her jaw dropped. She told herself to close her mouth, but her body wasn't paying attention.

He was as tall as she remembered. Lean, powerful and too good-looking by far. Not a tribal elder, or even a prince. No, he was much more dangerous. He was Arizona Smith—the man from her dream.

Chapter Two

"Arizona, this is one of my nieces. Chloe. She's the journalist. Chloe, this is Arizona Smith. I think you were watching him on the morning news show earlier today, weren't you?"

Charity's question hung in the air, but Chloe didn't answer. Arizona shifted uncomfortably in his seat at the round table. He was used to fans being tongue-tied in his presence, but Chloe Bradley Wright didn't look like the rabid fan type. Plus, she was staring at him as if he'd grown a horn in the center of his forehead. He brushed back his hair, casually letting his fingers touch the skin there, just to be sure.

"Hi, Chloe," he said, and held out his hand. In the past he'd found that polite, social niceties often put people at ease.

Her gaze dropped from his face to his hand. She still looked panicked, but she responded automatically. "Mr.

Smith. What a pleasure.'' Her attention shifted to her aunt. ''You didn't mention company for dinner. I think there's a roast, but it's not defrosted. I could put it in the microwave and—''

''All taken care of,'' Charity said, and patted the empty chair next to hers. ''Get yourself something to drink and join us. Arizona and I were just catching up on old times. He has some wonderful stories. I'm sure you'll be interested in them.''

Chloe didn't respond right away. Her gaze settled back on his. Arizona read concern in her eyes and something that looked like apprehension. He held in a sigh. No doubt Charity had been telling tales out of school again. The older woman loved to brag about his exploits. Okay, he was willing to admit that there had been a time when everything they said about him was true, but that was long ago. These days his life was practically boring. At least when it came to his conquests with women.

Chloe moved to the refrigerator. ''Would either of you like anything?''

''I'm fine, dear,'' Charity said.

''Me, too.'' Arizona motioned to the bottle of beer in front of him.

Chloe gave him a tight smile, then collected a diet soda for herself. She walked back to the table.

Arizona told himself it wasn't polite to stare, but Ms. Chloe Bradley Wright was very easy on the eyes. Tall, at least five-eight or -nine, slender with big brown eyes and a cascade of reddish-brown curls that tumbled to the middle of her back. She might not have a lot of curves, but she was woman enough to get his blood pumping.

If he had a type, she would be it. Fortunately he didn't have one, nor was he looking for anyone to keep him company during his brief visit to Bradley.

"I'm trying to convince Arizona to stay with us while he's here," Charity said, picking up the conversation where they'd left it when Chloe had arrived home. "I've explained there's plenty of room and he won't be any trouble at all. What do you think?"

Chloe was staring at him again. Whatever the reason for her attention, he found he liked it. She blinked twice, then looked at her aunt. "What? Oh, sorry. I was—" She took a sip of her soda. "It's just I've been staring at your picture all day. I can't believe you're sitting here in my kitchen."

Her words hung in the room like dust motes floating on a sunny afternoon. The silence lengthened. Chloe sucked in a breath and flushed, as if she'd just realized what she'd said.

"That came out wrong," she said quickly.

"Not to me it didn't." Arizona winked. "The fan club can always use a new member. Did I mention I often take care of initiation myself?"

He was teasing...for the most part. Chloe's flush deepened. Maybe the little town of Bradley would be more interesting than he'd first thought.

He glanced over and saw Charity's speculative gaze. Ah, so his friend was thinking about a little matchmaking. He drank his beer, unconcerned by her efforts. He'd dealt with much tougher than her in the past. As they said in Australia—no worries.

Chloe cleared her throat. "Now you've seen me at my worst, or close to it. I don't usually make a habit of putting my foot in my mouth. What I meant was I'm a reporter with *Bradley Today* magazine. The writer who was going to follow you around for the next couple of weeks and write the article won't be able to do it. Our editor assigned me this morning. I've been busy doing research."

A reporter. Assigned to him. He liked that. "Should be fun."

"Yes, well, I left a message at your hotel explaining the situation."

"I've been with Charity most of the day," he said. "I'll be sure to listen most attentively when I get back to my room."

"You do that. There'll be a quiz in the morning."

She smiled then. A real smile without thought or purpose. Her face lit up, her eyes sparkled and he found himself leaning toward her, already planning what he could do to make her smile again.

Chloe reached for her briefcase and unzipped the leather, unconstructed bag. "I believe we have an appointment at the gem exhibit at nine-thirty in the morning. Does that still work for you?"

In more ways than you know, he thought, but only said, "Yes."

"Good." She made a notation in her date book. "It will take me a couple of days to get up to speed. I have Nancy's research, of course, but I want to do some of my own. I'll try not to be a pain with all my questions."

"My life is an open book," he said.

Charity coughed. "*Really,* Arizona? Oh, good. I was afraid there were some stories you wouldn't want me telling, but with your life being so accessible and all..." She turned to her niece. "Later I'll tell you about the time a tribal elder's daughter paid him to teach her how to please her husband. It seems that there was a problem with—"

Arizona groaned. "Charity, have you no shame? That is private."

"I thought you were accessible. I thought you wanted to share yourself with the people."

"Not that much of myself. There are some things Chloe should learn on her own."

Chloe raised her eyebrows. "How kind of you to say that, but don't worry. I'm not interested in any lessons on pleasing the men in my life."

"They're all satisfied?"

"Completely."

In her tailored slacks and linen jacket, she looked professional and confident. He wondered if Charity saw the slight tremor in her niece's hand as she picked up her can of soda. Chloe was lying through her teeth. Which either meant she wasn't pleasing her man, or there wasn't a man to please. He found himself wanting it to be the latter.

Charity chuckled. "I'm sorry, Chloe. I'm giving you completely the wrong idea about Arizona. It's true that he can be a charmer when he wants to be, but for the most part he's a decent and kind man."

Arizona winced. "I thought you were my friend."

"I am."

"You're talking about me as if I were the family dog."

Chloe leaned forward and rested her elbows on the table. "So you don't want to be thought of as decent and kind? Secretly you long to be—" She pressed her lips together.

Indecent. His brain filled in the word and he shifted in his chair. What was going on between himself and Chloe? This didn't make sense. The banter was fine—he enjoyed people who were fun and funny. But the sexual innuendo wasn't his style. Too obvious. Was it the lack of female companionship in his life, or was it something else? Something about Chloe specifically?

Before he could analyze the situation, the front door opened and a female voice called out a greeting.

"That's Cassie," Charity said, rising to her feet. "My other niece. She's the baby of the family."

"That's hardly fair," Chloe protested. "She's younger by all of six months. You make her sound like she's still a teenager."

"Or that you're an old woman," Charity teased.

"Thanks."

A young woman entered the kitchen. Her gaze settled on Arizona. "I saw you on television this morning," she said and grinned. Her short dark hair accentuated her large eyes. Where Chloe was tall and slender, Cassie was a good five or six inches shorter, with plenty of curves.

A nice enough young woman, Arizona thought as they were introduced, but not intriguing. Not like her sister.

"So you're a famous explorer," Cassie said as she reached for a pitcher of iced tea and poured herself a glass. Heart-shaped earrings glinted at her earlobes.

"That would be me. Larger than life."

Cassie settled next to him and sighed. "Do women gush when they meet you?"

"Only if they're incredibly discerning." He glanced up and caught Chloe's smile.

"Are you married?" Cassie asked.

"Cassie!" Chloe frowned at her sister. "Don't be personal."

"Why not? Well, are you?"

"You proposing?"

Cassie sipped her tea, apparently unruffled by the conversation. "No. I'm involved with someone. But Chloe is single."

Arizona shot her a glance. So there *wasn't* a man in her life. Funny how that piece of information was suddenly fascinating.

"Thanks for sharing that particular detail," Chloe said and rose to her feet. Her aunt stood by an electric frying pan sitting on the counter. "Can I help?" she asked.

"I'm doing fine. I'm cooking Arizona's favorite for dinner," she said.

Chloe glanced in the pan, then over at him. "Pot roast?"

"Yup. You'd be amazed how hard that is to find in some places."

"I'll bet."

"There's chocolate cake and ice cream for dessert," Charity added. "Both you girls will be staying for dinner."

It wasn't a question. The sisters exchanged knowing looks, and Arizona was pleased that he wasn't the only one Charity bossed around.

"You don't have to if you have other plans. Although I would very much like the company." The latter comment he addressed to Chloe.

"Oh, we aren't busy," Cassie said. "I'm only seeing Joel and I can call him and cancel."

"Joel would be your young man?" he asked.

"Uh-huh. We're engaged to be engaged." She held out her left hand. A thin gold band encircled her ring finger. The diamond set there was so small it looked like a grain of sand.

"It's lovely," he told her.

She beamed.

Cassie started asking him more questions. He answered automatically, most of his attention focused on her sister. Chloe didn't rejoin them at the table. Instead she moved around the kitchen, doing odds and ends that to his mind looked like busywork. Almost as if she was staying as far away from him as possible. Did he make her nervous?

There was something between them, he thought. Some kind of a connection. He knew there were people who would dismiss a feeling that they'd met someone before. He didn't. He'd traveled too much and seen too many things he couldn't explain to overlook the obvious.

When he looked at Chloe there was heat and desire, but there was also something else. An intangible he couldn't explain but that he wouldn't ignore, either. He wanted to get to know her better. At least circumstances were conspiring to assist him in his quest. If she was going to be writing about him, she could hardly spend the three weeks he was in town avoiding him.

She turned and opened a drawer. As she choose forks and knives, one fell to the floor. She knelt down to pick it up. The movement prickled at the back of his mind. As if he'd seen her kneel before. But when he probed his mind, the image that appeared to him was of Chloe completely naked, kneeling on a bed of straw.

Not that he was complaining, but where on earth had that thought come from? He swore silently and forced himself to pay attention to Cassie and her list of questions. Thank God he was sitting down and no one could see the obvious and rapid physical response to his vision. Clearly he'd been without a woman for too long. He'd outgrown the appeal of a bed partner in every port, but he was still a man who had needs. At some point in time he was going to have to do something about them.

Cassie stopped her bombardment long enough to get up and fix a salad. Chloe walked over to the table and began setting it.

"Pot roast, vegetables, mashed potatoes and salad," she said. "Not very exotic fair. Are you sure you wouldn't like me to run to the gourmet store and grab a bottle of chocolate-covered ants or something. Just so you'll feel at home?"

Her voice was low and teasing. She stood close enough that he could inhale the scent of her. "I think I can handle this."

He wasn't talking about the food, but did she know that?

"If you're sure," she said and picked up his empty bottle of beer. "I'll get you another one."

Cassie sliced tomatoes into the bowl of lettuce and cut-up vegetables. She grinned at him. "So when was the last time you had three women waiting on you?"

He thought for a second. "It's been a couple of months. I was staying—"

Small bits of radish hit him in the face.

"Hey!" He looked up and saw Chloe prepared to launch another assault.

"That was an incorrect answer," she told him. "You should try again."

He eyed the piece of radish. "Charity, you're not protecting me from these bloodthirsty nieces of yours."

"You were just bragging how you can handle things. So you're on your own."

"I'm seriously outnumbered."

Chloe tossed him another piece of radish. This one he caught and popped in his mouth.

"No one here is impressed," she informed him, her eyes bright with laughter.

The teasing continued throughout the preparation of the meal. Arizona enjoyed watching the three women work together. They moved with an easy grace that told him they did this often. Their banter reminded him that on occasion his chosen life could be very solitary. Sure he loved what he did, but his lifestyle didn't allow for a home of his own, or many intimate connections. He had lots of acquaintances, but few friends.

He tried to distance himself from the situation, to observe instead of participate, but the trick didn't work this time. He kept finding himself pulled into the conversation. The sense of family was strong and he was the odd person out. As the three women joined him and began dishing up food, he realized he was the only man at the table. He liked that in a group.

When everything was ready, Cassie plopped herself next to him and smiled. "I have a ton more questions."

Chloe took the seat opposite his, while Charity was next to her. He rubbed his chin thoughtfully. "I don't know if I can answer anything without first getting an agreement that everything we discuss here is off the record."

There was a stunned moment of surprise followed by a burst of laughter. Both women looked at Chloe, who raised her hands in the air. "Fine. I won't take notes, record the conversation or make any attempt to retain it in my brain. I'm sure that important secrets will be shared here tonight, but the public will just have to stay uninformed."

"So how long are you in town?" Cassie asked.

"Three weeks."

"Where were you before you got here?"

"South America. I was making arrangements to ship the gems. Before that I was in India."

Chloe passed him the bowl of mashed potatoes. As he took it from her, she shrugged. "You'll have to forgive her. Cassie works with preschool children. She doesn't get out much."

Cassie gave her sister a mock glare. "Oh, and you've traveled the world yourself. I know you have a lot of questions, too. You're just pretending to be sophisticated."

Arizona leaned toward Chloe. "It's working," he said in a low voice.

Her dark eyes flickered with an emotion he couldn't quite register, then she smiled and looked away.

"What do you usually look for?" Cassie asked as he finished serving himself and passed on the mashed potatoes. "Bones and stuff?"

"I'm not that disciplined," he admitted. "I know it's

important to study the details of life in lost civilizations, but I don't have the interest. I want to learn about the unusual. The mystical and unbelievable.''

Cassie frowned. ''What do you mean?''

''Magic. Objects that cast spells or connect the wearer to whatever gods that society worshiped.''

Chloe put some salad on her plate and gave him an innocent smile. ''Remember the last Indiana Jones movie, Cassie? It's the one where they were looking for the Holy Grail—the cup Christ is said to have used at the Last Supper. Arizona looks for stuff like that.''

Arizona wasn't fooled. Chloe might have just been assigned the story, but she would have spent the day doing research. She had to know that he loathed being compared to that fictional movie character Indiana Jones. There was no way he could compete with that kind of hero and come out anything but second best. Tweaking the tiger's tail, he thought. She obviously wasn't a pushover. He liked that in a woman.

Cassie stared at him wide-eyed. ''Really? So you're interested in legends?''

''All kinds. Old stories, myths about the past.''

''Family legends?''

There was something about the way she asked the question. Chloe focused on her sister. ''Mr. Smith doesn't want to hear about that,'' she said, her expression tight. ''It wouldn't be interesting.''

A mystery, he thought as he glanced from sister to sister.

''Just because it didn't work for you doesn't mean it's not real,'' Cassie said. ''We have a family legend. The Bradleys do anyway. That's the family on our mother's side.''

''Cassie, I don't think—'' Chloe began, but her sister waved her off.

"Ignore her," Cassie said. "She's a cynic when it comes to stuff like this."

"I'm intrigued," Arizona admitted. As much with the idea of a family legend as with the mystery as to why Chloe didn't want him to hear it.

"The story is that several hundred years ago an old gypsy woman was being chased by some drunken men. They were throwing stones and yelling at her and she feared for her life." Cassie waved her hands as she talked, providing animation for the tale.

He spared a glance for Chloe. She stared at her plate as if it had suddenly started forming signs and symbols in the mashed potatoes.

"A young woman heard the commotion," Cassie continued. "She lived in a small cottage on the outskirts of town. I think she was being shunned or something but no one knows for sure. Anyway, she invited the old woman in and protected her from the men. In return the woman gave her a magic nightgown."

"Really?"

Cassie's humor faded. "I'm not making this up."

"I don't doubt you. It's just clothing isn't commonly used to carry magic. It doesn't age well, is easily torn or destroyed. But it's not unheard of. What's the magic?"

"This is the good part. Every woman in the family is supposed to wear the nightgown on the night of her twenty-fifth birthday. If she does, she'll dream about the man she's going to marry. He's her destiny and as long as she marries him, they'll live a long and happy life together."

"I see." Interesting story. He'd heard several like it before in different forms. It was a common theme. Related stories were the idea of sleeping with a piece of wedding cake under the pillow, or the stories about St. Agnes Eve.

"Any punishment for not sleeping in the nightgown?" he asked.

She shook her head. "I don't think so. Aunt Charity? You're the one who knows the most about it."

Charity shrugged. "There have been rumors of unhappy marriages when the woman didn't pay attention to her dream and married the wrong man, but I don't think there's a penalty for not wearing the nightgown."

"I'd like to see the nightgown," he said.

"Is that really necessary?" Chloe asked. "It's just a nightgown. I mean you've probably seen a dozen just like it."

"Ignore her," Cassie said, rising to her feet. "She's crabby because the legend let her down."

More intrigued because Chloe was obviously hiding something, Arizona leaned toward her. "What don't you want me to know?"

"Nothing." But her dark gaze avoided his. "It's just a story. It doesn't mean anything."

"It means something to your sister."

"Cassie has always been the dreamer in the family."

"Oh, and you're the practical one?"

This time she looked directly at him. "Absolutely. I only believe in things I can prove."

"Not magic?"

"Magic is skillful sleight of hand at best, smoke and mirrors at worst."

Before he could answer, Cassie returned to the kitchen. She handed him a soft cotton-and-lace nightgown. The fabric was old, but it didn't have the look or feel of something from a couple hundred years ago. He fingered the lace. Sometimes objects spoke to him. Not in words, but in images or sensations. A prickling along the back of his neck or a—

She stretched out on the straw and reached up for him. Her eyes were bright with passion, her lips wet from his kisses. Slowly, so neither of them could doubt his intent, he knelt beside her and placed one hand on the inside of her knee. Inch by inch he drew his hand up toward the most secret part of her. The nightgown offered only token resistance, tightening slightly before sliding out of the way.

As quickly as it had appeared, the image faded, leaving Arizona feeling aroused and slightly disconcerted. He hadn't really seen much of the woman's face. Just her mouth. But he'd formed an impression of her, one strong enough to identify her.

Chloe.

"What do you think?" Charity asked, her gaze far too knowing.

He hoped his expression didn't give anything away. He cleared his throat before speaking. "It's antique enough to pass muster in a vintage clothing shop, but this isn't more than fifty or sixty years old."

Cassie's mouth drooped with disappointment.

"Hey, that doesn't mean the magic won't work," he told her. "Who wears it next?"

"I do," Cassie said, then raised her eyebrows. "Of course my birthday isn't for about five months. However, if you want to talk about a recent experience, ask Chloe. She wore it last night."

"Really?"

Chloe flushed slightly. "It was my birthday yesterday. Big deal. I wore it. Nothing happened."

He studied her, the smooth skin, the high cheekbones and firm set of her chin. She was lying, but about what?

"No dreams at all?" he asked.

"None worth mentioning."

"Maybe you should let us be the judge of that. After all,

if you're so interested in my story, maybe you should share yours with me. Just to be fair.'' As he said the words, the image of her in the nightgown popped back into his head. No way, he told himself. It hadn't been him. He wasn't anyone's idea of destiny. The fates were smart enough to know that.

A timer dinged on the stove. Chloe rose to her feet. ''Saved by the bell, and I mean that literally. The cobbler is ready. Why don't the three of you go on into the living room. I'll serve the dessert and bring it to you.''

''Ah, Chloe, you're no fun at all,'' Cassie complained.

''I know. It's my lot in life.''

''Don't worry,'' Charity said as she linked arms with him. ''We can use the time to convince Arizona to stay here instead of at some boring hotel. What do you think?''

Cassie clapped her hands together. ''That would be great! Say yes, Arizona. I swear I won't bug you every minute with questions.''

''Just every *other* minute,'' Chloe muttered.

Cassie grinned. ''Actually, she's telling the truth, but would that be too awful?''

''Not at all,'' Arizona said.

He *was* tempted. He would have accepted the gracious invitation except for one thing. Chloe. Something about her called to him. He could still picture her in the nightgown and he was hard with wanting. If anything happened between them, he didn't want to worry about upsetting Charity by taking advantage of her hospitality and therefore be unable to make love with Chloe.

Talk about an ulterior motive, he told himself. If Charity knew what he was thinking, she would want him neutered for sure.

Cassie took the nightgown from him and folded it. ''We're supposed to wash it by hand using water from the first rain after the first full moon following the wearer's birthday. I've marked the full moon on my calendar. I don't want to forget. Chloe might not believe, but I'm determined to make sure the legend happens to me.''

Arizona stood up and caught Chloe staring after her sister with an incredible look of sadness on her face. He wanted to ask her what was wrong, but this wasn't the time, and even if it was, he didn't have the right. He was just a guest in the house. Of course there was the detail of the article Chloe wanted to write. She was going to spend the next three weeks chasing after him, and if she played her cards right, he just might let her catch him.

Chapter Three

"There is a perfectly logical explanation," Chloe told herself as she exited the freeway and headed for the university. "Things like this happen all the time. It's nothing to worry about. I'm not going insane."

She braked at the stop sign and shifted her car into neutral. Her mouth curved up into a smile. "The fact that I'm talking to myself is not an indication of mental imbalance. I've *always* talked to myself. The trick is to not answer. At least not out loud."

The intersection cleared. She shifted into first and accelerated. Okay, so she was still feeling very strange about the dream she'd had two nights ago. Being exhausted didn't help. She hadn't been able to sleep at all the previous night, what with trying to make sense of everything. Obviously she'd seen Arizona's picture somewhere in the past, and his image had been lodged in her subconscious. It happened all the time. Cassie had been talking about the nightgown legend for weeks before Chloe's twenty-fifth birthday. The combination of life pressures, family-legend expectations and Lord knew what else had created a very real dream. But it was only a dream.

The fact that Arizona had invaded her life the next day was merely coincidence. The world was full of them.

"I'm going to be fine," she said aloud. "This article is a great opportunity for me. I'm going to turn in a dynamite project, impress the socks off my editor and write my way into a job with a big New York publisher."

She drew in a deep breath. The spring air was warm, the sun bright, the sky clear. At the next stop sign Chloe glanced around at the budding trees and green lawns that marked the outskirts of the university campus. For the first time in months she had the top down on her little sports car. The wind ruffled her hair and made her want to laugh. She would get through all this. She'd always been a survivor. If nothing else, she would keep reminding herself that Arizona Smith was just a man. Okay, he was very good-looking and the sight of him made her heart race. And maybe when they'd shaken hands yesterday she *had* felt a slight electrical charge, not to mention the fact that she didn't even have to close her eyes to picture him naked, next to her, on top of her, touching her everywhere as he—

"Stop it!" she commanded herself. "Don't go there. It's way too dangerous territory. Keep it light, keep it professional."

With that she turned into the parking lot by the exhibition hall. She found a parking spot by the main walkway and put up the top on her convertible. She'd barely finished collecting her leather briefcase when a black four-wheel-drive Ford Explorer pulled into the spot next to her. As she stepped out of her convertible, she had the feeling her car looked like a gnat buzzing beside an elephant. Then the tiny hairs on the back of her neck all stood up and a shiver raced down her spine. She couldn't think about cars or even breathing because she knew. *He* was there.

Sure enough, a tall, handsome guy climbed down from the driver's seat and circled around the front of the Explorer. Arizona wore khakis and a long-sleeved dark green shirt. His hair needed a trim, his boots were scuffed, and none of that mattered because there was a glint in his green eyes that made her wonder if the devil was half so appealing as this man standing in front of her.

"Morning," he said. "I thought I saw you zipping by me on the freeway. You were talking to yourself."

Chloe tightened her grip on her briefcase, then faked a casual chuckle. "Dictating, actually. I'm a journalist. It's an occupational hazard."

"I see." His gaze traveled leisurely over her body. The attention was as tangible as a blast of hot air. She found herself wanting to move close and rub up against him, just to make the moment complete. Before she could make a total fool of herself, he turned his attention to her car.

"Nice," he said, pointing at the silver BMW Z3 convertible. "You ever pretend you're James Bond?"

Chloe rolled her eyes. She'd heard the question before. Yes, the car had been featured in Pierce Brosnan's first film as James Bond, but that wasn't why she'd bought it. Some of her trust money had become available a couple of years before, she'd needed a new car and she'd always wanted a convertible. She'd bought the car on a whim and had never regretted it even once.

But she wasn't about to explain that to Arizona. She was in a lot of danger with this man. He was the subject of a story she intended to write, so she had to get the upper hand. His respect for her professional abilities was required.

But she had a feeling he wouldn't care about her years of study or how many articles she'd written. He exuded power the way flowers exuded scent. He would respect someone who gave as good as they got. She was having enough trouble trying to forget about the dream and ignoring her unexplained attraction to him. She refused to let him best her in a game of wits.

She made a great show of glancing around the parking lot. "I don't know if you've noticed, Dr. Smith, but Bradley is firmly located in an area referred to as the Sacramento delta. This part of California is completely flat. So unless you plan on scaling a building or two, this four-wheel-drive monstrosity you've rented seems a great deal like overkill to me." She kicked the closest monster tire and smiled. "Of course, you're the expert in archaeology. Perhaps there's something I should know to explain this."

Their gazes locked. Chloe didn't dare back down. Better to have gone too far than not far enough, she told herself.

A slow smile pulled at his mouth. His eyes brightened with humor. "Yeah, yeah. You called me on that one. I couldn't help it. I hate little cars." He took her arm and led her toward the exhibit hall. "Let's get one thing straight. I prefer Arizona to Dr. Smith, okay? Let's keep things informal."

The victory was sweet, although not enough for her to ignore the tingling in her arm or the way her heart fluttered in her chest. "Works for me. I want you to feel comfortable."

He looked at her. "I do. I feel very comfortable."

If they ever made love, they would be in danger of experiencing spontaneous combustion.

She didn't know where the thought had come from, but she knew it was true. Dear Lord, the man turned her on. But she couldn't let him know.

"Good. Then you won't mind answering all my questions."

They'd reached the building. Arizona held the door open for her. "Not at all. We can talk about anything you'd like."

The hallway was dim and it took a minute for her eyes to adjust. They stood facing each other. "I have a whole list of things I want to ask you."

"I think I'd rather talk about you."

It took a minute for his words to sink in. Chloe's body screamed a gratified "Yes!" when she finally absorbed the meaning of his statement. Her brain resisted. Was this teasing or testing? She didn't allow herself to think it might be an invitation. He couldn't possibly know about the dream. Did the attraction go both ways? The thought both excited and terrified her.

"That's not very subtle," she told him, pleased that her voice was calm. Shrieking would have been so unattractive.

"I can be if that's what you would prefer."

"What would you prefer?"

She hadn't meant to ask that question, but it was too late to call it back. Once the words were out, she really wanted to hear the answer.

The devastating smile returned. "I'd like to take you to an island in the South Pacific. Somewhere isolated and romantic."

"I'm sure you have just the one in mind."

"Of course. You'd like it. The indigenous population has a society based on a female deity. The social structure is matriarchal. In their eyes, men pretty much have one use."

Chloe was grateful for the dimness of the foyer. She could feel herself flushing. Based on what she'd read about him, he was probably telling the truth about the island. Despite herself, she laughed.

"I should be insulted," she told him.

"But you're not."

"No, I'm not." How could she be, when every cell of her being responded to him. Not just because he was good-looking. In fact, that was the least of his appeal. Much of what drew her was his energy. She felt like a cat seeking out the warmth of the sun. She wanted to bask in his glow.

"Don't you have some gems you want to show me?" she asked in an effort to change the subject.

"Absolutely." He led the way down the hall toward the exhibit hall.

She fell into step with him. "You're not what I expected," she admitted.

"So you've been doing your homework. Did you think I'd be more scholarly?"

"No, although I'm sure you're the expert everyone claims. I guess I didn't think you'd be just a regular guy. I try not to form too much of an impression of someone before I meet him. I don't want to be writing the article in my head too early. But in your case, that was more difficult than usual. There's a mythical element to your press clippings."

"Tell me about it." He stopped suddenly and turned to face her. "Despite the press trying to make it seem otherwise, I'm not Harrison Ford or Indiana Jones." His mouth twisted. "I can't tell you how many times those comparisons have been made."

"How often do you come out ahead?"

"Good question." His features relaxed a little. "We're running about fifty-fifty. You wouldn't believe the people who have trouble understanding that he's an actor portraying a fictional character. What happens in the movies has very little to do with real life. But people have expectations."

"You don't want to disappoint them," she said guessing.

"Of course not. But I'm not a larger-than-life character. Who can compete with a movie legend? This is real life. I don't get a second take to make sure the line is said just right."

"I would guess that the fans who most want you to be like Indiana Jones are the ladies," she said.

He groaned. "They bring me hats like his. And whips."

Chloe wasn't sure what to say to that. "I see."

He winked. "Of course some of them have been quite satisfied with reality."

I certainly was.

She jumped. Had she said that or just thought it? Her gaze flew to his face. He was watching her expectantly. Her heart, which had stumbled a couple of beats, resumed its steady thudding. She must have just thought it. Thank goodness. Arizona could never know about that night—or her dreams.

"Chloe, I'm sorry. I was just teasing. If it bothers you, I'll stop."

His statement didn't make sense for a second. Then she realized she'd been quiet and he probably thought she'd been insulted by his comment. "It's fine," she told him.

He shrugged. "Seriously, there was a time when I enjoyed all the press and comparisons. I worked hard to live up to the hype."

"A girl in every port?"

"Something like that."

"What happened?"

"I grew up. It got old. I've learned that quality is the most important part of a relationship."

That surprised her. "So you're a romantic at heart?"

He shoved his hands into the front pockets of his slacks.

"Yes. But not the way you mean it. If you're asking if I believe in love, the answer is no."

That didn't make sense. "You said you believe in magic."

"Of course. One doesn't have anything to do with the other. Magic exists. Love is the myth."

"No way. I've never seen magic at work, but you only have to look around to know love is everywhere. Parents and their children, couples who have been together fifty years, kids with their pets. How can you deny all that evidence?"

He stepped toward the wide double doors that led to the exhibit. "It's surprisingly easy," he said, pulled a key from his pocket, turned the lock and pushed open the right door.

As she moved to step inside, she was instantly assaulted by cool air. The light was even more dim inside, with only an illuminated path to guide them. A shiver rippled up her spine, but this one was from nerves, not attraction. Chloe instinctively fingered the heart-shaped locket she wore around her neck.

"This way," Arizona said with the confidence of someone who could see in the dark.

They'd taken about two steps when a voice stopped them. "You can't come in here," a man said. "The exhibit isn't open yet." Seconds later a bright light shone in her eyes, blinding her.

"It's okay, Martin," Arizona said. "This is Chloe Wright. She's a journalist. I brought her by to show her the exhibit."

The light clicked off and a security guard stepped out of the shadows. "Oh, sorry, Dr. Smith. I didn't know it was you." The fifty-something man smiled. "Let me know if you need anything."

"I will, Martin, thanks."

When they were alone again, Arizona motioned to the dark draperies on either side of the lit path. "The entrance is going to have blown-up photographs showing some of the ruins, that sort of thing. Robert Burton, a friend of mine, is composing appropriate music. Whatever the hell that means."

Chloe chuckled with him. "Probably something with a South American flavor."

"Probably."

They continued down the walkway toward bright lights. Dark drapes gave way to glass cases exhibiting tools, bowls and animal hides fashioned into primitive clothing. Arizona briefly explained the significance of the items.

"I constantly offend my colleagues," he admitted, not looking the least bit concerned by the fact. "I know I should be interested in this kind of thing." He motioned to a row of cutting knives. "They are the basis for understanding how a people lived day by day. But I'm a true romantic. I find the living more interesting than the dead, even the long-dead, and I prefer magic to reality. I don't care what they used to skin their kill. I want to know how they prepared for the hunt. I want to learn the rituals and hear the songs." He shrugged. "As I'm frequently reminded, religion and magic have their place, but a good knife in the hands of a skilled hunter can keep a family alive for the winter."

Chloe studied the honed cutting edges. "But religion feeds them as well—their souls rather than their bodies. That has to count for something."

"Exactly."

Arizona beamed at her as if she were a rather dull student who had finally come up with the right answer. She barely noticed, being too busy wondering where on earth that thought had come from. She was way too pragmatic to be concerned about the state of anyone's soul.

"I'm glad you see my point," he told her. "However, there are a few people I can't seem to convince. They're much more into the physical than the spiritual. We need to go through here."

He led the way into a brightly lit alcove. There was a closed door at the far end. He knocked once. Another security guard stepped out. "Yes, Dr. Smith?"

"Jimmy, I made arrangements to show Ms. Wright the gem collection. You ready to unlock the cases for me?"

The guard, a young man of Chloe's age, nodded seriously. "Yes, sir. Let me get the keys and disable the alarm."

When he disappeared back into the room, Arizona winked at her. "Jimmy is in charge of the gems. He's very proud of that. He'll be accompanying us. With him around, we can unlock the cases and you can actually touch the stones."

"I'd like that." She stared at him. "How long have you been in town?"

"A couple of days. Why?"

"You seem to know everyone's name. Or is that just a habit with security guards?"

"I told you. I'm interested in the living."

Jimmy joined them, cutting off any further chance for conversation. He led the way to the last room. The walls were plain black. Tall glass cases formed a staggered line down the center. Spotlights illuminated their precious cargo.

Arizona nodded at the first case. "We'll start at this end and work our way down." As Jimmy unlocked the case, Arizona sighed heavily. "I found them, but do they trust me with them now?"

"Sorry, sir," Jimmy said without cracking a smile. "I'm following the rules."

Chloe moved close to the display. The door opened and Arizona reached inside to pick up a huge pink stone. It was the size of an orange, with an irregular shape. He held it with a reverence that made her nervous about taking it from him when he offered it to her.

"This will heal you," he said. "Arthritis, stomach trouble, anything internal. I don't think it would work on a broken bone, although I could be wrong. Some of the incantations were written down. We've found pieces on tablets and animal hides. The tribe is obscure. The language is tough. Not related to other Indian tribes in the area. I don't have any of the incantations with me, so just think good thoughts while you hold it and hope for the best."

She took the stone from him. It was heavier than it looked. The top was bumpy, but the bottom was smooth and fit perfectly into the palm of her hand. She studied the way the light glinted off the facets.

"They didn't find the stone this way, did they?" she asked.

"No. It's been cut. There are definite markings. That's one of the mysteries. The tools we found aren't strong enough or sharp enough to have done this, so how did it happen?"

She handed him back the stone. "Do you have a theory?"

"Of course. But you're going to have to come to my lecture series to hear what it is."

He put the stone back in the case, waited until Jimmy locked it, then moved to the next exhibit.

There were stunning gems used in religious ceremonies, more healing stones, some of undetermined purpose. Arizona talked about them all, as if they were well-loved friends. When they were at the last case, he removed a huge diamond nestled in a flower-shaped bed of gold. The object was so heavy, she had to use both hands to hold it.

"Close your eyes," Arizona instructed. "Focus on the stone."

Chloe did as he requested. Instantly, the diamond began to glow. She frowned. That was impossible. For one thing, she had her eyes closed. How could she know if something was glowing or not? For another, she didn't believe in the mystical. But she could feel the heat and would have sworn she saw the light.

"This is a loving stone," he said. "It would have been used in ancient weddings to bind a couple together."

Instantly she could see the cave, the two of them entwined on their bed of straw. Which was crazy, right?

As the image filled her brain, the stone definitely brightened. Chloe stiffened and opened her eyes. She stared at the diamond. Nothing about it had changed. It wasn't glowing at all, and now that she was paying attention, there really wasn't any heat.

Arizona took the stone from her and returned it to Jimmy. After thanking the guard, he led her out of the exhibit hall. There was a small garden behind the building. Stone benches surrounded an inverted fountain.

Still confused by what had happened, she settled on one of the benches. He took a seat next to her.

"What did you think?" he asked.

"It's very impressive. I can see why you enjoy your work and why you have such a following. You've brought a great find to national attention."

He dismissed the compliment with a wave. "I haven't done anything that special. I followed a few clues, refused to give up when other people did, but I'm no hero. There are a lot of great scholars out there. I'm just some guy interested in pretty rocks and religious icons.''

''You're selling yourself a little short, aren't you?''

''Not really. When I met Joseph Campbell I was so impressed, I couldn't talk. He was my idol. I don't say that lightly. I've met many impressive people, but he was the best.''

Interesting. She made a mental note. That information could add some depth and human interest to her story. ''Are there any important people you haven't met yet who intrigue you?''

His smile was slow and lazy. It should have warned her. He relaxed back in the bench. ''Yesterday I would have said yes, because until yesterday I hadn't met you.''

It was a line, she reminded herself. But it was a good one. ''Not bad.''

His smile didn't fade, but something dark and dangerous crept into his expression. ''I wasn't kidding, Chloe. I know you felt it, too. The energy when you were holding the diamond. Did the stone glow when you closed your eyes? That's supposed to be significant.''

She tried swallowing, but her throat was too tight. When coughing didn't clear it, she decided to ignore both the sensation and the question. She opened her briefcase and pulled out a small handheld tape recorder.

''I'd like to ask you a few questions,'' she said.

He eyed the machine. ''Obviously we're on the record.''

''We have been all morning.''

His gaze sharpened. ''Really? That surprises me.'' He crossed his ankle over his opposite knee. ''Ask away.''

The sun was warm, but the heat filling her body came from the inside. There was something about him, about his relaxed posture. She angled away from him, but even so, the bench was suddenly too small. She felt confined and much too close. She could inhale the masculine scent of his body. Her mind didn't want to focus on questions or interview techniques. She wanted to move closer still; she wanted to run away.

Neither possibility was wise, she reminded herself, so she dug out a list of questions she'd prepared the previous night when she couldn't sleep.

"You traveled with your grandfather for most of your formative years," she said.

"That's right. He showed up one day when I was about three or so, and took me with him. One of my first memories is riding a yak somewhere in Tibet." He stretched out his arms along the back of the bench. His strong tanned fingers lay within inches of her shoulder and she tried not to notice.

"Grandfather traveled in style," he continued. "At heart, he was an adventurer. Fortunately the family had money, so he was able to go where and when he wanted. He'd run guns into Africa before the Second World War. He knew heads of state, from Nixon to obscure tribal elders in kingdoms the size of a grocery store. He would decide to spend a summer somewhere or maybe a winter, but we never stayed longer than a few months. Grandfather loved to be moving on."

Chloe knew this from her research. "He arranged for tutors?"

Arizona nodded. "Sometimes several at once. I studied for hours every day. When I was fourteen, he put me in university, Oxford, then I moved to Egypt for a year or so. India, South Africa. I have an assortment of degrees." He grinned. "None of them practical."

"Are you an adventurer, too?"

"In a manner of speaking. I've tried to be more methodical, to use what I know to discover the past. Grandfather wanted to travel for the sake of being gone. I want to accomplish something."

She looked at him. From where she was sitting, he looked like a fairly normal guy. Perhaps he was a little too good-looking, but otherwise, he seemed to be much like the rest of the world.

"You're staring," he said. "Is there a reason?"

She shook her head. "You're so different from anyone I've ever known. My family is one of the founding families of this town. My mother's maiden name is Bradley. The Victorian house has been ours for generations. I've traveled some, but not like you. Bradleys have been in this valley for more than a hundred years."

He shrugged. "Roots aren't a bad thing."

"I know. I'm not unhappy with my life. I'm just wondering what it would be like to have lived yours." She tried to imagine always moving around, never knowing where one was going next. The thought wasn't pleasant.

She remembered the running tape and the fact that this was supposed to be an interview. "Okay, next question. I know your mother died shortly after you were born. When did your father pass away?"

If she hadn't been studying him so closely, she wouldn't have noticed the subtle stiffening of his body. "My father is alive and well. At least he was the last time he called me."

"But you grew up with your grandfather. He took you away when you were three."

"I know."

"Why didn't you stay with your father?"

"It just worked out that way."

The journalist in her jumped onto the detail. Questions sprang to mind. Had there been a problem? An estrangement? Some legal issues? Why had Arizona's father let his only child be taken from him and subjected to such an odd upbringing?

"You're going to pursue this line of questioning, aren't you?" Arizona sounded more weary than annoyed.

"Yes. I'm figuring out which way to go."

He didn't answer. Instead he raised his head to the sun. "It's warmer than I thought it would be," he said.

"We're about ten degrees above normal for this time of year."

"I should have dressed for it." He reached for his right cuff and undid the button.

All the questions and strategies about how best to handle the interview fled from her mind. The entire world disappeared as she focused her attention on those long fingers and his casual act.

He finished rolling up the right sleeve and started on the left. She knew what she was going to see there. Despite the fact that she'd only met the man yesterday and that he'd been wearing long sleeves then, too. Despite the fact that none of the photos in her research files showed him in anything but long sleeves. She knew about the scar because she'd seen the man naked in her dreams.

That wasn't real, she reminded herself. It hadn't really happened. So when he rolled up the sleeve, there wasn't going to be a knife scar on the inside of his left forearm. Except she knew that was exactly what she was going to see.

She stopped breathing.

He made one fold of the fabric, then another. The tail of the scar came into view. She told herself this wasn't really happening, except it was and she didn't know how to make it stop.

He caught her stare. "It's not so bad," he said, motioning to the scar. "Want to hear how it happened?"

"I can't," she said, her voice tight. "I can't. I have to—" She couldn't think of a real excuse so she didn't bother making one. Instead she gathered up her notes and her tape recorder and thrust both into her briefcase.

It was too much to take in. The dream and the man and the fact that she'd known what the scar looked like before she'd even seen it.

"I'll be in touch," she managed as she scrambled to her feet and headed for the parking lot.

"Chloe? Is something wrong?"

She held him off with a wave. As soon as she was on the far side of the garden, she began to run. It was only when she tried to fit her key in the lock that she realized she was blinded by tears she could neither explain nor understand. What on earth was happening to her?

Chapter Four

Chloe finished stacking the folders into neat piles. She'd already dusted her computer, rearranged her pencil cup and answered all her messages. Even the boring ones. Still, the busywork wasn't enough to keep her mind from scurrying around like a frantic chicken, scuttling from place to place, or in her case, subject to subject.

She'd tried lecturing herself on the importance of being professional. She'd scanned a couple of articles on maintaining one's cool during interviews. She'd taken countless deep breaths, tried a bit of stretching in the ladies room and had even sworn off coffee.

It wasn't helping. The truth was she was scared.

Something strange was happening to her. She didn't want it to be true, but she could no longer ignore the obvious. Fact number one. Before yesterday, she'd never met Arizona Smith. She didn't think she'd even seen a picture of him or known who he was. Fact number two. Night before last she'd had a long, detailed, highly erotic dream about Arizona. A dream so intense just thinking about it sent a quiver of excitement through her belly. Fact number three. In said dream, she'd pictured Arizona naked. She *knew* what the man looked like naked. That was fine. All men sort of looked the same without their clothes. The basic working parts had a lot in common. But it was more than that. She knew about his scars. The one on his knee and the one on his forearm. Fact number four. That very morning she'd had confirmation that her dream had some basis in reality. After all, the scar had been exactly as she remembered it.

Fact number five. Maybe she was going crazy.

Chloe folded her arms on her desk and let her head sink down to her hands. She refused to consider insanity as an explanation to her problem. It had to be something else. Something logical. Maybe along with seeing his picture and not remembering it, she'd also read an article that mentioned his scars.

Or maybe the nightgown was real.

That last thought made her shudder, but in a whole different way than when she thought about making love with Arizona. Anything mystic was just too weird for her. She didn't want the nightgown to be real. She didn't want to know her destiny and she sure didn't want to have to get involved with a man like Arizona Smith. He had a woman in every port. He didn't even believe in love.

She straightened in her chair. He was wrong about love. It did exist. Unfortunately it wasn't worth the pain it brought along, but it was definitely real.

"I don't want this," she murmured to herself. "I want my life to be normal, like everyone else's."

She suddenly remembered she was in the office. Talking

to herself in the car was one thing, but in front of others, especially co-workers, was quite another.

This has gone on too long, she told herself firmly and silently. She had to pull herself together. She reached for the pad of paper she always kept by her phone and then grabbed a pen. She would make a list. List making always helped.

First, she would pretend the dream never happened. Every time she thought about it, she would push it to the back of her mind. Eventually she would forget. Second, she was going to act like the professional she was. No more personal conversations, no more freaking out because she saw a scar. She didn't even want to imagine what Arizona must think of her.

"Professional," she muttered. It was time to work on her article.

She glanced at the list she'd made, figured she could remember both items on her own and tossed the paper into the trash. Next, she reviewed the background material Nancy had left her. There were a couple of points that hadn't been clear. Chloe picked up the phone and dialed the reporter's home number.

When Nancy answered, Chloe introduced herself and politely asked about her pregnancy. They talked about work for a few minutes, then Nancy mentioned Arizona.

"I've been seeing the man everywhere on the local news. Is he as impressive in person?"

Chloe thought about her own reaction to Arizona and bit back a sigh. "Unfortunately, yes."

The two women laughed.

"Gee, Mark and I have wanted children for a long time, but now I'm feeling a little left out of it. I'm getting stretch marks and a daily afternoon backache while you're out playing with the new guy in town. It's not fair."

"But in a couple of months you're going to have a baby, and all I'll be left with is a story." And a broken heart.

The last thought came without warning and Chloe firmly ignored it. She was not going to get involved enough to get her heart broken. In fact she wasn't going to get involved at all.

"Speaking of the story," she said. "I have a few questions on a couple of your sources."

"I figured you would. My system of taking notes is tough for people to follow. You'd think after all this time I'd be more organized, but I'm not."

Chloe went through her questions and wrote down Nancy's replies. When they were finished she said, "From what I can tell you were angling your story toward telling about the man and his myths."

"Right, but I was never happy with that. Have you thought of something better?"

"I don't know if it's better, but I have another idea. I'd like to write about the man *behind* the myths. Arizona has traveled all over the world. He has a strong belief in the mystical and spiritual. From what I've seen he has an image the media loves. But who is the man underneath? How does he decide what he's going to pursue? What are his influences now and what were they in the past?"

"I like that," Nancy said. "I think the readers will like it, too. Arizona is getting tons of media attention so there's no point in rehashing old material. Everyone will be tired of it by then. But this is new and fresh. Have you run it by Jerry?"

Chloe glanced at her watch. "I have a meeting with him in a couple of hours."

"He's going to think it's great." She laughed. "Actually what you're going to hear is a noncommittal grunt, which means he thinks it's great. If he hates it, he tells you to your face.''

''I know that one firsthand. Okay, Nancy. Thanks for your help.'' They said their goodbyes and hung up.

Chloe turned on her computer and prepared to type up her notes. Usually she could focus on her work, but today there was a voice nagging in the back of her mind.

''This is too ridiculous,'' she said softly. ''I won't get a moment's peace until I fix this.''

With that, she picked up the phone again, consulted a pad of paper and dialed.

''Room 308,'' she told the receptionist. ''The guest's name is Arizona Smith.''

She waited while the call was connected. It was possible that he hadn't gone back to the hotel yet. He might be out all day. If that was the case, she would leave him voice mail asking him to get in touch with her. No matter how long it took, she was going to have to talk to him and apologize for her behavior that morning. There was no point in trying to explain—she wasn't about to tell him about her dream or the fact that she'd known about his scar even before he'd rolled up his sleeve. But she at least had to atone for her rudeness in running off.

The receiver was picked up, cutting off her train of thought.

''Smith,'' he said by way of a greeting.

''Hi, it's Chloe. I'm sorry to bother you.''

''No bother.''

His voice sounded normal. She took that as a good sign. ''I'm calling to apologize for what happened earlier today. I don't know why I ran off like that.'' She crossed the fingers of her free hand, hoping the superstitious gesture would make up for the small lie.

''I understand. Sometimes I have that effect on women.

They lose control and rather than let me see how overcome they are, they run off.''

His voice was so calm and serious it took her a minute to figure out he was teasing. She chuckled. ''Yeah, right, that was it exactly. Overcome by your substantial charms, I had to retreat to the relative sanctuary of my office so that I could recover.''

''Are you better now?'' he asked.

''Much, thank you.'' They laughed together, then she said, ''I'm serious. I don't know what came over me. It was terrible to leave like that. I promise it won't happen again.''

''It better not. You won't get much of a story if you keep running out on the interview.''

''Can I make it up to you? Would you please come over for dinner tonight?''

He hesitated. Chloe swallowed as her good humor disappeared like feathers sucked up into a tornado. Of course. Why hadn't she thought of that? ''You have other plans,'' she said, making it a statement, not a question. Who was she, this other woman?

''Actually, I don't. Yes, I would love to join you for dinner. However, your aunt already issued the invitation and I accepted.''

''Aunt Charity phoned?''

''First thing this morning.''

Chloe knew she shouldn't be annoyed at her aunt. After all, Charity called the old Victorian mansion home, and she had every right to invite whomever she liked. But the tension was there all the same.

''That's great,'' Chloe told him. ''I'll see you then. This time I promise not to freak when you show off your scars.''

''If you're very good I'll even let you touch them.''

She thought about the one on his leg and couldn't suppress a shudder of anticipation. "You've got yourself a deal."

Chloe pulled into the driveway. Mr. Withers, the seventy-year-old misogynist caretaker sat on his rider-mower, going back and forth on the front lawn.

"Evening, Mr. Withers," Chloe called out as she stepped up to the front porch.

Mr. Withers offered a wave that was more dismissal than greeting and muttered something under his breath. Probably something mildly offensive, Chloe thought with a grin. The old man had been around since long before her mother had been born. He'd always taken care of the house. If either of the sisters dared to try to engage him in conversation they risked being called mindless ninnies. Chloe had always wanted to ask what other kind of ninnies existed—didn't the definition of the insult imply a mindlessness? But she didn't think Mr. Withers would appreciate her humor.

"Have a nice night," she told him as she stepped into the house and was rewarded with another grunt.

She shut the front door behind him, effectively cutting off most of the noise from the power mower. "I'm home," she yelled in the direction of the kitchen.

"It's Chloe!" Cassie came racing down the hall and slipped to a stop in front of her. "I want to hear everything, but so does Aunt Charity so you have to wait until we're all together. But plan on spilling lots and lots of details. Oh, and *he's* coming to dinner. Isn't that great?" She took a deep breath before continuing. "He is so amazingly cool and good-looking. How can you stand it? I mean, spending the day with him. Did he look into your eyes and say something wonderful? Don't you think he's just incredibly interesting?"

Chloe put down her briefcase and slipped out of her linen

jacket. After linking her arm with her sister's she led them both to the kitchen. "I don't even know where to start," she admitted. "I swear, Cassie, sometimes you act like you're barely sixteen instead of nearly twenty-five."

Cassie tossed her head, making her short dark hair dance around her face. "I'm blessed with an enthusiastic nature," she said, not the least bit insulted by her sister's comment. "I enjoy life and all that it has to offer. Arizona Smith is a very interesting man and I'm enjoying his company. We can't all be jaded reporters. I'd rather be the romantic dreamer I am any day."

They reached the kitchen. Cassie stepped away and got them each a soda from the refrigerator. Chloe settled at the kitchen table. "Where's Aunt Charity?" she asked.

"Taking a shower. The spaghetti sauce has been simmering for hours." She pointed to a pot on a back burner. She plopped down opposite her sister. "Tell me everything."

Chloe obliged, telling her sister about the gem exhibit and recounting Arizona's stories.

Cassie sighed. "It's so romantic. What a great way to spend the morning. But you probably just sat there taking notes, not even noticing the man. You're hopeless." Cassie tucked her short hair behind her ear. "I swear, when I have my twenty-fifth birthday and I get to wear the nightgown, I'm not going to waste a perfectly good opportunity dreaming about nothing! I plan to have a wonderfully romantic dream."

Chloe smiled as her sister talked. She was glad they were back together again. The three years they'd spent apart in high school had been difficult for them both. She fought against a familiar flash of anger. Their parents should have planned better, she thought for the thousandth time. If they had, the two sisters wouldn't have been separated and put into different foster homes.

She shook off the old memories and concentrated on the evening ahead. She'd promised herself that she would act like a real professional, that she wouldn't let thoughts of the dream interfere.

"What time is Arizona coming over?" she asked.

Cassie glanced at the clock above the stove. "In about an hour."

"I'd better get changed."

Cassie followed her up the stairs. "Are you all right? Is something bothering you? You got a funny look on your face a second ago."

"I'm fine." They reached her bedroom first and both women entered. They sat on the bed facing each other. "I was just thinking that I'm glad we're back together. High school was hard."

Cassie's good humor faded a little. "I know. I hated that the courts forced us to live apart. But we're together now — at least until you run off to the big city to write for one of those New York magazines." Cassie held up her hand. "Don't even say it. I know the drill. This is what you want and you have every right to pursue your dreams. But I'll miss you."

Chloe leaned toward her. "You could come with me. We could rent an apartment together."

Cassie shook her head. "No. I don't want to leave Bradley. I like it here. I adore my job."

"You're a nursery school teacher."

"Exactly, and I love it. The kids are great. I know you don't understand—you want more for me. But this is what *I* want and you have to remember to respect that."

"I know." Chloe sighed. It was a familiar discussion.

One she'd never won. "I just think you could do so much more with your life."

"And I think working with children is the most important thing I *can* do. Besides, even if I was tempted to run off to New York with you, which I'm not, I couldn't. What about Joel?"

Chloe forced her expression to remain pleasant and her hands still, when all she wanted to do was grab her sister by the shoulders and shake some sense into her.

Joel and Cassie had been dating since high school. They had an "understanding" that they would become engaged and then marry.

It was all a quirk of fate, Chloe thought grimly. While she had been sent away to another city when their parents had died and the two girls had been put into foster care, Cassie had stayed in town. She'd gone to the local high school and had started seeing Joel.

"If you can't say something nice," Cassie warned.

"Joel is the most boring man on the planet."

"That's hardly nice."

"You don't know what I was going to say. It's a real improvement."

"Oh, Chloe, we can't all be like you. I think it's great that you want to leave Bradley and make something of yourself. That's your life and you're going to be wonderful. But it's not my life. I want to stay here. I want to have a family. Joel wants to marry me. I love him. I've been dating him for nearly nine years and he makes me happy. Let it go."

Chloe bit her tongue and nodded her agreement. There wasn't anything else she could say. Cassie was right—they each had to live their own lives.

Her sister stood up. "I have to go make myself beautiful for our guest and I suggest you do the same." She paused in the doorway and leaned back dramatically, the back of one hand pressed against her forehead. "Maybe he'll tell us about the time he saved the virgin from the angry volcano by single-handedly fighting off a dozen hostile natives with his bare hands."

"I'm sure that will be the first story to cross his lips."

"I knew it." Cassie waggled her fingers and left.

Chloe stared after her. The two sisters couldn't be more different. Part of the reason, she knew, was because they weren't related by blood. When her mother had had trouble conceiving, her parents had gone on a long waiting list for adoption. As sometimes happened, Amanda Wright had later found out she was pregnant. The doctors had warned her she was unlikely to have another baby, so they hadn't pulled their application. Seven months after Chloe had been born the Wrights received a call telling them there was a one-month-old girl available, if they wanted her.

Growing up, Chloe couldn't remember a time when Cassie hadn't been around. The girls had been inseparable. That had made those three years apart even more difficult.

She stood up and walked to the closet, not sure what she was going to wear tonight. Something pretty, but professional. She was going to ask Arizona questions to make up for her lapse earlier that day. As she studied her wardrobe, she heard Cassie's enthusiastic but off-key singing drifting down the hall. She smiled. Cassie was one of those rare people who absolutely believed the best in everyone and always told the truth. She led with her chin and sometimes she got hurt. But that never changed her feelings about herself or the world.

Chloe wondered what it would be like to have that much faith. She was too cynical to believe in people. Especially those she didn't know well. That's why she was a decent journalist. The thing was if she wanted anyone else to believe that, she was going to have to write a dynamite article. Arizona Smith and the secrets of his life were her ticket out of Bradley.

Arizona swallowed a drink of beer and wondered why the sight of an attractive young woman cooing over the scar on his arm didn't do a thing for him. Cassie bent over him and made tsking noises.

"I can see where they first stitched you up in the field," she said. "There are still a few puncture wounds."

Her fingers were cool and smooth as she stroked his skin. He waited, hoping to feeling a tingle or a flicker of interest. Nothing. Less than nothing. He was restless.

Cassie straightened and smiled. "Any other scars?"

She'd noticed the mark on his arm the second he'd walked into the house. As near as he could figure, the sight of it had sent Chloe screaming out of his presence. Funny, he'd never thought it was that scary looking, but then he was a guy. Maybe Chloe was squeamish.

Cassie's gaze was filled with curiosity and good humor. She reminded him of the little sister he'd never had. He couldn't help teasing her a little. "I do have another scar on my leg. I'd show it to you, but I'd have to take my pants off to do it."

"Oh, I don't mind," Cassie said quickly.

Arizona watched her, but there was no guile in her expression. Had she really meant what she'd said?

Footsteps interrupted his thoughts. He looked up and all the attraction that had been missing when Cassie had touched him slammed into him with the subtlety of an aircraft carrier taking out a forty-foot yacht.

Chloe stood just inside the kitchen. She wore a sleeveless dress in pale peach. The soft-looking fabric clung to her curves in a way designed to make a man forget to breathe.

Her long hair had been pulled back into a braid. His fingers itched to tug the curls free.

"You might want to rethink your comment, Cassie," Chloe said to her sister. "I believe you just told Arizona you wanted him to take his pants off."

"I do." Suddenly, Cassie seemed to realize the implications of what she'd just said. She blanched, then color flooded her face. "Oh, no. I didn't mean— That is to say, he has a scar and—" She glanced from him to Chloe and back. "I didn't mean anything else. We were talking and—"

Chloe chuckled. "We know what you meant. Just be careful. Not every strange man is going to understand you're not issuing an invitation."

Cassie nodded.

Arizona leaned close to her. "I won't take offense if you'll explain to your sister that I'm not really strange."

Chloe took the seat opposite him. "Yes, you are, and I'll thank you not to corrupt my little sister."

"Little by how much?" he asked. "Charity told me you're about the same age."

"Chloe is six months older," Cassie told him. "I was adopted."

"So I heard." He looked from one to the other.

Charity came into the room and walked to the stove. "The sauce is nearly ready," she said, lifting the cover and stirring. Instantly a spicy tomato aroma filled the room.

"I'll do the garlic bread," Chloe said.

"I'll take care of the salad." Cassie headed for the refrigerator.

"Should I offer to help or will I be told to just stay out of the way?"

"The latter, of course," Charity told him, her eyes twinkling at him as she glanced over her shoulder.

He leaned back in his chair. It didn't matter how many cultures he visited, or where he traveled in the world. Some customs remained the same. The ritual dance of women preparing a meal was one.

Whether the women were barefoot by an open fire, in a log house, a stone kitchen or a Victorian mansion, they moved with a grace and rhythm that was as old as the species. Conversation ebbed and flowed as they performed their magic. He supposed he enjoyed watching because no one did this for him very often. He was a frequent guest, but never a member of the family.

He caught Chloe's eye and they shared a moment of connection across the kitchen. The rest of the room disappeared until she was the only one left. Then Cassie touched her arm and she turned away from him. He was again on the outside. He envied her the place she held in this special world.

The dinner dishes had been pushed to the center of the table, but no one was in a hurry to pick them up. Arizona tore apart the last piece of garlic bread as Cassie raised her hands in frustration.

"How can you say it's not true?" she asked. "The nightgown has been in the Bradley family for generations."

"It's just a nightgown," Chloe insisted. "How can you say it has magic powers? As I've said before, there is no such thing as magic or destiny. It's all smoke and mirrors."

Cassie shook her head. "Aunt Charity, you talk to her."

"She won't listen to me," the older woman said. "Arizona, you have a go at it. Chloe is our resident cynic."

"I'll try." He leaned forward and stared at the beautiful woman sitting across from him. He would rather carry her up to bed, but that hadn't been offered as one of the options, so he thought about the various feats of magic he'd experienced personally.

"Several years ago I was in India," he began. "A boy had been mauled by a tiger stalking the village. The cat nearly took off his leg. Although the bone wasn't broken, he lost a lot of blood."

He tried not to notice the way her eyes darkened as her pupils widened with the storytelling. He tried to ignore the scent of her body, the slender curves beneath her dress or the way he *knew* how great it would be between them, almost as if they'd been lovers before.

"If he'd been near a hospital, he might have had a chance," he continued. "But the village didn't even have a nurse, let alone medical facilities. My grandfather and I knew the boy was going to die and we could only offer painkillers to ease his passing."

He paused, remembering his own fear from that night. He'd been thirteen or fourteen, and he could relate to the screams of fear and pain from the injured child.

"That night the village performed an old ceremony of sacrifice and worship. They came together to heal one of their own. I wasn't allowed to attend—I was considered too young. But I heard it. The singing and chanting. I smelled the incense. I don't know what they did but it worked. When I went to visit him the next morning, I was afraid he would already be dead. Instead, I found him sitting up. His wound had nearly healed. He was talking and laughing because the pain was gone. Within a week, it was as if it had never happened. Since then, I've witnessed many things I can't explain."

"Wow," Cassie breathed. "That is so cool."

Chloe rolled her eyes. "Every supermarket tabloid has a story about people being abducted by aliens. Do you believe that, too?"

So she was a doubter. Somehow that made the challenge more interesting. "I saw the boy. When I see aliens abducting people from cornfields, I'll believe that as well."

"I want to know what has made you believe in all this."

"I want to know what has made you such a cynic," he responded. "Do you mean to tell me that in all your twenty-five years there hasn't been one incident you can't explain? One event or circumstance that makes no sense, but that you can't deny?"

Their gazes locked. Something flickered in her eyes. Something that called out to him and if they'd been alone...

But they weren't, he reminded himself. They had two very interested onlookers.

"My, look at the time," Chloe said. "If we don't get these dishes soaking, they'll never come clean."

With that she sprang to her feet and started to clear the table. The other two women moved to help her. Cassie shooed Arizona back into his seat when he tried to assist. His gaze followed Chloe. She was hiding something. He could feel it.

There was a mystery behind her pretty face and he had every intention of solving it.

Chapter Five

"I look like a bridesmaid," Cassie complained.

Chloe fluffed her sister's hair. "You look beautiful. I love that dress."

"It's too young. I should change into something else. Why can't I look sophisticated, like you?"

Chloe faced front and studied their reflections in the mirror. They stood in her bathroom, both ready to go out for the evening. Cassie wore a long-sleeved, silky dress of pale pink that fell to midcalf. Lace edged the oversize collar. Her thick hair had been smoothed away from her face, exposing the gold heart earrings she always wore—the earrings that matched Chloe's locket—a legacy from their mother.

Chloe was willing to admit that while Cassie didn't look like a bridesmaid, there was definitely something virginal about her dress and her expression. She was still untouched by the ways of the world. Chloe thought about her own heartache and figured her sister was lucky to still be so unaware of the emotional pain that awaited her.

Chloe turned her attention to her own reflection. In contrast to her sister's innocence, she looked ready for sin. She'd pulled her long curls up on top of her head, securing them in a large clip. The ends fell to the back of her neck and danced against her bare skin. Her dress was simple. A scoop-neck, long-sleeved velvet dress. The soft burgundy fabric came to midthigh, exposing a lot of leg.

Overtly sexy wasn't her usual style, but then neither was a man like Arizona. She was attending a reception in his honor. She figured she needed all the help she could get just to maintain some kind of power base in the relationship. If only she weren't so attracted to him, she might have a fighting chance. But she *was* attracted. She shivered at the thought of being near him again. Of seeing him and talking to him. Lord help her if he asked her to dance. She would probably become a giant puddle right there on the dance floor.

"I hate being short," Cassie said with a sigh.

"You're five-five. That's average, not short. Besides, I would love to be petite."

"Me, too." Cassie patted her hips. "Instead, I'm curvy. You get to be tall and slender and beautiful. If you weren't my sister, I think I'd hate you. I might just hate you anyway."

Chloe smiled and kissed her cheek. "You know you love me. I love you, too. So we're even."

The doorbell rang downstairs. Cassie glanced toward the door. "That will be Joel. You know we're going out to dinner before we come to the reception, right?"

"Why? There will be food at the party. You can eat there."

Cassie slipped out of the bathroom. "You know how

Joel is. He's concerned that with Arizona's reputation and his world travel, the university will be serving something exotic. Joel doesn't eat exotic things. We'll go to our regular restaurant and join you later."

Chloe resisted the urge to roll her eyes. What on earth was Cassie doing with Joel? Why couldn't she see she was simply settling? There was a whole world out there just waiting to be seen. But instead of speaking her mind, Chloe forced herself to smile. They'd had this discussion a hundred times. Cassie knew her sister's opinion on the subject, and she was old enough to make her own decisions.

"Don't change your mind about coming," Chloe said. "I really want you there."

"I wouldn't miss it. I promise." She waved, then left to meet her date.

Chloe lingered in the bathroom for a few minutes, touching up her makeup and spraying on perfume. As a rule, she didn't put much on her face during the day. A little mascara, sunscreen and powder. But for events like this, she went all out. At least she had the satisfaction of knowing she looked her best. She would need the confidence to face everyone at the reception.

"It's really dumb to lie to myself," she said, and she collected her tiny evening purse. Okay, she would tell the truth. She wanted to look her best to give herself the confidence to face Arizona...and because she was female enough to want to knock his socks off. It wasn't going to happen, of course, but a girl could dream.

Thirty minutes later, she accepted the car claim ticket from the valet and stared up at the front of the hotel. The welcome reception was being held in the grand ballroom. Bradley wasn't that big a town and most events like this were held here. She knew the approximate layout of the room, at least half the guest list and who was likely to get drunk and embarrass themselves. She was here both as a reporter and as a guest. The former role meant that she would need to spend at least part of the evening talking to Arizona.

"Talk about a hardship," she murmured under her breath. She made a promise to herself that no matter how good he looked in his tux, she would not swoon, then she squared her shoulders and headed for the ballroom.

The huge room was much as she expected. Bright lights glittered from a dozen chandeliers. There were crowds of people in tight conversation groups. Her name was checked against the list of invitees, then she was admitted.

Chloe made her way to the bar in the east corner and ordered a glass of white wine. It was false courage at best, but she had a feeling she was going to need all the help she could get.

As she sipped the tart liquid, she glanced around. While she told herself she was just checking out who was wearing what, she knew she was actually searching for him. *Damn.* She couldn't even pretend she wasn't interested for five minutes. What hope did she have of pulling off the professional act? Well, she was going to have to figure out a way. Maybe if she walked around for a while and chatted with some other people she might figure out how to pull this off. If she—

"I thought you were never going to get here."

The voice came from behind her, but she didn't have to turn around to identify the speaker. Even if she hadn't recognized him from how he sounded, her body instinctively knew. Was it his scent, his heat or something more basic than that? She wasn't sure. All she knew was that there wasn't going to be enough time to get her act together.

Fake it until you make it, she told herself as she turned so they were facing each other.

He'd had a recent haircut and shave. She filed the information away as she drank in the sight of him. Strong, handsome features, green eyes that twinkled with amusement and what she hoped was appreciation. He wore a black tux, obviously tailored, and a crisp, white shirt. He was tall, dangerous and too sexy by far. The only thing that gave her hope of surviving the evening without making a fool of herself was the fact that he seemed to be studying her as completely as she had studied him.

"Well," he asked and did a quick turn, like a fashion model. "What do you think?"

"You clean up very nicely, Dr. Smith."

"I could say the same, but it wouldn't do justice. You always look lovely, but tonight you're radiant."

He brought her free hand up to his mouth and kissed her knuckles. The old-fashioned gesture nearly drove her to her knees. She had to consciously remind her body to keep breathing.

"We are," he said as he tucked her hand into the crook of his arm, "a fabulous-looking couple. Everyone will be jealous. It's our duty to walk through the crowd, spreading our attractiveness among them. They will expect it. They might even throw money." He gave her a wink.

His outrageousness made her laugh and his easy smile calmed some of her nervousness. "How noble of you," she told him. "I'm terribly impressed by your concern for the little people."

He leaned toward her. "Seriously, I expect you to protect me. I hate parties like this. Everyone wants to impress me with their exotic travels. Some even bring pictures. I never know what to say. I don't do the celebrity thing very well."

His confession both surprised and pleased her. "I'll do what I can to keep you safe."

They began to circulate through the room. Chloe had

been prepared to introduce Arizona to the local dignitaries, but he already seemed to know them. He greeted the mayor and most of the city council by name.

"How do you do that?" she asked when they'd excused themselves to go sample the food. "How do you know who everyone is?"

Arizona collected an empty plate for each of them and led her to the buffet line. "I met the mayor and her husband at the airport. There was a city council meeting yesterday and I attended."

Chloe glanced at the food spread out before them. There was nothing more exotic than some enchiladas, but Cassie had probably been right to let Joel take her out to dinner. He would have fussed over the fact that there wasn't a steak in sight.

"I have a terrible time remembering people's names," she said as she took some salad. "I keep a detailed card file so I don't mess up at press conferences."

"I'm lucky," he admitted. "It's easy for me to remember names and faces. I only have to meet someone once and I know them. It works. People like to be remembered."

Especially by someone like him, she thought. It wouldn't matter if he was at a dinner at the White House, or in some small village. He would always be the center of attention. Even now, she knew people were watching him, trying to figure out an excuse to talk to him.

The adoration should have made him unbearable, but Arizona handled it with grace and humor. She suspected that was true for most of his life. Was there anything he didn't do well?

"How's the story coming?" he asked as they settled into two chairs to eat. "Are you going to dig up the skeletons in my closet?"

"Do you have any?"

"No, but wouldn't it be fun if I did? Maybe I'm Elvis." He curled his upper lip and tried to look sexy.

She laughed.

He pretended to be wounded. "I wasn't trying to be funny. If there weren't so many people around, I would sing for you."

"I can't wait."

"Dr. Smith?" A beautifully dressed middle-aged woman stopped in front of him. Chloe recognized her as the chairperson of the cultural council. It had joined forces with the university to sponsor Arizona's visit and lecture series. "It's nearly eight o'clock. The university president is about to introduce you and we'd like you to say a few words."

"No problem." He stood up and set his plate on a tray, then winked at Chloe. "You'll be able to tell which one is me up there," he said, pointing to the small stage at the far end of the room. "I'll be the one stuttering."

She smiled. "I'll wave."

"Great." He winked. "Don't go giving all your dances away. I want one."

"No problem," she said lightly, while every cell in her body screamed that he could not only have all her dances, he could have her, too. Anytime, anywhere.

So much for acting professional.

As Arizona was led to the podium, the crowd moved in that direction as well. Chloe found herself swept along. She caught bits of conversation around her. Everyone was talking about him. The men wanted to be him and the women wanted to make love with him. She couldn't blame either group. He was just that kind of man—a force of nature.

She supposed her physical reaction was something to be expected. It wasn't a crush, exactly, but really close. Still, she could control it. At least enough to get her job done. Tonight they would dance together, and she would probably lose her head a little, but in the morning everything would be back to normal. At least that was her fantasy.

The university president greeted the crowd. Chloe tried to listen, but her gaze kept slipping to Arizona. He was tall and powerful as he stood in front of everyone. There was an ease about him. He was the kind of man you could talk to and instinctively trust.

It took her a few minutes to realize that she was the center of some attention and speculation. She heard her name mentioned and when she turned in that direction, the woman who had been speaking blushed and looked away.

Chloe sucked in a breath. People had noticed Arizona with her. Of course. How could they not? He'd been at her side since she'd arrived. They were talking about them. She could *feel* it.

Arizona started to speak. He thanked the crowd for attending and soon had them laughing at one of his stories. Chloe watched him with a combination of trepidation and pride. He was going to come back to her when he was done up there. He'd as much as told her and she believed him. He might have a woman in every city around the world, but for tonight, he would be with her.

He did return, and as he did, the band started playing. He swept her into his arms without asking. She didn't mind. Where else was there to be?

They moved together easily, like an old married couple dancing to a familiar song. There were others on the floor, but she felt as if they were alone. Still, when they circled around, she caught interested stares and heard murmurs of speculation. One woman glared at her in obvious outrage. She wasn't sure if she should be irritated by the other woman's anger or flattered.

"What are you thinking?" he asked.

She wore pumps with two-inch heels. Even so she had

to tilt her head to meet his gaze. "That I've never been out with the most popular boy in school before. Some of the cheerleaders are a little cranky."

"I don't believe you didn't date the football captain."

She liked the feel of him next to her. His body was strong and warm. It was also exactly as she remembered it from her dream, but she didn't want to think about that.

"You should," she told him. "I wasn't very popular in high school. I was too tall and too skinny. These things—" she glanced down at her modest breasts "—didn't bother making an appearance until nearly eleventh grade. I didn't think I was ever going to get breasts. Big eyes, big lips, too much hair. I've sort of grown into my looks. But it's a recent thing."

"You've done a fine job."

"Well, thank you, sir. What about you? How does it feel to be the archaeological equivalent of a rock star?"

She thought he might pretend to misunderstand the question, or give her a teasing response. Instead, he looked slightly uncomfortable and asked, "Do you really want to know?"

"Yeah, I do." Even though she found it hard to concentrate, what with them being so close and all. If she closed her eyes, she found herself mentally drifting back to that night in the cave when they'd made love. If she kept her eyes open, she got lost in his dark gaze and never wanted to surface again. It was a tough choice.

He solved her dilemma by wrapping his arm more tightly around her waist and drawing her closer. His cheek rested against her temple.

"Women have always been available," he said. "I don't claim to understand what combination of genes and luck make that true. It started when I was about thirteen and it hasn't let up yet. When I was younger, in my teens and early twenties, I took advantage of that fact.''

He pulled back enough for her to see his face. His expression was earnest. ''I was smart enough to be careful, so no one got pregnant and I hope no one got hurt. But it wasn't my finest hour. Fortunately, it got old very quickly. I learned it was more fun when I got to know the lady in question and took the time to develop a relationship to her.''

He pulled her against him again. She liked being close. For reasons she couldn't explain, being with him made her feel safe.

''A wise old woman, and I do mean that, helped me see the light. She was a shaman and had to be close to a hundred years old. Anyway, this wise old woman once told me that every time people make love, they give away a piece of their soul. If one makes love with the same person again and again, eventually they exchange souls and that is what was intended for married couples. But if one makes love with many people, one will find oneself with nothing left to give to the one who matters. Worse, we end up with no soul of our own.''

''I hadn't thought of it that way, but the theory has merit,'' she said.

''I agree. *Now.* At the time I was all of eighteen, and if I remember correctly, all I could think about was getting her great-granddaughter into bed, so I wasn't the most appreciative audience.''

The music stopped. They broke apart and applauded. ''Let's go get some fresh air,'' Arizona said.

She allowed him to lead her to the open patio at the far end of the room.

The night air was clear and balmy. She reminded herself she was working and should be trying to get a story from him. But she couldn't think about anything but the man standing next to her. There was something about him—something that called to her. If she was the kind of woman who believed in destiny, she would be willing to admit he was the one for her. But she wasn't and he wasn't. Still, he was a very good time.

"You're beautiful," he said, leaning against the railing and drawing her against him.

She supposed she could have resisted, but she didn't want to. She wanted to be next to him, to feel his arms around her again. It was almost like dancing, but they were alone in the shadows and the only music came from inside her head.

His face was so familiar, she thought. It was as if she'd known him forever. Had they really made love or had it just been a dream? Did he own a piece of her soul?

"What are you thinking?" he asked. "Sometimes you look at me and you get the strangest expression on your face. I always wonder if I have spinach in my teeth."

"It's nothing," she said quickly. There was no way she could tell him she'd been thinking about that dream. He would want to know the details. He was already intrigued by the story of the Bradley family nightgown and the legend. She didn't dare think what he would make of her story.

"It has to be something," he insisted. His expression turned teasing. "I have ways of making you talk."

"Some spell or curse?"

"Nothing that drastic."

He tilted his head toward her. Instinctively she raised hers. This was not professional, she reminded herself, then she decided she didn't care. They'd been heading toward this moment since they met. She wanted to kiss him. She *needed* to kiss him. She had to know if it was the same as she remembered.

His mouth brushed against hers. They weren't standing all that close. His hands rested on her waist, hers were on his forearms. For a second—as her body registered the sensations of his heat, the firm softness of his mouth—she couldn't do anything more than absorb what was happening.

Then she felt it. The absolute electrical jolt that shot through her. It was hotter and brighter than lightning. It was recognition and need and passion and color, as if every part of her being responded to this man. Even more terrifying, it was familiar.

She knew what he was going to do even before he parted his lips. She knew the taste and feel of him. She knew how his hands would slide up her back, how she would step into his embrace, how their bodies would fit together. The knowledge only increased her desire. She wanted him because being with him was so incredibly perfect, she thought as his tongue slipped into her mouth.

Her breasts swelled, that secret place between her legs dampened. She felt his hardness press against her hipbone. They breathed in sync. She tilted her head one way, he moved the opposite, so they could deepen the contact. Reunited lovers kissing for the first time.

It was better than she remembered, she thought, then wondered how she could remember kissing a man she'd never kissed before. The dream didn't count. It wasn't real. Then she stopped thinking because her brain shut down. She could only feel him next to her, holding her, touching her. Their bodies fit perfectly together. She wrapped her arms around him and buried her fingers in his cool, soft hair. His shoulders were broad, as was his chest. Every part of him had been put together with her pleasure and enjoyment in mind…or so it seemed.

Tongues circled and danced and mated. She wanted more

from him. She wanted to feel him inside of her; she wanted him to claim her and mark her in the most primitive, primal way of all.

At last, he drew back slightly, breaking the kiss. His breathing was as labored as hers. He rested his forehead against hers and exhaled.

"Pretty amazing," he said, his voice low and husky. "Even better than I thought, and I thought it would be great."

"Me, too."

He tucked a loose curl behind her ear, then brushed his thumb against her cheek. His eyes were bright with passion. She could feel the need radiating from him. Faint tremors rippled through his hands.

"Chloe, I—"

He lowered his head and she knew he was going to kiss her again. She also knew that this time they might not stop at kissing.

"There you two are. We've been looking everywhere. Isn't the ballroom lovely? They always do such a great job with the decorations."

Cassie's voice cut through the quiet of the night. Instantly, they stepped apart. Chloe touched a finger to her mouth and wondered if her lips were swollen.

"Hi," she managed, hoping that her expression wouldn't give her away. The last thing she needed was Cassie's knowing glances, or getting the third degree when they were both home later.

Cassie gave her sister a quick smile and turned to Arizona. "I wanted Joel to meet you." She looked at her boyfriend. "Joel, this is Arizona Smith."

The two men shook hands. While Arizona looked elegant in his tailored tux, Joel was obviously ill at ease in his too-small navy suit. He had the disgruntled air of a man who would rather be home watching a movie on cable.

Chloe suppressed a sigh. Joel was perfectly decent. A pleasant enough man, with short blond hair and pale blue eyes.

"Did you catch the Giants' score?" Arizona asked. "When I left my room, they were ahead three to two."

Joel's sullen expression eased. "Dodgers tied it up in the eighth, but that was when we got here and had to park the car. I don't know what it is now."

"I'm sure they have a television in the bar," Arizona offered.

"Great." Joel turned his attention to Cassie. "Would you mind if we checked?"

"Of course not." She gave a little wave, then took Joel's hand. "We'll see you later."

"Save me a dance," Arizona called after her.

Cassie giggled.

Chloe watched her go. "It's only the beginning of the baseball season and already he would rather watch a game than anything. What on earth does she see in him?" She leaned against the railing, then straightened abruptly. "Wait a minute. How did you know Joel was interested in sports?"

Arizona shrugged. "Many men are and he looks like the type. I wasn't trying to get rid of him, but I figured if he watched the last inning, he wouldn't sulk when Cassie wanted to dance."

"Good thinking. I wish…" Her voice trailed off.

"That he were a different kind of man?"

"Exactly. She deserves better."

"But he's the one she wants."

"Is he?" Chloe wasn't so sure. "He's the only man she's ever dated. How is she supposed to know what she wants? She should get out there and experience life. She deserves someone who will love her and cherish her. Someone intelligent. Not Joel.'' She rubbed her temple. ''It's an old argument and one I've never won. After all, it's her life.''

''You and Cassie are very close.''

It wasn't a question.

''We always have been.''

''It's none of my business, but why are you so angry at your aunt Charity?''

She couldn't have been more shocked if he'd suddenly grown horns. Her first instinct was to ask him how he figured it out. Her second was to tell him to mind his own business. Her third was to wonder if she was that obvious.

''I don't know,'' she said at last, glad the shadows on the patio would hide her face. She didn't want him to know what she was thinking. She did know why she was angry with her aunt, but she wasn't ready to deal with it. She might never be ready.

''Want to talk about it?''

His perceptions suddenly annoyed her. How did he always know what she was thinking? How dare he always know the right thing to say or do! ''Only if you want to talk about why, if your father is still alive, your grandfather raised you.''

''Touché,'' he said. ''I'm sorry. I should learn to leave tender ground alone. I'm sorry.''

She ducked her head. ''No, I'm being snippy. I'm the one who should apologize.''

''Okay.''

She looked up at him.

He grinned. ''I'm waiting,'' he told her.

''I apologize.''

''That's it? That's all you're willing to say? No declaration of your unworthiness? Of how gracious I am to put up with you? Nothing about—''

She lightly slapped his arm. "Stop it."

He stepped back in mock alarm. "Violence. I don't know what to say. I'd been about to suggest we find a quiet room somewhere and make wild passionate love together, but now I'm not sure I can trust you not to take physical advantage of my person. I guess we're just going to have to dance, instead."

She didn't know whether to laugh, agree to the love-making, or slap him again. "You make me crazy."

"That was the plan all along, Chloe."

"I figured as much."

He held out his hand and she took it. Then she followed him back into the main room to have that dance.

Chapter Six

"Oh, my goodness, the man has a fan club!" Cassie said as she pointed at the computer screen.

Sure enough, an Internet search on Arizona's name had unearthed an assortment of references, including a link to a fan club.

"We have to check this out." Chloe clicked the arrow on that entry. She was at her home computer, continuing her research on Arizona, which she was starting to think was just a way of avoiding starting the actual writing. Once she figured out the first sentence of the article, she knew the rest of it would come fairly easily. But so far she was in the dark about her beginning.

Cassie pulled up a chair and sat down next to her. "I can't believe it. I've never known anyone with a fan club before." She laughed and touched her sister's arm. "We could write him a letter. You could talk about how great he dances. Maybe you could talk about the other stuff, too.''

Chloe glanced at her sharply. ''What other stuff?''

Cassie puckered up her lips and made kissing noises. ''I saw what you two were doing out there on the patio last night. I figured we had better come interrupt before things got too hot and heavy. There wasn't a whole lot of privacy.''

''Nothing happened. It was just a kiss.'' She flinched, half-waiting for lightning to strike her down. It had been a whole lot more than the kiss—which was part of the problem. It should have been pleasant or even very nice. Instead it had burned her down to her soul. She wasn't even sure if she was relieved or disappointed that he hadn't followed up that first kiss with a second. Once they'd gone back inside to the reception, Arizona had been swept away by interested guests and Chloe had finally left alone around midnight.

''It looked like some major passion to me,'' Cassie said, and leaned her elbows on the desk. ''I wish Joel would kiss me like that.''

''Doesn't he?''

Cassie shook her head. ''Joel and I have a very comfortable relationship.''

''Comfortable is okay for year thirty of marriage, but you guys are still dating.''

''I know.'' Cassie shrugged. ''I don't want to talk about it.'' She pointed at the computer screen. ''Look.''

The computer had located the web site for Arizona's fan club. There were photos of him, a bulletin board on which to leave messages, letters to Arizona and a map showing all the places he's visited.

''Imagine how much money we'd make if we could get

a picture of him naked,'' Cassie said thoughtfully. ''We could sell copies. What do you think?''

Chloe laughed. ''I think he would probably want to be cut in on the profits. Are you going to be the one to ask him?''

''It might go better if you did that.''

Chloe ignored her. She clicked on various pages of the web site and made notes. ''These people need to get lives.''

''It's romantic. He's a very exciting man. You know, you should post your article here when you finish it. I'm sure they'd really like it.'' She sighed. ''He's just so great. Gracious and funny. I really like him. I think you do, too. Wouldn't you like to travel around the world with him? He's just—'' She clapped her hands together. ''He's exactly the kind of man I want to dream about when I wear the family nightgown. Don't you agree?''

Chloe felt a surge of irritation. She was having enough trouble controlling her raging desires without her sister throwing logs on the fire. ''Number one, you're supposed to be engaged to Joel. Number two, I actually have work to do and that would be a lot easier without your editorial comments.''

Cassie stared at her for a second, nodded, then rose to her feet. ''Sorry. I leave you to your research.'' She walked out of the room without looking back.

Chloe returned her attention to the web site, then groaned. She was turning into a witch.

With a couple of clicks, she logged off the Internet and returned to her word-processing program. After saving her work in progress, she rose to her feet and headed down the hall. Cassie's bedroom door was open. Her sister was curled up on the bed reading a book.

Chloe watched her. She didn't know exactly what to say. At this point, she wasn't willing to risk the truth. She didn't want to admit that part of her problem was that she *had* dreamed about Arizona, and it was making her insane.

"I'm sorry," she said at last. "I had no reason to snap at you. I have a lot on my mind and I'm just not myself."

Cassie looked up. "I know. This article is very important to you. It's your ticket out."

Chloe entered the large room with pale pink walls and a lacy bedspread on the full-size mattress. "I wouldn't go that far."

Cassie patted the bed, indicating that her sister should have a seat. "It's true. Come on, Chloe, it's time for you to leave. It's what you've always wanted. Sometimes I think you've stayed because of me, but I'm practically your age and I've been all grown-up for a long time. Aunt Charity and I will be fine without you. Of course we'll miss you, but it's time for you to move on. We can take care of the house until you're ready to come back."

Chloe reached out and squeezed her sister's hand. "You're way too nice a person. Why do you put up with me?"

"Beats me."

Chloe smiled. Then her humor faded as the familiar guilt took its place. She knew that Cassie would take care of the house for her. Cassie wouldn't think twice about it, but she, Chloe, was annoyed that it was an issue. Their parents had been wrong, she thought, as she had dozens of times in the past. They should have left everything to the girls equally. Instead Chloe had inherited the house and a small trust fund. Cassie had inherited a large trust fund—equal in value to Chloe's inheritance—but not equal in spirit. The message had been clear. Their only blood heir had received the family home.

Chloe knew that Cassie put on a brave face; she never said anything. But Cassie was the real traditional one in the family. She was the one who believed in the legend—she was the one who loved the house. It should have been hers. She also knew that on some level Cassie had been hurt by the will. But Chloe didn't know how to talk to her about it.

There was a knock on the open door.

"Chloe, there's a call for you," Charity told her. "It's Arizona."

Cassie made kissing noises again. Chloe rose to her feet. "I'm ignoring you," she said as she crossed to her sister's desk and picked up the extension. "Hello?"

"Chloe, it's Arizona. I hope I'm not interrupting."

"Not at all." If the nerves soft-shoeing inside her stomach were anything to go by, she was very happy to hear from him.

"Something's come up. I've been doing some research about a lost tribe up in the Pacific Northwest. I just got a call from some friends of mine working up there. They've found something I need to take a look at. The lecture series doesn't start for a few days and I don't have much holding me here, so I thought I would go and see what they've found."

"I see."

He was leaving. She'd always known that he would—it was the nature of the man. But she hadn't expected it to be so soon. The nerves in her stomach fizzled into a cold knot of disappointment.

"I'll work on the article while you're gone and save any questions I have until you get back," she told him, hoping she sounded calmly professional.

"That's one scenario," he agreed. "However, I thought it might be interesting for you to come along. You could observe what I do firsthand."

She wanted to jump up and down shrieking "Yes, yes,

oh yes!'' at the top of her lungs. Instead she drew in a deep breath. ''An interesting idea.''

He was probably coming on to her, a voice in her head said. As lines went, it was a good one, but still a line.

''I hope you don't think I've made this up simply to get you alone in the wilderness. Actually I'm just not that creative, otherwise I would have. But the artifact is legitimate. I can give you a number to call to check it out.''

He could read her mind. Why was she not surprised?

Of course she wanted to go. Desperately. She wanted to spend as much time with Arizona as possible and she refused to question her motives. ''I'll need to run this past my editor,'' she said. ''Can I call you first thing in the morning?''

''Sure. I'll be hoping for a yes.''

Me, too, she thought. ''I'll be touch. Bye.''

When she hung up the phone, Cassie was dancing from foot to foot. ''You're going away with him. This is *so* cool. You'll be in wilderness. It'll be romantic. Maybe you'll see him naked and we can get that picture for his fan club!''

Chloe's heart was pounding and she wanted to jump up and down like her sister. Instead she shrugged. ''It would be okay to go. I think it will add some dimension to my article.''

''Article-smarticle. I'm talking about adding some dimension to your life! Chloe and Arizona sittin' in a tree. K-I-S-S-I-N-G.''

''I'm ignoring you,'' Chloe said as she walked out of the room.

''Confess,'' Cassie called after her. ''You *want* to see the man naked.''

''I'm sure he's not that impressive.''

''Liar!''

But Chloe didn't know if the accusation came from her

sister or her conscience. After all, she *had* seen Arizona without his clothes, and it had worked for her in a big way.

"I'm not sure what he's going to look at," Chloe continued nervously. "But I think seeing an archaeological dig and watching him work will add depth to the story."

Jerry didn't even look up from the papers he was reading. Her editor made a grunting noise low in his throat. She wasn't sure what that meant.

"So you want me to go?" she asked.

Finally, he spared her a quick glance. "Yes, I want you to go. Keep track of expenses. The magazine will reimburse you for the reasonable stuff. Don't go ordering any expensive wine with dinner. Don't sit in poison ivy."

"I think I can handle that."

"Good." His gaze narrowed. "How's the guy? Is the piece gonna be decent?"

She thought about telling Jerry all she'd learned about Arizona, about the fan club on the Internet, the inherent charm, the way he actually believed in magic. But she didn't think her boss really cared about the details. He would find all that out when he read the article.

"It's going to be great," she told him.

"Better be." He grimaced. "Nancy said you were on the right track and I trust her. Not that I should. Pregnant. Do you know she actually expects time off after the kid is born? I asked her what for. She says she wants to breastfeed. Can you believe it? Like a bottle's not good enough. What is it with women today?" He shook his head in disgust and glared at her. "Don't you have a story to write? Packing maybe? Get out of here."

"Yes, Jerry." Despite herself, Chloe grinned. Jerry acted so tough all the time, but he would be the first one at the hospital after Nancy gave birth. He would be cooing like everyone else over the newborn.

She made her way back to her desk. She had her permission. She was really going away with Arizona. Out into the wilderness, where anything could happen.

Chloe stared at the clothes folded neatly on top of her bed. "I don't know what to take," she admitted. "I've never been camping."

Cassie sat in the chair by the desk and smiled. "You'll do fine. Take jeans and underwear. Shirts and sweaters. You'll want to layer if it gets cold, but you won't want anything bulky."

"Arizona says we'll have to hike in the last part, so I have to carry everything with me."

Cassie leaned forward, picked up the blow-dryer and waved it in the air. "In that case, I'd leave this behind. It's big, heavy and you're not going to have electricity."

"I know. I just thought—" She shuddered. "I don't know what I was thinking. It was a hideous mistake to agree to this. I'm completely out of my element."

"You'll be fine. Arizona will keep you safe."

Chloe didn't know whether to laugh or scream. What her sister didn't understand was that Arizona was part of what she was afraid of. But she couldn't say that to Cassie without going into detail. And how was she supposed to tell her sister that she had indeed had a dream the night of her twenty-fifth birthday and that the man in her dream had been someone she'd met the very next day? How was she supposed to confess that every time she was near him her body went up in flames, and that all the time they were apart, he was all she could think of?

Besides, not all of her fears were about Arizona. Some of them were about herself. She didn't know what was wrong with her. She felt herself changing. Nothing was as it should be. She wanted… Chloe sighed. That was the problem. She didn't know what she wanted.

Cassie stood up and walked to the bed. She opened Chloe's cosmetic bag and dumped the contents.

"Toothbrush and toothpaste," she said. She rummaged through the rest of the items, then eyed her sister's long hair. She picked up a wide-toothed comb and a cloth-covered rubber band. "Don't worry about makeup." She fingered a tube of sunscreen. "This has moisture in it." She added a tiny bottle of shampoo to the small pile. "Arizona will bring soap, I'm sure. Use his."

Chloe stared at the half-dozen items. "How do you know this stuff?"

"I work with preschoolers. If nothing else, I've learned to improvise." She pointed to the piles of clothing. "Want me to do the same on that?"

"Please."

As Chloe watched, her sister sorted through jeans, shirts and sweaters. She picked up a waterproof windbreaker, a thin, high-tech fabric pullover guaranteed to keep Chloe warm, two flannel shirts, a spare pair of jeans and underwear.

"Take extra socks," Cassie told her. "Your feet might get wet."

"That's it?" Chloe asked.

"It is if you really have to carry it on your back. I know this from personal experience. I've baby-sat too many kids who didn't want me to bring the stroller. I told myself it was just a quick trip to the mall and that they didn't weigh all that much. After about five minutes I learned they got heavy very quickly, and I always regretted my decision."

"I'll take your word for it," Chloe said. "You're obviously the expert."

"I might have some shampoo samples," Cassie said. "You know those little flat packages? Let me check, because they would be lighter than this bottle. I'll be right back."

After she'd left, Chloe looked at the small pile of clothing and wondered what on earth she was getting into. Would she and Arizona be alone for any part of their trip? That thought both terrified and excited her. She didn't know what was going to happen.

Nerves fluttered in her stomach. Actually, that wasn't true. If they were alone together for any length of time, she knew *exactly* what was going to happen between them. Was she ready for that?

She wasn't sure. She thought about her sister and wished she could tell her what was really going on. She would like someone else's opinion on her best course of action. Unfortunately, Cassie was a classic romantic and would only see the potential for love, not the probability of heartache. Chloe might firmly believe that love wasn't for her, but that didn't mean her emotions couldn't be engaged under the right circumstances. So far, Arizona had everything going for him.

She thought about having a few words with Aunt Charity. No, Chloe told herself. That would never work. She couldn't confide in the older woman. Arizona had been accurate and perceptive when he'd picked up the fact that there was trouble in the house. Chloe didn't trust her aunt. Maybe it was childish, but she'd never forgiven her for not being there.

Chloe walked to the window and gazed out at the lawn. There had been a time in her life when she'd·wondered if she would ever see this perfect view again. She reached up and fingered the locket hanging around her neck. Her thoughts drifted back to that horrible time when she and

Cassie had lost their parents in a car accident. One minute everything had been fine, the next they were alone in the world. They'd clung to each other until the courts, unable to find their legal guardian, had split them up and sent them to different foster homes.

Three years, Chloe thought grimly. The family lawyer had looked for three years until he'd finally found Aunt Charity, their father's sister. As soon as she'd been told what had happened, she'd flown back to America and had brought the girls home. Cassie had been grateful, but for Chloe the rescue had come too late. She'd been all of two months from her eighteenth birthday when she could have returned home on her own.

Chloe knew that logically it hadn't been Aunt Charity's fault that she'd been traveling the world. No one expected her to sit at home in case her brother died unexpectedly. But logic hadn't helped Chloe get through those years apart from Cassie and away from the only home she'd ever known. So even though she desperately wanted someone to talk to, she wasn't about to confess all to her aunt.

So she was going to have to be a grown-up and take care of herself. That or she was going to have to accept the consequences of her actions.

"I knew I had them," Cassie said, walking back in the room. She held out a handful of cosmetic samples. "I found a couple that are face cleaners as well as two shampoo packs, so take them all."

"Thanks. I really appreciate the help. I would have packed all wrong without you."

"No problem."

Chloe looked at her sister. Cassie had a very innocent expression on her face. She stood with her left hand tucked behind her back.

"What have you got there?"

"Nothing."

"Don't give me that. What is it?"

Cassie grinned wickedly. "Well, it won't take up much room in your backpack and it will certainly give you two something to talk about over roasting marshmallows."

She pulled her hand free. A condom rested on her open palm.

Chloe felt color flare on her cheeks. "I didn't know that you and Joel had been intimate."

"Oh, we haven't been," Cassie said easily. "But I do like to be prepared in case we ever decide we're ready. So, do you think one is enough for you and Arizona, or do you want to pack the whole box?"

Chloe stared at the protection and didn't know what to say. It was absurd to assume she and Arizona would become lovers. They hadn't known each other that long. But like her sister, she had been raised to be prepared.

"Nothing's going to happen," she told her sister firmly, even as she took the condom and stuck it in her small cosmetic bag.

Cassie grinned. "If you're very lucky, you just might prove yourself wrong!"

Chapter Seven

"You ready?" Arizona asked.

Chloe glanced back at the four-wheel-drive Explorer heading down the mountain. Then she looked at him. Her expression was two parts apprehension, one part honest-to-God fear.

But she didn't answer him right away. Instead she squared her shoulders, then adjusted her backpack, raised her chin and smiled. "Sure. This is going to be fun."

"Liar," he told her.

Her smile broadened. "Okay, maybe I'm exaggerating. I confess, I do wish there was another way into the site or the dig, or whatever you call it, but I'll survive. I appreciate the opportunity to see what you actually do with your day." She paused. "Also, we'll be able to continue our interview while we're hiking. At least until I'm so out of breath I can't ask questions. But your lecture series starts in three days. Will we be back in time?"

''That's not a problem,'' Arizona told her while he ignored the flicker of guilt. There *was* an easier way into the valley, but he wanted them to hike in. There was something going on between them—something he'd never experienced before—and he wanted time to explore that. His visit to Bradley was limited already. There were so many drains on his time.

If he were going to be completely rational, he knew there was no point in pursuing whatever attraction might flare between them. There was no way to make a relationship work. He'd sworn off casual affairs and even if he hadn't, Chloe didn't strike him as the type to give herself easily. Logic dictated that he should just answer her questions and ignore the rest of it. However, he'd never been one for logic. The unexplained caught his attention time after time. He wanted to know the whys. He couldn't pass up a good mystery. In this case, there was something between him and Chloe and he was determined to find out what. These couple days alone might be his only chance.

She pulled a small tape recorder out of her jeans pocket. ''I'm ready if you are,'' she said.

''Then let's go.''

He checked the placement of the sun and figured they had about six hours of daylight. Chloe wouldn't be able to hike much more than that anyway. Not that she wasn't in great shape. But she wasn't conditioned for long hours on the trail.

There had been a surprisingly long stretch of relatively dry weather, so the ground was only damp underfoot. Towering trees lined the trail. The low-lying plants were bright green. Wildflowers and berry bushes were in full bloom. The air smelled clean and crisp. It was a perfect afternoon.

He started walking nearly due east.

''Where are we going?'' Chloe asked as she kept pace

with him. At this point the trail was wide enough for them to walk side by side.

"There's a valley on the other side of this low range," he said, pointing ahead. "We'll reach the top of the rise tonight. That will be where we camp. Tomorrow we'll head into the valley. The site is there. Just curious—was that information for you or the article?"

Her brown eyes twinkled. "Both. I have so many questions, I'm not sure where to start."

"Does it matter?"

"I suppose not." One corner of her mouth turned up slightly. "So, Arizona Smith, why don't you wear a hat?"

Involuntarily, he reached up and touched his bare head. "I don't need one here. There's no need to protect myself from the sun."

"I see. I thought all bush types wore hats. They do in the movies." Her voice was teasing.

He shook his head. "That's part of my problem. I wore one nearly all the time. Before." He grimaced. "That movie. It changed everything. After that my lecture series became more popular. I appreciated that, but I hated the billing. A few places advertised me as a 'real-life Indiana Jones.'"

"Did your audiences expect you to show up with a bull-whip?"

"You'd be surprised." He thought about the women who would come to his lectures and sit in the front row. Their adoring gazes had nothing to do with him—who he really was. They were only interested in the persona.

Not like Chloe. He glanced at her. Her stride was long, her posture straight. She was gorgeous. Today she wore her curly red hair pulled back in a braid. She was tall and lean and he wished they were lovers so that he could suggest they stop for an hour or so and make love right here…out in the open.

"Do you have anything in common with Indiana Jones?" she asked.

"Sure. We're both men. His finds are more spectacular. How can anyone compete with the Ark of the Covenant or the Holy Grail? I think I had better luck with women. We're both teachers, although none of my students have ever fallen for me."

"I doubt that," she said. "I would guess more than three-quarters of your students are female and almost none of them are there because they need the class for their major."

He opened his mouth to protest, then realized she was right. His classes *were* predominantly female. "None of them have come on to me." He held up a hand before she could protest again. "Trust me, I would have noticed that."

"I'm sure they were working up to it."

"I hope not. They're a little young."

"You're not all that old."

"Old enough."

Old enough to know what he wanted, he thought. It wasn't just that Chloe was pretty. His attraction to her was as much about the way she made him laugh and her intelligence as it was about her body.

"I assume you know you have a fan club on the Internet," she said.

He groaned. "I might have known you would find that."

"You're not proud?" she teased.

"Of course not. It's humiliating. These people—"

"Women," she interrupted. "They're women, Arizona. I checked the membership directory. We're talking at least ninety-five percent women."

"Great. Men, women, Martians, it doesn't matter. I still

don't get it. I'm not brilliant, I'm tenacious. I've studied and I've had some luck. Yes, I've made a few finds, but I'm not going to change the world. I don't know what they see in me."

"Don't you?" Chloe stopped and looked at him. "I can't tell if you're serious or if you're fishing."

"I'm not unaware that some people find me physically attractive," he said formally, wondering if it was possible to sound like more of a jerk than he did.

"Good to know," she said solemnly.

"You're teasing me."

"A little. This is the first time you've ever been pompous."

Pompous? Was that how she saw him? Perfect. He'd sure done a great job charming her. Talk about a crash and burn.

She touched his arm. The light contact seared him all the way down to his knees. His groin ignited. The wanting was as powerful as it was instantaneous.

"I do understand what you're saying," she said and dropped her hand to her side. "Who do you consider a hero?"

"Easy question. Joseph Campbell. He wrote several books, but the best known is *The Hero of a Thousand Faces*. He explored the idea that storytelling is universal to the human condition. All races and cultures have stories about the beginning of the world, the creation of man, stories that tell how boys become men. I was very young when I first read his work. He's the one who got me interested in the mystic."

"I'm not discounting his place," Chloe said. "But what about the things you've found? All those treasures might have stayed hidden for generations."

"Granted, but while I've brought some tangible artifacts to light, he explained why we have the dreams we do. I've visited my fan club web site. It's very flattering, but I'm not the hero in that. They've created a myth about someone who doesn't really exist. In my mind, Joseph Campbell is someone who truly is a hero. His ideas changed lives. I know he changed mine.''

He motioned for her to continue walking, then fell into step with her. The air was cool, but the sun warmed them.

''There is a certain amount of fame that comes with some of my discoveries. It's my least favorite part of what I do. I get through it by reminding myself it's fleeting. In a couple of weeks no one will care who I am until the next discovery.''

''That sounds cynical, although realistic. Would you rather the world ignored your finds?''

''Good question. The answer is no. I want them to understand and appreciate. I know enough to realize I can't have one without the other.''

She looked at him. ''Why do I suddenly suspect you like it much better in the bush where no one knows who you are and you're treated like just another visitor?''

''You'd be right. I've traveled all over the world. My best memories are of people I've connected with, not of standing behind a podium talking to a cheering crowd.''

''So do the women ever throw you their panties?''

He tugged on the end of her braid. ''I'm not the kind to kiss and tell.''

She laughed. ''I'll take that as a no.''

''It's probably best.''

''So have they shown up in your room unexpectedly?''

''Why this sudden interest in my personal life?'' he asked, although he was pleased that she seemed focused on that. He would hate for the attraction to be one-sided.

''Ah, so that was a yes.''

He chuckled. ''Yes, once or twice.''

"How was it?"

He thought back. "The first time was in a small village on an island in the South Pacific. I was all of eighteen and the woman was at least thirty. Her husband had died and she was about to remarry someone much older. I think I was her last fling."

"And?"

"And what? I was a kid. I had no concept of quality, so I made it up in volume. She taught me they weren't interchangeable."

"I see. And the second time it happened?"

He drew in a deep breath. "I was on a lecture tour in Europe a couple of years ago. There was a particular young woman who developed a crush on me. I didn't encourage her at all, in fact I barely knew who she was. One night I came in late and found her waiting for me in my bed."

Chloe's eyes widened. "What did you do?"

"I explained that I was flattered, but not interested. When she wouldn't leave, I got another room for the night, then in the morning, I changed hotels."

Chloe burst out laughing. "The most trouble I've ever had with the opposite sex is when old man Withers, the seventy-year-old misogynist who takes care of the grounds of the house, calls me a ninny. He calls all women ninnies."

"Are you going to put that in the article?" he asked. He hadn't requested that any part of their conversation be off the record. Perhaps he should have. When he was around Chloe he thought of her as a woman first and someone he would like to get to know second. He rarely remembered she was a journalist.

"I'm not out to make you the bad guy," she said. "I want to show a different side of you and connect that with your work. Neither my editor nor I is interested in a hatchet job."

"I appreciate that."

"I find it interesting you're asking me this after the fact. Isn't that dangerous?"

"Yes."

"You're not concerned?"

"You've just explained that I shouldn't be."

They were still walking side by side. Their hands brushed. Without thinking, Arizona laced his fingers with hers. Chloe stumbled a step, but didn't pull away.

"But how do you know you can trust me?" she asked.

Was it his imagination or was her voice a little breathless? He wanted to know that she was reacting to him the same way he reacted to her. He wanted to know that she felt it, whatever the *it* was, too.

"Gut instinct," he said. "I've met a lot of people in my life and I've learned how to read them."

Her hand was small but strong. He liked the feel of her next to him like this, walking together on the trail. He found himself eager to show her the site, to explain his world to her. He wanted her to enjoy their time together, to be impressed by him, to think he was nearly as exciting as his image.

"Is there anywhere on this planet you haven't been?" she asked.

"If you're talking continents, I haven't been to Antarctica. Otherwise, I would guess I've hit most of the major points."

"Why am I not surprised?" She gave him a quick, sideways glance. "You can be a little intimidating," she admitted. "I've interviewed fairly powerful people in the past. Government officials, celebrities. You're the first one who has made me feel like the country mouse come to town for a visit.''

He leaned close. ''You don't look anything like a country mouse. In fact, there's nothing rodent-like about you at all.''

''Gee, thanks.''

Gently, reluctantly, he thought, although that could just be wishful thinking on his part, she pulled her hand away from his. ''Back to business,'' she told him. ''I have a lot more questions.''

''Ask away.''

''About your travels. From what I've been reading, most of them were financed privately. You don't work with a particular foundation or for a university.''

''That's true. There's a rather impressive family trust fund that has paid my expenses. I've had opportunities to work for charitable organizations, helping them raise funds. I do that frequently. When I do guest lecture series I tend to donate my fees to the local children's hospital and women's shelters. I've done specific tours for museums, and then they keep the proceeds.''

''You don't keep any for yourself?''

''I don't have to.'' At her look of confusion, he shrugged. ''My family has a lot of money. I don't need more so why wouldn't I give some of it away?'' He replayed his last couple of comments in his mind and frowned. ''I'm not some do-gooder,'' he said. ''I was taught it was my place to give back. But don't make me out to be a saint. I'm very much a man with as many flaws as the next guy.''

''I see.''

Her words didn't give anything away, and he couldn't tell what she was thinking. He almost didn't want to know. Better to imagine she was thinking about being with him, touching him, holding him close. Because that was what he wanted her thinking. He wasn't willing to explore the realization that it was much easier to deal with Chloe wanting him than her actually liking him.

They stopped around one o'clock to take a break. Chloe let her backpack fall to the ground, then rotated her shoulders.

"Cassie warned me it was going to get heavier as we walked, but I didn't believe her. I see now I was wrong."

"Sore?" Arizona asked.

"I'll survive."

She watched him release his pack as if it weighed nothing. It had to be twice the size of hers, but then he was not only male and stronger, but used to this sort of thing.

The afternoon was warm, but not too hot. She eyed the clear sky. "I thought the Pacific Northwest was known for rain."

"It is. Looks like we're going to get lucky." He hesitated just long enough for her breath to catch. "With the weather."

"Of course," she murmured. With the weather. What else? Certainly not with each other. It wasn't her fault that she found the man wildly attractive. The more she got to know him, the worse it got. It wasn't enough that he was good-looking. No, he had to be smart, funny and kind as well. She was going to have to be very careful when she wrote her article, or she was going to come off like some teenager with a major crush.

"Ready for lunch?" he asked.

He sat on a fallen log and reached for his backpack. Chloe settled next to him. She had two canteens hanging from her pack. They'd stopped at a rapidly flowing stream about a half hour before and refilled their water supply.

"Here you go." He handed her two protein bars, a small plastic bag filled with what looked like cut-up dried vegetables and fruit, and an apple.

"Goody, five-star cuisine," she said as she eyed what was supposed to pass for a meal.

"Don't wrinkle your nose at me, young lady. There are plenty of vitamins and minerals there, along with enough calories for energy."

"I didn't say anything."

"You didn't have to."

Usually she was more difficult to read. Was she so open around him, or could he just see inside of her? "I wasn't complaining. This is different from what I'm used to. I don't have your 'bush' experience. What with how you grew up and all."

"It wasn't like this," he said as he stretched out his long legs in front of him and crossed them at the ankles. Worn jeans hugged his powerful thighs. "My grandfather didn't believe in living with physical discomfort. We always traveled first class."

"There are a lot of places you can't get a jet or a limo."

"True. We used carts and camels, boats, whatever was necessary to get us where he wanted to go. But he arranged for the best. Plenty of staff along to handle the luggage and the details."

Chloe tried to imagine that kind of life. On one hand, it sounded very exciting, but on the other she would miss having a place to call home.

"Did you like living like that?" she asked.

"I suppose every kid dreams of running away to live a life of adventure. I did that and more. I have experienced things most people just read or dream about. But there were things I missed."

He stared into the grove of trees, but she knew he was

actually seeing a past she could only imagine. How had his world and his life shaped him? What would he have been like if he'd grown up as the boy next door?

"I never had my own room, so I didn't collect things the way a lot of kids do," he said. "I didn't have a lot of friends. In some places there weren't boys my age around, or if there were, they were busy with school or helping the family. We moved around so much, I would just get to know someone and then it would be time to leave."

"I hadn't thought of that," she admitted. "It sounds lonely."

"Sometimes it was. I had tutors. They were usually with us for a couple of years at a time, so that was something I could depend on." He shrugged. "Growing up like that is all I know. I can't pass judgment on it without something to compare it to. I don't think it was better or worse, just different. I experienced the world from a different point of view. If we planned to settle in one place for a few months, I usually enrolled in the local school."

He looked at her and grinned. "When I was a teenager I used to complain about not having fast food or high school girls around."

"So despite everything, you were very normal."

"I like to think so." His smile faded. "I always wanted a brother or sister. Someone around my own age to talk to and be with. Grandfather tried, but he wasn't a peer. I envy you and Cassie for being so close."

She couldn't imagine anything in her rather dull life that someone like Arizona would be interested in, but the idea of a sibling made sense.

"She's my best friend," she said. "We're so different, we can't help arguing sometimes, but none of that really matters. We love each other so much."

"It shows." He ripped open the protective covering on

one of his protein bars and took a bite. After chewing he asked, "So how are you different?"

She nibbled the dried vegetables and found they tasted better than they looked. "You have to ask? Cassie is a dreamer. She believes in fairy tales and magic."

"That's right. And you're the completely practical one."

"Exactly. She wants a very traditional life. Husband, children, a home." She stopped talking and pressed her lips together. A home. The house. That beautiful Victorian house that their parents had left to her instead of leaving it to the two girls equally.

They'd probably been afraid the sisters wouldn't be able to work out a way to share. No doubt they'd been trying to prevent the house being sold. But their will had reinforced Cassie's feeling of not truly being a part of the family.

"Is there anything wrong with wanting a traditional life?" Arizona asked.

"No, and it makes sense for her. Cassie just wants to fit in. She wants to have roots."

"Doesn't she now?"

"I don't know that she thinks so." She shrugged. "It's complicated. Cassie—" She automatically reached inside the neck of her T-shirt and pulled out the locket she always wore.

Arizona reached over and touched the heart-shaped piece of jewelry. "Connections with the past," he said. "She has the matching earrings. And her memories. Your parents chose her. Isn't that enough?"

His dark eyes saw too much, she thought. She felt as if he could look deep down into her soul and that made her nervous. Was she enough for him? Sometimes she didn't think she was enough for herself, let alone someone else. But then she was used to being confused. It was becoming a constant in her life. She didn't understand her relationship with Arizona any more than she understood why the man had appeared in her dream. She didn't know what she wanted from him, what she felt about him, or what he expected from her.

She jerked her thoughts back to their conversation. "I have the house," she said. "I wish they'd left it to both of us instead of just me."

"So she would have that connection?" he asked.

She nodded.

He touched the locket again. His knuckle brushed against her throat. A warmth flowed through her, just as it had when he'd taken her hand while they'd been on the trail.

"It's not the house," he said. "It's here." He placed his fingers against her forehead, then moved them lower, to just above her left breast. "And here. No one can take that away from her. Or you."

He wasn't talking about the house anymore, she realized. There was something in his eyes, something dangerous and irresistible. She wanted to lean closer. She wanted him to kiss her. She wanted to feel his arms around her, holding her close, making her safe. With Arizona she felt safe…and that had been missing from her life since her parents had been killed.

But instead of leaning toward him, she straightened, putting distance between them. Who was this man who invaded both her dreams and her life? What did he want from her? And how on earth was she supposed to resist him and his power?

Chapter Eight

Stars filled the night sky. Chloe stretched out on her sleeping bag and stared up at the vast expanse of lights above her head. Bradley wasn't a big town, but it was close enough to Sacramento that the city lights washed out most of the stars, even when the weather didn't interfere. Or maybe her life had gotten so busy, she didn't take time to look at the heavens anymore. She would guess most people suffered the same fate. Now, gazing up and admiring the beauty of the stars, she wondered what other wonders filled what she considered her very ordinary life.

"It's a beautiful night," Arizona said as he stepped back into camp. He dropped onto his sleeping bag only a few feet from her own.

"I was just thinking that," she said and tried to ignore the fact that she was going to have to do as he had done and venture out into the wilderness to do her business.

It was bad enough to have to do that during the day when

she could see whatever was lurking around, but at night—she would be defenseless. She didn't want to act all wimpy and girllike, but she couldn't help picturing herself from a critter's point of view. A pale white expanse of tempting flesh just hanging there, begging to be bitten or scratched or…

Stop thinking about it, she ordered herself silently. But it was one of the few times she envied men their ''equipment'' that let them pee standing up.

''So what did you think of dinner?'' Arizona asked in a tone that warned her he expected a positive response.

''Great,'' she lied cheerfully. ''I had been worried that freeze-dried food would taste gritty and odd when it was mixed with boiling water, but I was wrong.''

Actually, it wasn't a lie. The food at dinner had easily been worse than she'd imagined.

''I liked it, too,'' he said. ''Beats grubs any day.''

She dismissed him with a wave. ''You didn't eat grubs. This afternoon you said your grandfather liked to travel in style. I'm sure he brought along a chef to cook his favorite dishes.''

''You're right.'' His teeth flashed white in the light of the campfire.

''I figured. You thought dinner was pretty gross, didn't you?''

''Wretched comes to mind. I think they forgot to cook the rice before packaging it. Tell you what. When we get back to civilization, I'll take you out for a fancy dinner.''

''You've got yourself a deal.''

Their gazes locked. Despite the few feet between them, she felt his heat. She was in trouble now.

She forced her gaze away and returned her attention to the stars. ''Do you know anything about the constellations?'' she asked, hoping he would go along with the change in subject.

''I do now because I've studied them, but when I was a kid, I would make up stories. Sometimes the village elders would tell me what the different stars represented. I learned that all different cultures have their own view of what the heavens mean. I suppose some of that is because the sky looks different in different places.''

Chloe told herself she should dig out her tape recorder and turn it on. But she didn't want to break the mood. Besides, she wasn't having trouble remembering anything Arizona said to her. She didn't even have to close her eyes to hear his voice in her head.

''The changing stars can tell about the coming seasons. The harvest sky is different from the planting sky.''

He continued talking. She listened to the words and wrapped herself in the stories he wove. He was so different from anyone she'd ever known. And yet the heart of him was familiar to her. Was it the dream? Was it her imagination, trying to create a connection so she could pretend her attraction had some basis in emotion and not just in physical awareness? But it was more, she reminded herself. She didn't just want him...she actually liked him.

There hadn't been many men in her life. Normally she didn't make time for them. She didn't want all the bother of trusting someone only to have him let her down.

''What are you thinking?'' he asked.

She inhaled deeply and smelled the wood smoke from their fire, along with the lush scent of the forest growth. ''That for me, the sky is always constant. The stars might change with the time of year, but I've never seen a different sky. I've just realized that's the perfect metaphor for the differences between us.''

''Is that bad?'' he asked.

"No, it's a fact that we can't change, but I don't think it's a value judgment. We don't have anything in common."

"I would disagree with that."

She turned to face him. In the darkness of the night, his body was little more than murky shadow. "I'm surprised you'd think that."

"Why? We're both intelligent, curious about our world. We both ask questions. We laugh at the same things. We're very much alike."

"I hadn't thought of it like that," she admitted. "I was more focused on our life experiences. For example, the first day of school. I was a very mature five and a half, while Cassie hadn't quite turned five. My mother bought us matching dresses, but in different colors. I've seen the pictures and we were too adorable for words."

Arizona smiled. "I'll bet."

"Bradley Elementary," she continued. "It's built on the site of the original Bradley schoolhouse, founded by my family back in the late 1800s. There's even a plaque by the auditorium. I don't think your first day of school was anything like that."

"You'd be right." He closed his eyes for a minute, then opened them. "I was in Africa and I attended a tribal school. Interesting, but not educational. I didn't speak much of the language. That afternoon my grandfather started making arrangements for me to have tutors."

"That's my point," she said. "Different experiences."

"Even if I'd been living in the States, I don't think I would have been in a matching dress."

She laughed. "Probably not."

He propped his head on his hand. "Tell me about your first kiss."

"Oh my. First kiss. I was fourteen, I think. At a girlfriend's birthday party. Also my first boy-girl party. We were playing Spin the Bottle. His name was Adam. He was shorter than me, but very cute. All the girls had a crush on him. It was brief and not very romantic, but I hugged the memory close for months. And you?''

"Penelope. We were both twelve and in Cairo. Her father was a peer of the realm, but don't ask me his title. I don't remember. He was in the British embassy. Penny and I met at a very dull party where we were the only children. I remember it was hot and she smelled like roses.''

Chloe flopped onto her back. "You had your first kiss in Egypt and I had mine in Cynthia Greenway's basement. What is wrong with this picture?''

"Nothing.''

"Easy for you to say. Next you'll be telling me that your first lover was some fabulously beautiful courtesan arranged for you by your grandfather. That she was a Christmas present.''

Arizona was silent.

Chloe sucked in a breath, turned back toward him and stared. "You're kidding?''

He cleared his throat. "Actually, it was a birthday present, and courtesan is a strong term. She was experienced.''

"How polite. And you were all of sixteen?''

"Seventeen.''

"I'll bet you had a really good time.''

"I did. I was young and at the time I didn't know there was a difference between having sex and making love. She taught me a lot about mechanics but nothing about the heart.''

Chloe was grateful for the darkness. At least Arizona wouldn't be able to see her stunned expression. She didn't consider herself a prude, but apparently she was. This was too far out of her realm of experience. She didn't know what to say.

"You're shocked," Arizona said.

"A little. That sort of thing doesn't happen in Bradley."

"What does happen?"

"Are you asking about my first lover?"

"Yes."

She sat up and pulled her knees into her chest. "I haven't thought about Billy in a long time." Mostly because she didn't let herself think about him.

"You don't have to talk about it if you'd rather not."

"No, I don't mind." Actually, she didn't, which surprised her. Maybe enough time had passed. Maybe she'd finally healed.

"When my parents died," she began, "Cassie and I were sent into foster care. She stayed in Bradley, but I was sent to a family in a neighboring town. They had a son, Billy. He was a couple of years older than me. The first few months I stayed in my room and kept to myself. I'd lost my parents and Cassie. We wrote and saw each other when we could, but it was different. We didn't feel like sisters anymore."

"How was the family you were with?"

"They were very kind to me. They tried to understand what I was going through. They gave me time. Eventually I started participating in family events. One day I looked up at the dinner table and realized Billy was sitting across from me. He smiled and I smiled back. A few pieces of my broken heart mended at that moment."

"Sounds romantic."

"It was fairly typical. We went on dates, then started going steady."

"Did his parents know?"

"Yes. We tried to keep it from them for a while, but we

weren't very good at sneaking around. I think the first time Billy and I made love was in the back seat of his car." She smiled at the memory. "It wasn't very comfortable."

"The car or the act itself."

"Both. We didn't know what we were doing. It was quick. The sex itself was always much more for him than me. I liked the holding and being close. It didn't matter if it was physically satisfying because I loved him, so it was perfect."

"I'm sure it got better."

She smiled. "Not much." Her smile faded. "We weren't together long enough for us to get really good at it."

She didn't want to think about that, she reminded herself. So instead she recalled what it had been like to be with Billy. He'd been so attentive and eager—both for her and to please her. He'd always touched her as if she were the most precious creature alive. Perhaps to him, she had been.

But the sex itself hadn't moved her. Perhaps she'd been too young, or they'd been too inexperienced. She'd never felt that ultimate pleasure, either with him, or the two young men she'd been intimate with during college. It was a sad state of affairs that the best it had ever been had been in a dream…with the man just a few feet away from her.

"So Billy was your first boyfriend and your first lover," Arizona said. "Were you in love with him?"

"Yes. Deeply. He stole my heart and I've never been sure I got all the pieces back from him."

Arizona pushed himself up into a sitting position. They faced each other. "So you believe in love, but you won't believe in anything magical or mystical."

"They're not the same. I've experienced love." She might have experienced magic—in the form of her dream— but she wasn't ready to admit that to him.

"I don't," he said flatly.

It was the second time that night that he'd stunned her into silence. He'd mentioned it before but she hadn't really believed him. Everyone had to believe in love. Her mind raced, but she couldn't form any words. Finally she managed to blurt out, "How is that possible? What about all the weird stuff you research? You'll put your faith in a rock or a story, but not in the depth of human emotion?"

"Exactly."

"Are we talking about romantic love or all of it? What about parents caring for their children. Most would die for them. Isn't that a demonstration of love?"

"Yes. I would agree that many parents have strong feelings for their children. In most cases I would be willing to call that love."

His careful qualification of his answer made her curious, so she filed that information away to ask about another time. She didn't want to get away from what they were already talking about.

"So it's just the issue of romantic love you have problems with," she said.

He nodded.

She was still having trouble believing this conversation. Arizona believed in things she couldn't even begin to understand, but not love. But love was a fundamental part of the human condition.

"What are you so afraid of?" she asked.

He leaned toward her. "Do *you* believe in love between a man and a woman?"

"Of course. I plan to avoid it, but I know it exists. I've experienced it."

"With Billy?"

"Yes."

"Anyone else?"

She shook her head.

"So why do you want to avoid loving a man?"

She struggled to find the words to answer his question. "If you don't get close, you can't get hurt. So I avoid getting close."

His face was in shadow. She didn't know what he was thinking about. But she anticipated what he would ask next and braced herself for the pain.

"How did Billy hurt you?"

"He betrayed me."

"With another woman?"

If only it had been that simple. "He died." She wrapped her arms around her knees and pulled them closer to her chest. "It all gets twisted in my brain and I can't figure out what happened when."

She drew in a deep breath. "I went into the foster home when I was nearly fifteen. Billy and I began dating toward the end of my sophomore year of high school. The next fall, he started getting sick. It took the doctors a while to figure out that he had leukemia. He fought it for a long time. They used drugs and chemotherapy. He was in and out of the hospital. He promised to love me forever. He promised to get better. I believed him because I couldn't face the alternative. Then one day, he died."

She closed her eyes against the memories, but that didn't help. Her throat tightened. "I know he didn't die when my parents did. If he had, he and I wouldn't have met. But that's how I remember it. My parents dying, then Billy. All the time he was suffering and slipping away all I wanted was my family. My parents. If they couldn't be there, I needed my sister with me."

She felt the tears on her cheeks. How long had it been since she'd cried over Billy? "I used to pray every night that he would get better, that the lawyer would find Aunt Charity so Cassie and I could be together again. It didn't help. Billy passed away in October of my senior year of high school. He was all of nineteen. I was seventeen. Aunt Charity showed up four months later. Four months too late in my mind.''

Maybe it was the tears in her eyes, because she hadn't seen Arizona move, but suddenly he was crouched next to her and pulling her close. She went into his arms. She needed his strength and warmth to chase away the coldness of the past.

"I'm sorry," she whispered. "I don't usually get like this.''

"We all have our demons.''

"I don't believe in that.''

"I'm talking about emotional demons, Chloe. The kind that live inside. We all have them, whether we want them or not.''

His arms wrapped around her as he pulled her next to him. She rested her head on his shoulder.

"Do you still love him?'' he asked.

"No.'' Her voice was muffled against his neck. "I did for a while, but we were so young. I don't know that the relationship would have lasted as long as it did if he hadn't been sick. That added a level of intensity that fueled whatever we were feeling. But he was a good person. I admired him, his courage, his determination. I just wish I hadn't believed him when he told me he wouldn't leave me.''

"The people who are supposed to love us the best always end up hurting us.''

She closed her eyes and focused on being next to him. He smelled of wood smoke and the unique fragrance that was his own. "That sounds like the voice of experience talking.''

"It is. When we first met, you asked about my parents.

You assumed, because I was raised by my grandfather, that they were both dead.''

"You said your father was still alive.''

"He is. The reason my grandfather took me is that my father abandoned me to nannies. He blamed me for my mother's death. Apparently the labor was hard and long, and she wasn't very strong. He couldn't bear to be around me." He took a deep breath. "Emotionally and physically, he turned his back on me. I'm lucky. My grandfather was there to pick up the slack. But I spent the first fifteen years of my life trying to figure out why my father hated me. My grandfather finally took pity on me and explained it."

The ache inside of her deepened. "I'm sorry."

"There's no need for that. I've put it behind me and moved on. But it might make it more clear as to why I'm not a huge believer in love. Even when it comes to parents loving their children. I've seen a lot of neglect in my life, and I've experienced it firsthand."

She raised her head and looked at him. "We are quite a pair, aren't we?"

"It's not so bad."

He shifted until he was reclining on the sleeping bag, then pulled her down next to him. She settled into his arms, her head on his shoulder, her hand resting on his chest. She should have been self-conscious in such an intimate position, but it felt right. Perhaps it was the privacy of being alone together in the middle of nowhere; perhaps it was because they'd both just bared their souls. She didn't care which. At this moment in time, there was nowhere in the world she would rather be than here, with him.

A thought occurred to her. She raised her head and looked at him. "You know everything we've talked about tonight is private. I won't be using it in my article."

He touched the tip of her nose with his index finger. "Yes, I knew that. I trust you, Chloe."

"I'm glad." She settled down again. "So what was it like growing up with your grandfather? Were you close?"

"We were as I got older. When I was a kid I think he thought of me more like a puppy than a person. I know he cared, but he wasn't the most responsible parent. I wanted to be able to depend on him and I couldn't. He would pay attention to me for a while, then ignore me for weeks at a time. At least the staff always took care of me."

"I can't even imagine what that was like. At least Cassie and I had our parents for the first fourteen years of our lives, and we had each other." She pressed her lips together. No doubt all the fans on the Internet and everywhere else thought the same thing she had—that Arizona's life had been like a movie. All good times and laughter, played out in exotic locations. But the truth was different.

"While there are some things I would have liked to change, I don't regret how I was raised," he said. "Like I said before, it's all I know."

"Think of all you missed. Life in the suburbs can be pretty exciting. Barbecues, mowing the lawn, school dances." Her voice was low and teasing.

He chuckled in response. "You make it sound so tempting." He shifted his arm and rested his hand on her head. Long fingers stroked her hair. "I haven't lived any part of the American dream. Sometimes I wonder how I would have been different if my grandfather hadn't come to get me."

"You would be a different person. We're shaped by our experiences."

"The old nature-versus-nurture argument. But you're right. I would be different. How did we get on this topic of conversation?"

"We started out talking about firsts. First kiss, first love." She frowned. "If you don't believe love exists, then you've never loved anyone."

He stiffened slightly. "I cared for my grandfather very much. He was important to me. I have friendships that matter. But romantic love, no."

He spoke the words so easily, yet her reaction to them was anything but casual. Her heart tightened in her chest and her throat closed. She wanted him to believe in love, which was insane. What did it matter to her? His stay in town was very temporary. Even if it wasn't, she wasn't interested in any kind of entanglement.

"We are a sorry pair," she said lightly, as much to conceal her emotions from him as to convince herself that she was fine. "You don't believe in love. I believe in it, but I want to avoid it at all costs. I refuse to hurt that much again."

"Just think of the heartache we're saving ourselves."

"Agreed. Except…" Her voice trailed off.

"Except what?"

"I can't help wondering what we're missing. Look at Cassie. She's so different from me. She leads with her chin and wears her heart on her sleeve. There are probably other clichés that apply, but I can't think of them right now. The point is she just puts it all on the line."

"Is she happy with her boyfriend?"

"Good question. I don't know. I hope so. I think she's settling for Joel, but then I'm not the one in the relationship."

"Sometimes people would rather accept what they can get instead of spending their time wishing for the moon."

It felt so good and right to be in his arms, she thought. She didn't ever want to leave. If the price of this moment was another day of hiking in the Cascade Mountains, then it was a small payment. She liked the heat of him, the scent of him, the feeling of safety, the way her body was slowly coming alive.

"According to your fan club on-line, you're something of a superhero, Arizona. Are you telling me you couldn't get me the moon?"

"Hey, I'm just a guy."

"Oh, but what a guy."

She made the statement without thinking. Arizona raised himself up on one elbow and stared down at her. Light from the fire flickered on his face. His gaze locked with hers. Sometimes she didn't know what he was thinking, but this time she had no trouble reading his thoughts.

The heat between them flared instantly as her body went up in flames. She knew what he was going to say even before he spoke.

"I want you."

Those three words stole her breath. Every part of her melted in anticipation.

"I want you," he repeated as he traced a line from her cheekbone to the corner of her mouth.

It wasn't going to mean anything, she told herself. It was impossible that this would be for more than one night. In the end, it wouldn't be more real than the dream. Was that enough for her? Could she live with those rules and not have regrets?

Her first lover had been Billy. Her second, a boy in college. She'd hoped he would help her forget her first love, but the plan hadn't worked. The lovemaking had been disappointing. The only time in her life she thought she might have experienced ultimate pleasure had been during the dream about Arizona. What if reality didn't live up to that billing?

What if it was better?

She continued to look at him as she realized it didn't matter. She didn't want to be with him because of her body, she wanted to be with him because of her heart. It wasn't love, she reminded herself. She wouldn't do that again. But it was respect and caring. Wasn't that enough?

"I've never made love in a sleeping bag," she said at last.

"Actually, I haven't either, but I understand it can be done. There are, however, certain limitations."

"Like what?"

He smiled. "Let me show you."

Chapter Nine

He bent down and pressed his mouth against hers. His lips were warm and firm. He moved with a sureness that told her he remembered their previous kiss. The one at the reception. Unfortunately her memories stretched back to another time when they'd made love in a cave on the side of a mountain.

She told herself not to think about that. The dream was just that—fantasy. This was real, this man who held her in his arms and moved his mouth back and forth as if seeking the most perfect fit. But even as she tried to push the past away, it intruded and she wondered if reality could stand up to what she'd experienced that night.

One of his hands moved behind her shoulders. He gently pulled her braid out from under her back, then tugged on the rubber band holding her hair in place. With his fingers, he freed the long curls and combed them into place around her face.

When he was done, she reached up and wrapped her arms around him, drawing him closer. She wanted to feel him press against her. She wanted to absorb his heat and his strength.

He tilted his head slightly, then opened his mouth and pressed his tongue to her lower lip. She instantly parted for him. He slipped inside, a quick, confident movement that made her wonder what else he would do well. Would he know how to touch her? Would he find the right places to stroke and tease, discover the proper cadence to send her soaring into perfection?

She couldn't answer the question and when his tongue touched hers, she didn't care. The warmth flowed through her, as if her body were melting against his. She moved one hand to his head, to hold him in place. His hair was soft and cool beneath her questing fingers. Her breasts swelled, her nipples puckered. An aching tingle began between her legs. She wanted this...wanted him.

He shifted, sliding one leg between hers. His rock-hard thigh pressed against her feminine place. The pressure teased her with promises of what would come later. Gently, slowly, almost as if she didn't want him to notice, she began to rock her hips up and down, sliding herself against him. The action both eased and increased the feeling of tension filling her.

"Chloe," he breathed against her mouth. "I want you so much."

His hands cupped her face. He lifted his head slightly, so they could look at each other. His expression was hard, his muscles tense. His breathing came in heavy bursts. Against her hip she felt the proof of his desire.

A quiet pride filled her. She didn't know why this man wanted her. No doubt he'd met other, more exciting, prettier women. Some probably had been smarter, some funnier, but none of that mattered to her. He was in her arms, holding her close. He wanted to make love with her and she clung to that reality with every fiber of her being.

He kissed her cheek, her jawline, then forged a damp trail to her ear.

"I want you," he repeated. "It's like being a teenager again. I feel like I'm going to explode." He rubbed his hardness against her hip, then groaned. "I could lose control right now."

Boldly, not sure where the courage sprang from, Chloe slipped one hand down his chest to his jeans. She placed her hand flat against the throbbing ridge. He swore once, then bit on her earlobe. Arousal shot through her, brought on by the feel of him against her palm, the word he'd muttered and the sharp nip of his teeth.

"You're going to make me embarrass myself," he told her.

"Then we'll just have to do it again until you get it right."

"That won't be a problem."

His slow, masculine smile made her toes curl. She wondered where on earth she'd gotten the courage to say these things to him. Was it the dream? She wasn't sure and she didn't mind. With Arizona she wanted to be bold—she wanted to be the kind of woman he would want and admire.

He cupped her face in his hands and kissed her again. This time he didn't wait—this time he plunged inside instantly and she was ready for him. Her tongue met his. They brushed against each other, circled, stroking. She inhaled his breath. Her body softened against his hardness, dampening, swelling, readying. She continued to move herself up and down against his thigh. Her panties were wet and she had the feeling that if she could just figure out the right spot or rhythm, something wonderful would happen.

One of his hands moved down her neck to her shoulder. From there he traveled across her chest to her right breast. She arched against him, encouraging him to touch her there. Her skin tingled, her nipple was hard, her body ached with a need that threatened to overwhelm her.

He slid over the curve, then cupped her. Through the layers of her clothing—bra, T-shirt, sweatshirt—she felt him move in a circle, as if discovering all of her. Chloe was pleased with her long, slender legs, could live with her butt and hips, but she'd always felt self-conscious about her small breasts. She thought they were fine, but compared to those she saw in magazines, she knew she was bound to disappoint some men.

But not Arizona. She wasn't sure how she knew this. He didn't say anything and she wasn't sure she believed that she could read his thoughts by how he touched her. Yet the rounded curves fit perfectly into the palm of his hand and she knew that was exactly how he liked it.

His hand moved lower until he reached the hem of her sweatshirt. He tugged on the garment, pulling it up. They broke apart enough to help him free her of the fleece. Her long-sleeved T-shirt followed. Instantly the cool night air nipped at her skin. She shivered, knowing that soon he would be on top of her, touching her everywhere, warming her through to her bones.

He knelt, straddling her legs. With a quick movement, his sweater and shirt joined hers in a pile on his sleeping bag. His green eyes glowed as if lit from within. His breathing was as rapid and ragged as her own.

She gave a nervous laugh. "So what do the forest creatures think about what we're doing?" she asked.

He grinned. "That humans have a funny way of staying warm at night."

He stretched out beside her and pulled her close. Her

head cradled in the crook of his arm. Their mouths met. With his free hand, he tangled his fingers in her hair, then stroked her bare shoulder. Shivers rippled through her—shivers that had nothing to do with the air temperature and everything to do with anticipation.

She didn't notice him unfasten her bra, but the undergarment loosened, then fell away. "So beautiful," he breathed against her mouth as he used his index finger to circle the underside of her breasts.

Her nipples puckered and her breath caught in her throat. She wanted him to touch her there on the tight peaks. She wanted to know if it was going to feel as good as it had in the dream.

He broke away from their kiss and moved down her neck. Her upper body arched toward him in anticipation. He didn't disappoint her. His mouth closed over her left nipple.

Soft, wet heat encircled her. He teased the taut bud with his tongue, then gently scraped it with his teeth. A moan escaped her, then another. She grabbed his head, her actions a silent plea for him to never ever stop what he was doing.

His fingers mimicked the action of his mouth, then he switched. As the dampness between her legs increased, her hips began to move with a will of their own. She needed him.

"I never thought—" She began, but couldn't finish the sentence. There wasn't enough air in her lungs. She'd never thought it could be like this. It *was* better than the dream. So much better. And yet it was all familiar.

She didn't want to think about that. If she got caught up in trying to figure out what had really happened the night she'd worn the nightgown, she would miss what Arizona was doing to her now. She didn't want that. She wanted to live in the moment, because life had never been this perfect.

He licked the valley between her breasts. At the same time, he unfastened her jeans. Large hands tugged at the fabric and slowly pulled it down.

She'd taken off her boots when she'd first sat on the sleeping bag, so her jeans came off easily. He tossed them on the growing pile of clothing. He knelt between her legs and kissed her belly. Until that moment, she hadn't realized he'd pulled her panties off, too.

But there wasn't time to worry or protest. Because before she could figure out what was going to happen next, he'd kissed her right on top of the soft auburn curls protecting her femininity. His fingers urged her legs apart, then gently parted her woman's folds. With an unerring accuracy, he touched his tongue to that single point of pleasure.

Chloe gasped and came up into a nearly sitting position. No one had ever done anything like that to her before. She didn't know what to make of it, but she was sure she liked it. Even as she braced her weight on her hands, she parted her legs more.

His tongue was magic. He circled her and danced over her. He began a fast rhythm, then slowed until she thought she might scream. Tension filled her. Tension she'd felt before, but not like this. In the past, she'd experienced mild anticipation. Now she knew she was going to die if he didn't finish what he'd started.

Even as he continued to pleasure her, she couldn't help watching him. His head bent low as he loved her so intimately. The play of the firelight on his bare back. Broad shoulders, long legs tucked under him. Bare feet. When had he taken off his shoes and socks?

Then she decided she didn't care. As long as he never stopped what he was doing. As long as—

She collapsed onto her back and exhaled his name. Pleasure raced through her, making her tense more, making her want to plead and demand and scream. All her attention focused on the places he touched. Not only on his tongue teasing her so deliciously, but also on the single finger he'd inserted inside of her.

He went in deep, exploring her, urging her on. Her hips jerked, driving him in more, needing him. His tongue moved faster, then stopped, letting her concentrate just on his finger. In and out, rubbing against her, forcing her to a place she'd never been.

She tried to catch her breath. Her heels dug into the sleeping bag, her fingers grasped at the quilted fabric. More. She needed more.

He read her mind. His mouth pressed against her again. He flicked his tongue back and forth. The finger inside of her circled and plunged. The movements conspired together to force her to the edge. Every part of her body tightened in anticipation. Then he stopped. One heartbeat. Two. She knew he was making her wait, building the anticipation. A whimper escaped her.

He touched her again—in tandem. His tongue, his lips, his hand. And she exploded.

She knew what was happening, but she couldn't control it. The moment was too perfect. She bucked and grabbed his shoulders, begging him not to stop. He continued to move, faster and lighter, drawing it all out of her until every cell of her body had filled itself with the passion and pleasure.

Slowly, very slowly, she relaxed. He pulled his mouth away and sat up. Perspiration coated her body. Her legs trembled. She would never be the same again.

"You are incredible," he said.

She opened her eyes and stared at him. "Me? I was just along for the ride. You're the one who—" She broke off and motioned vaguely with her hand. What did one say at a moment like this?

"You're very responsive." He rubbed his hands along her thighs, then up her belly. "I knew just where you were the whole time. That made it easy to know what to do."

Nice to know, even if she hadn't been doing it on purpose. Definitely better than the dream, she thought as he slipped off his jeans and briefs. Comparing what she'd felt then to what had just happened was like saying a cup of saltwater was just like an ocean.

The sight of his arousal springing free caught her attention and forced all other thoughts from her mind. He was exactly as she'd known he would be. His chest, the scar on his forearm—she raised herself on one elbow to look—and the one on his knee. Familiar yet different. She didn't have an explanation and right now she didn't care.

"We have a dilemma," he said as he knelt between her legs again. "I want you very much, as you can tell."

He glanced down and she followed his gaze to his very impressive maleness. The thought of him filling her made her tummy tighten in anticipation.

"I want you, too," she whispered.

He leaned forward and kissed her, then he touched her cheek with the back of his fingers. "I didn't bring you up here to make love with you. I'm willing to admit I'd hoped we might end up right here, but I would have politely accepted a rejection on your part."

"Okay." She wasn't sure what he was getting at. "I'm confused."

He exhaled sharply. "What I'm trying to say is that I want to protect you. I brought condoms with me. But I don't want you to get the wrong idea. I really respect you. I think you're great, and I—"

She pressed her fingers over his mouth and smiled. "No

problem. I'm glad that you wanted this to happen. And to be completely honest, I brought them, too.''

His eyes widened. ''You brought condoms?''

She blushed. Thank goodness it was too dark for him to see. ''Well, it's wasn't exactly my idea. Cassie gave me one.''

That satisfied male smile returned. He reached for his jeans and withdrew the square plastic package. After putting on the protection, he pressed the tip of his arousal against her, then leaned down to whisper in her ear.

''Just one?'' he said. ''That wouldn't have been nearly enough.''

Chloe's giggle of delight only increased Arizona's need. He'd hoped making love with her would be terrific, but even his imagination hadn't come up with anything even close to this glorious reality. He'd meant what he'd told her before. He *had* practically been able to read her mind when he'd been touching her. Maybe it was just instinct, but there hadn't been any of his usual concerns when he was with a woman. He'd known exactly where to touch, how fast, for how long. He'd known when she was getting close and what she wanted to make it perfect for her.

Now, even before he entered her, he knew exactly how it was going to be. She would threaten to swallow him completely and he would surrender himself to her.

She reached up and touched his face. ''Be in me,'' she breathed. ''Please.''

With that, he entered her. He moved slowly, not wanting to hurt her. But she was already so aroused. Her tightness stretched to accommodate him. He had to grit his teeth against the pleasure. All he wanted was to explode right there, but he couldn't. He wanted to make it good for her, too.

He opened his eyes and stared into her beautiful face. Dark eyes stared back at him. She was smiling.

"You feel great," he told her.

"You, too."

He pulled out, then pushed in again. Back and forth, moving a little faster each time. Her eyes widened. She clutched at him.

"It's happening again," she said, sounding shocked.

"It's supposed to "

"I don't "

Her fingers dug into his back. She raised her legs and wrapped them around him. "Arizona, please!"

He knew what she wanted…what they both wanted. Fast and hard.

He plunged in and withdrew, pumping his hips, taking her with him. She whimpered. Her breathing came in little gasps. He could feel her collecting herself. He swore silently, willing himself to hold back, to give her what she craved.

Suddenly, she dropped her feet to the ground and pushed up against him. He buried himself inside of her. She grabbed his hips and held him in deep.

Her gaze still locked with his, she climaxed around him. Her body rippled, massaging him, drawing him in more, forcing him to give in to the incredible passion surging through him. She milked him until he exploded.

When they had both recovered, he stretched out next to her and pulled her close. He wanted to tell her it had never been like that for him before, but wondered if she would believe him. Even to his mind, it sounded like a line.

The problem was, he meant it. He hadn't felt anything like this before. There had been a connection, a oneness. The words of the old shaman came back to him. "When you mate with a woman, you give away a piece of your soul.''

That's what had happened, he realized. He and Chloe had exchanged parts of their innermost selves. He'd never wanted that before—mostly because the thought scared him. But with Chloe, he didn't mind. He liked the thought of having a part of her soul to carry with him, and for reasons he couldn't explain, he trusted her with a piece of himself.

They were quiet for a long time. Chloe enjoyed the silence. She needed to catch her breath, both physically and emotionally. She wasn't sure of everything that had happened between them. It had definitely been better than the dream, which was a little terrifying. The good news was, she reminded herself, at least the best it had ever been was now a real-life experience and not something she'd thought up in her head.

''What are you thinking about?'' Arizona asked.

Chloe's head rested on his shoulder and her hand stroked his chest. Somehow they'd found their way inside her sleeping bag. ''That it's never been like this before.''

''For me, too. Pretty spectacular. And that was just our first time out. Imagine what we could do with a little practice.''

There was something to think about, she thought. ''No, you don't understand. After Billy, there were two young men in college. I'm not a virgin, but I've never climaxed before.''

She instantly regretted her confession, but he didn't get all weird on her. The hand stroking her hair never slowed and his breathing remained even.

''I wouldn't have guessed,'' he told her, ''but I'd be

lying if I said I wasn't glad. I wanted to make it perfect for you.''

''Oh, it was, and then some.''

''Good.''

She was on her side, facing him. Her right leg rested on top of his. She bent her knee and rubbed her foot up and down along his shin. Her thigh brushed against a raised ridge in his skin.

''You have a scar.'' She made a statement rather than asking a question.

''I was cut with a knife when I was about fifteen. We were in India. A man got sick and had a high fever. He was delirious and thought we were trying to take him away. Several of us grabbed him to hold him down, but he got in a couple of good thrusts. I was in the way of one of them.''

He spoke so matter-of-factly, she thought. As if that sort of thing happened every day. ''I don't have any scars,'' she told him. ''We'll have to bond over something else.''

He kissed her forehead. ''I think we've done more than our share of bonding tonight.''

They had, she thought, realizing he was right. They'd bonded in the most intimate way possible. ''I knew it was going to be like this,'' she said without thinking.

The words hung in the silence of the night. She stiffened, waiting for the inevitable questions, but Arizona never asked. He only held her tighter against him.

I knew it was going to be like this.

The statement filled his head until it was all he could think about. She'd thought about them being together. She'd assumed it was going to be amazing. He didn't know why that should matter so much to him, but it did.

Who was this woman who had made a place for herself inside of him? Was he crazy? They couldn't get involved.

She was three different kinds of home and hearth. He'd never lived anywhere longer than six months at a time and he had no intention of changing his ways. He didn't want to settle down. Except for the occasional loneliness, he liked his life. Especially tonight.

He shifted until he was facing her, then he kissed her. The passion flared more slowly this time. Her arms wound around his neck as she opened her mouth to him. As if she read his mind.

Connected, he thought, distracted by the need building. They were connected. Maybe the thought should send him running for cover. It usually did.

"I want you," he murmured against her mouth. "I want to be in you. I want to feel you under me."

Her breathing quickened as her body responded to what he'd said.

They were well matched. She was tall for a woman, and he liked that. He liked the feel and smell of her skin, the brush of her legs against his. He liked her small, tight breasts and the tautness of her nipples. He liked the way her long hair spilled over her breasts, both exposing and concealing them. He liked her.

Something had happened between them. He knew that now. He didn't want to get involved, but he couldn't walk away from her. Not yet. Not tonight and maybe not for a couple of days. He wanted her too much.

As he reached for another condom, he told himself he was risking a lot. Maybe he should back off now.

He tried his surefire method for disconnecting. He pictured Chloe about thirty pounds heavier with a baby in her arms and another clinging to her skirts. He imagined a house, a yard and a minivan in the driveway. In his mind's eye, he saw the suburbs, his nine-to-five job and a medical and dental insurance plan. Then he waited.

But the arousal didn't go away and the vision didn't make him cringe. When she reached her hand between them, he allowed her to guide him inside her. They both groaned as he slid home.

As he began to thrust into her, he moved his hands all over her body. He liked her like this, but the thought of her with rounder hips, gently aging, didn't distress him as it should have.

He reminded himself that he came from a long line of men who got love all wrong. His grandfather, his father and him. He would never settle down, so this was just make-believe. Not love. Never love.

As her legs encircled him, he told himself this was all he was ever going to have. And for now it was enough.

Chapter Ten

Despite the hard ground, Chloe found herself drifting off to sleep. Perhaps it was a result of the physical exercise from hiking all afternoon. Or maybe it was because her body had been so thoroughly satisfied by Arizona's lovemaking. She decided she didn't much care. As long as he snuggled next to her, his arms around her making her warm and keeping her safe.

She lay on her side with him behind her, spooning against her. One arm rested heavily on her waist. She placed her hand on top of his and savored the feel of him. Her mind drifted and images formed. Images of Arizona. They hadn't know each other very long, but already the man was very much a part of her life.

She slept dreamlessly until well after midnight. Then she sank deeper and deeper into the dreaming place. Unrelated bits and pieces flitted through her mind until they came together to form a picture. Chloe found herself walking toward a vehicle. But instead of her sleek, sporty convertible, she unlocked a Suburban.

"Come on, you two," she called over her shoulder. "We're going to be late." But she wasn't angry as she spoke. The scene had been played out a hundred times before and they'd never once been late, although the children did love to dawdle.

A girl of maybe six or seven and a boy of four trotted after her, then climbed into the truck. Chloe stepped in after them. She checked to make sure they were wearing their seat belts, then carefully adjusted her own so that it encircled her very pregnant belly.

As she backed out of the driveway, she glanced up and saw the Victorian house where she'd lived her entire life. An upper floor curtain moved and Aunt Charity waved at her. Chloe waved back. Aunt Charity would take care of making dinner tonight, as she had for the past couple of weeks. Chloe was running behind on her book deadline, and she wanted to get the project out before the baby came. Plus there was the party on Friday, for which she wasn't close to ready. Her daughter needed a costume for the school play; she and Arizona had to make plans to celebrate their anniversary. It was overwhelming.

As she turned onto the main street, she found herself smiling. Yes, at times life overwhelmed her, but she'd never been happier or more content. She and Arizona were so right together. As if they truly were each other's destiny.

As she drove into traffic, the two children in the back began to sing. Chloe joined in. The words were a familiar rhyme. Then the sound faded and she found herself drifting out of the dream. She tried to call out a protest. She didn't want to leave. It was perfect there. She wanted it to be real. She wanted him to be her destiny.

Chloe awoke with a start. Cold night air caressed her

cheek and for a moment, she didn't know where she was. Something long and strong and warm cradled her from behind, trapping her in an unfamiliar cocoon.

She opened her mouth to scream, then the memories clicked into place. She was fine. She was in the forest with Arizona. They were hiking to an archaeological dig so he could look at some artifacts. They weren't married, she wasn't pregnant. Nothing was different from the way it had been yesterday or a month ago.

Until the last lie, she'd nearly succeeded in calming herself. But now her heart rate picked up and her body trembled. She wasn't the same. Everything had changed since Arizona had dropped into her life. Now they were lovers. How was she supposed to resist him? The way he touched her, the way he made her feel—no woman could walk away from that kind of magic.

She closed her eyes and willed herself to calm down. She was overtired. She was reacting emotionally to a difficult situation. That was what the dream had been trying to tell her—that things were different now. She wasn't really going to marry Arizona, live in Bradley and have three children. That was crazy. She was going to move to New York and write for a major magazine. She wasn't going to get married because loving someone meant opening herself to pain and Chloe had sworn to never do that again. It hurt too much.

"I'm fine," she whispered to herself. "It was just a dream. It's not true."

She repeated the sentences over and over. Slowly, her body relaxed. It wasn't real. He wasn't her destiny. In a couple of weeks he would disappear from her life as abruptly as he'd entered it and she would go on as before.

"There's nothing to be afraid of," she told herself. "Nothing at all."

Arizona shifted in his sleep and pulled her closer. She allowed herself to press against him. Unexpectedly, tears sprang to her eyes. She felt them fill her eyes, then spill onto her temple. What on earth was wrong with her? She was fine. It had just been a strange dream.

And then she knew. The truth dawned and with it a growing horror. She wasn't crying because she was afraid the dream would come true...but because she was afraid it wouldn't.

They walked in to the dig a little after one in the afternoon. Chloe hadn't known what to expect. Her entire experience with archaeology had been a visit to the La Brea tar pits in Los Angeles when she'd been ten or twelve. She vaguely recalled some motorized life size replicas of a woolly mammoth family caught in tar outside, and some fossils on the inside. Behind the buildings was the actual site itself, but that memory was a blur.

Here she'd expected to see a few open pits with college students delicately removing bits of bone using dental instruments. Instead, she and Arizona crested the rise and looked down into an entire village.

To the left were the tents used by the scientists and workers. To the right were obviously ancient stone huts, some reduced to crumbled remains, others standing tall with open places for windows and doors. A couple hundred yards back from the village was an open dirt area with a large circle painted in white.

"What do you think?" Arizona asked.

"It's huge," she told him. "I'd pictured something smaller."

"Most people do. They're studying a society here, not digging up dinosaur bones. Some of the finds are from two or three different Indian tribes. That's what everyone came to study. But about three months ago, they started unearthing a much older civilization...and one that was more advanced. No one knows who they are or where they came from. They're the ones who interest me.''

As he spoke, he started down the side of the rise. Chloe followed him. While she was pleased they'd arrived and she could put down her heavy pack for a few hours, in a way she was sorry to be around other people. Instead, she wanted to be alone with Arizona.

This morning could have been awkward. Between her very strange dream and their physical intimacy, she'd been prepared for stiff conversation and averted gazes. Instead, Arizona had awakened her with a kiss. She'd felt perfectly comfortable lying there in his arms. They'd had breakfast and dressed, but in the process of rolling up their sleeping bags and packing up clothes, they'd become tangled in each other. The lovemaking had been hot and fast, leaving them both satisfied and out of breath. Not a bad way to start the morning.

But all that would be different now, she told herself. There were other people around. She had to remember they were both here to work.

A tall, skinny man with a scruffy beard looked up at their approach. He wore thick glasses and baggy clothes. He had a clipboard in one hand and a handheld tape recorder in the other.

''Arizona!'' he called when he spotted them. ''I heard you were coming to check out what we found.''

''Hey, Jeff. Good to see you.'' They walked over to him and the two men shook hands. ''This is Chloe Wright. She's a reporter.''

Jeff shook her hand and winked. ''He's all flash, no substance. Don't let him fool you into thinking otherwise.''

Chloe found herself smiling at the rumpled man. "I'll do my best to remain objective."

Jeff returned his attention to Arizona. "We've found more artifacts. Some tools, bowls, nothing that will interest you." He slapped his friend's back. "The amulet is in here."

He led Arizona toward one of the larger tents. Chloe fell into step behind them. As they walked, she glanced around and tried to get a feel for all the activity. Long wooden tables had been stacked with bowls, stone disks and knives. There were open crates and two women filling them with the stone objects.

Every time they walked by someone, Arizona called out a greeting. He knew them all by name. He had a few teasing words for each of them. Chloe was reminded of the reception, where he'd known as many guests as she did, and she'd lived in Bradley all her life. She supposed it was just his personality. He enjoyed getting to know people and they wanted to know him.

"In here," Jeff said, motioning them inside one of the largest tents.

Arizona let his backpack slip to the ground before entering and Chloe did the same. There were more tables set up in here, she noticed as they entered. The objects littering the surface were small and delicate. Some were wood, a few cloth. Despite the canvas flaps rolled back to let in both air and light, the area smelled musty.

"We found it in what we thought might have been a wooden box. Unfortunately, it disintegrated when we moved it. But the amulet is intact. There are a dozen or so stone beads. Very round with a tiny hole through the center. We figured it was part of a necklace of some kind. How they made the stones so small and perfect is anyone's guess."

Jeff stopped in front of a table in the rear of the tent. "I've already finished the paperwork. You just have to sign for it and promise you won't lose it."

Arizona smiled. "I'll be careful."

"I know. That's why I'm releasing it to you." He glanced at Chloe. "We have some sandwiches left over from lunch if you want them."

Her stomach growled. "Sounds great."

"Help yourself when you're done." He picked up a rectangular acrylic case that was about six inches square and handed it to Arizona. "Good luck. I'm curious to hear what you figure out." With that he waved and left the tent.

Arizona lifted the cover and stared down at the small round stones. Chloe moved closer. One of the stones was larger than the others, and more oval than round. There was some kind of carving.

"A child sign," he said, and put the oval piece in the center of his palm. "That's a sleeping baby or young child."

She looked down and saw what looked like a cross between a crude drawing of an infant in a cradle board and a baby seal. The ridges underneath looked fluid to her.

"Water?" she asked, pointing.

"Probably. These dots up here—" He indicated the top half of the stone "—are stars. The tiny crescent is the moon. The water indicates a journey or travel. The birth of a baby, or a prayer for a baby to be brought to the family? Maybe a wish for a dying child to have safe passage to the next life." His voice was low and intense. "I'll have to start researching this fairly soon. I'm not going to have much time."

He muttered a few more sentences, then seemed to get lost in what he was studying. Chloe didn't mind. She moved away and bent over a few of the tables, trying to figure out what had been unearthed.

This was, she acknowledged, a different world from her own suburban life. Arizona was unlike anyone she'd ever met. Yet there were many things about him that called to her. His kindness, his intelligence, his humor. She found him physically attractive—she liked the feel of his body next to and on top of hers. She respected him.

She glanced back and saw him carefully weighing the round stones and the amulet itself, then making notations on a card. Their relationship just wasn't about sex—at least it wasn't for her. And that thought terrified her. If it was only physical, it would be so much easier to put into place. As it was, she was confused. What did it mean that Arizona had entered her life? What was she supposed to do now? The obvious answer was that she was supposed to enjoy the fun while it lasted, then forget about him when he left. It made sense. What other choice was there?

But what about the dream? Had that meant anything? Was it a premonition or just wishful thinking on her part?

"I don't want a traditional life," she reminded herself. "I don't want to fall in love again. I don't want to care. If you love people, then they can hurt you."

She'd experienced the latter firsthand. Her parents hadn't meant to die and leave her, but they had. So had Billy. She was tired of caring and then being left alone. She wasn't going to take that kind of chance again.

She heard footsteps and turned. Arizona walked over and gave her a sheepish grin. "Sorry. I got caught up in this." He shook the acrylic box. "Breakfast was a long time ago. You must be starving. Let's go grab a couple of sandwiches."

"Sounds good."

They went outside and found the food. A few of the

graduate students came by and talked to Arizona. As expected, he knew all of them by name. When a couple of the young women looked at Arizona with admiring eyes, Chloe had to fight down a surge of irritation. She wanted to slide closer to him and lay claim to him. But she didn't. As far as she could tell, Arizona barely realized they were female, let alone attractive and obviously smitten. For someone who could read a life's story in a single carved stone, he was amazingly dense when it came to women. It was, she acknowledged, a fine quality in a man.

At last, when they were alone, Arizona leaned forward and rested his elbows on the wooden picnic table. "Is it what you thought?" he asked, indicating the site.

"It's bigger and there's more activity. I'm glad you brought me. This will add a lot to my article." She touched the box lying between them. "What are you going to do with this?"

"I'll do some research. Most of what I need is available through Internet links with university libraries. I have to figure out what the carvings mean. Once all this gets dated, I'll look at other cultures from that time. There are often similarities." His eyebrows drew together. "My problem is I don't have a lot of time. Once the lecture series is finished in Bradley, I'm leaving for the South Pacific. I'm doing some work there this summer."

She'd known he wasn't going to stay. Why would a man like him want to spend any time in a small town? But she hadn't really thought much about his going away so soon.

"Are you excited about the island?" she asked, trying to pretend his plans didn't matter to her. After all, she reminded herself, they shouldn't.

"I've been there before. They have a rich oral storytelling tradition and I'll be recording and annotating many of their tales." His gaze lingered on her face. "You'd like it.

It's a strictly matriarchal society. The men exist to do the hard physical labor, but all the decisions are made by the women. I find it restful. There aren't any pressures to act macho.''

"Oh, right. I would guess you like it because the women there probably wait on you hand and foot."

His smile was modest. "There is that. But it's also very beautiful."

"I'm sure it is." She forced herself to keep smiling. Later, when she was alone, she would try to figure out why her chest was suddenly tight and it hurt to breathe.

"What's next for you?" he asked. "After the article, I mean."

"More work. I've put together some of my best writing. When I finish this story, I'm going to go to New York and see if I can get a job there. At least that's the plan."

"Sounds like a good one."

"I've wanted this for a long time." Chloe frowned. She *had* wanted this for as long as she could remember. Growing up, she'd dreamed about leaving Bradley and making it in the big city. But right now, the idea of being away from everything she'd ever known only sounded lonely.

"Have you ever thought about doing something else?" he asked.

She stared at him. He hadn't shaved that morning and stubble darkened his cheeks. His hair was slightly mussed, his clothes as wrinkled as hers. Yet he was the most handsome man she'd ever met. What was he asking? Was he hinting that he might like her to come along? Would she be willing to do that? What about her career? What about not getting involved?

"I can be flexible," she told him.

"That helps," he said, and though she waited, he didn't add anything.

Chloe fought against the disappointment. She was being a fool, she thought. Wanting something didn't necessarily make it happen. What was wrong with her? She wasn't usually this scattered. Maybe it was because Arizona had become so important to her in a relatively short period of time. It made everything so confusing.

Jeff sauntered over to the table. The two men spoke. Chloe watched Arizona. When he smiled, her lips curved up. His hands moved as he talked, and she remembered those same hands on her body. She was glad she was with him. She wanted to talk with him, hear his stories, be close.

The realization hit her with all the subtlety of lightning splitting a tree in two. She felt just as ripped apart inside. The reason she felt so confused and unsettled wasn't because Arizona was so appealing, or because the circumstances were new. It was because she'd fallen for him. She, a woman who constantly resisted getting involved, had fallen for a man who specialized in leaving everyone else behind.

A rumble of a distant engine cut through the silence of the afternoon. Arizona glanced at his watch. Two-thirty. Right on time. Jeff shook his hand.

"Let me know what you find," he said, pointing to the acrylic box. "Good luck this summer."

"You, too," Arizona said, then watched his friend head back to the main part of the dig.

"What's that noise?" Chloe asked. She rose to her feet and stared up at the sky. "A helicopter?"

"It's our ride home," Arizona told her. "The lecture series starts the day after tomorrow. There isn't time to hike out. We should be at the airport in about forty minutes. We're on the five o'clock flight to Sacramento. You'll be home by bedtime."

The noise got louder.

"We could have used a helicopter to get here?" Chloe asked.

"Sure. What did you think that circle was for?" He pointed to the huge white spot on the dirt. "It's the landing pad."

"I see." She turned to him. "So why exactly did we hike in here? I mean, what was the point?"

There was something stiff about her posture. Her face was unreadable.

"Are you angry?" he asked. She didn't answer. He scrambled to explain. "I thought it would be fun."

"For you," she said curtly.

"For both of us. The weather promised to be excellent, it's a pretty easy hike. I wanted to spend time with you. I thought you wanted the same."

He could feel the shifting emotional ground underfoot and struggled to stay upright. It was clear that he'd done something wrong, but for the life of him, he couldn't figure out what.

"Which part was more enjoyable?" she asked. "Was it watching me try to be a good sport my first time camping out, or did you like getting it on better?"

"Chloe, no. It wasn't like that. I enjoy spending time with you. I thought you felt the same. With our schedules, we haven't been able to be together as much as I would have liked. I thought this was a good way to make that happen. I wasn't trying to trick you into anything. I didn't force you last night."

Her expression softened slightly and he saw the pain in her eyes. How in God's name had he hurt her? He took a step toward her. She held up a hand to stop him.

"Don't sweat it, Arizona. You're a hundred percent right. You didn't force me. I practically begged for it."

"Chloe, don't."

"Don't what?" Her dark eyes spit fire. "Don't tell the truth? So I assume you had a radio with you the whole time? You could have called in the helicopter if something had gone wrong."

"Sure. If we'd had an accident."

"Or if I hadn't been good enough in bed."

With that she swung on her backpack and walked away. He collected his belongings and ran after her. The helicopter was on the ground, making it difficult to talk. He grabbed her arm and forced her to stop and face him.

"What's going on?" he asked. "How did we get here?"

"I don't like being made a fool of. You tricked me."

"I'm sorry I didn't tell you about the helicopter, but I'm not sorry about what happened. I don't think you are either." She flinched, but he kept on talking. "Don't make me out to be the bad guy. What we shared out there wasn't just sex and you know it. It was very special. I'm not going to regret that. I'll admit I didn't make you any promises. I don't do commitments, but if I remember correctly, they're not your style either. So why are you so upset?"

Her gaze was steady. Strands of red curls fluttered around her face. "I don't like being the entertainment."

His temper flared. "It was never like that and you damn well know it." He ground his teeth together. "Fine. Let's play it your way. I brought you along to have my way with you. It was great. Thanks, babe. Now can we go home?"

Something dark and ugly flashed in her eyes. Regret came on the heels of his anger and he was instantly sorry. But before he could say anything, Jeff pulled open the helicopter's door and motioned for her to step inside. Arizona followed.

They fastened their seat belts. The pilot glanced over his

shoulder and when Arizona gave him a thumbs-up, guided them into the air.

Normally Arizona enjoyed flying. Helicopters hugged the ground, allowing him to see things not visible from planes. But today the scenery didn't interest him. He looked at the woman sitting stiffly next to him. Her gaze was firmly fixed on the window.

"Chloe?"

She didn't respond. It was noisy and she might not have heard him. Or she was ignoring him. Arizona leaned back in his seat and folded his arms over his chest. They were stuck with each other until they arrived back in California. At some point in the journey he would get her attention and explain it all to her.

He waited until they were seated in the first-class section of the plane. While other passengers were busy stowing luggage and finding their seats, he leaned close and reached for her hand. She tried to pull back, but he wouldn't let her.

"Chloe, you have to listen to me."

She stared out the window. "No, I don't."

"Unless you start humming loud enough to drown out my words, you're going to hear me anyway, so why not listen?"

He took her silence as grudging agreement.

"I'm sorry," he told her. "I was a complete jerk. I should have told you about the helicopter and given you the choice. I really didn't take you out in the woods just to take advantage of you. Obviously I hoped we would become lovers, but my main goal was to spend time with you."

She didn't say anything, but he thought she might have relaxed slightly. He rubbed his thumb over the back of her hand. "I'm not sorry we made love. I've wanted you from the first moment I met you. You're beautiful and exciting. I'm lucky to have met you. I'm arrogant enough to think you might have wanted me, too. Even if you didn't, the lovemaking was spectacular enough to have changed your mind."

A faint smile tugged at her lips. She turned to look at him. "Even if you do say so yourself."

He shrugged. "You weren't going to say it."

She took a deep breath, then let it out. He squeezed her fingers. "I didn't set you up."

"I know," she said softly. "It's just, when I realized we could have flown in, I felt really cheap and stupid."

"I'm sorry. I didn't want that."

She nodded. "It's okay. How long can I throw stones? I had a condom with me, too."

"I remembered that, but I wasn't going to mention it."

"Probably a wise idea." She studied him. "I'm fine. I understand and I'm not angry."

"Or hurt?"

"That will take a little longer to get over."

"I'm sorry."

"It's okay. You don't have to keep apologizing. I'm fine. We're fine."

But they weren't. He could hear it in her voice. "You're not telling me something. What is it?"

She was silent for so long, he thought she wasn't going to answer. Finally she shrugged. "It's nothing. I just wish…"

Her voice trailed off.

What did she wish for? That things were different? That they were different? Did she want more than he was capable of giving? Women usually did. Normally that made him feel annoyed with them, but with Chloe he felt a sense of panic, that if he couldn't provide what she needed, he would lose her.

But how could he lose what he didn't want and had never had?

"We're fine," she repeated. "We both went into the situation aware that it was temporary. Neither of us wants to get involved and we're not. We had fun. What's not to like?"

She gave him a big smile and squeezed his hand. It didn't work. She was hiding something. But as surely as he knew the sun would come up in the morning, he knew she wouldn't tell him if he asked.

As the plane taxied to the end of the runway, he leaned toward her. Chloe rested her head on his shoulder. He couldn't escape the feeling that he'd really messed things up between them, but for the life of him, he couldn't figure out what…or how. And until he knew that, he couldn't begin to make things better.

Chapter Eleven

Chloe pulled into the driveway and stayed sitting in her car. This was *not* how she'd wanted the past couple of days with Arizona to end. She'd hoped they would be fun and pleasant and something she could be excited about remembering. The worst part was she couldn't exactly explain what was wrong.

It was something about the helicopter, she knew. He'd asked her to hike in with him and there had been no need. She understood what he'd told her, that he'd wanted time for them to get to know each other and that they would have a good time together. But...

But why did it hurt so damn much? She rested her head on the steering wheel and drew in a deep breath. She felt stupid. Which didn't make sense. No wonder Arizona was confused—she couldn't make sense of it herself. She'd agreed to go into the wilderness with him. She'd even brought along a condom. So the fact that they'd become lovers shouldn't be such a huge shock. She'd wanted it, too. But telling herself that didn't make the pain in her chest go away.

She got out of the car and pulled her backpack from the small trunk. She'd barely made it to the base of the rear steps when the back door opened and Cassie stepped out onto the porch.

"You're back! I'm so excited. I've been sitting here waiting. I want to hear every single detail. Start at the beginning and talk slowly."

Chloe stared at her sister's happy face. Cassie grinned like a Cheshire cat. "Was it wonderful?" she asked. "Did you two do the wild thing?"

Without warning, Chloe burst into tears. One minute she'd been fine, but the next sobs choked her as tears poured down her face.

Cassie was at her side in an instant. "Oh, Chloe, I'm so sorry. Come on. Come inside. I don't know what's wrong, but I do know that we can fix it together."

Chloe found herself led into the kitchen. Cassie took her backpack from her and set it in the corner. She settled her sister in one of the kitchen chairs, disappeared for a second, then returned with a box of tissues. While Chloe tried to bring herself under control, Cassie started heating milk for cocoa.

The familiar smells made Chloe want to weep more. Their mother had often made cocoa to help them through life's troubles when they were growing up. It remained a tradition today. Chloe wished that her problems were as simple as they had been all those years ago. The warm drink frequently worked when she'd done poorly on a spelling test or had been teased by a boy in school, but she doubted it was going to help tonight.

Still, she took the mug Cassie offered and when her sister

took the seat across from her, she tried to smile. "It's not so bad," she said. "I'm fine."

"Oh, I can tell." Cassie tucked her thick, dark hair behind her ears and leaned forward. "Start at the beginning and tell me what's wrong."

"I don't know where to begin." She took a sip of the steaming liquid. The rich chocolate taste comforted her. "It's all so complicated. I never meant—" She broke off and glanced around. "Where's Aunt Charity?"

Cassie frowned. She'd never understood Chloe's reluctance to trust their aunt. "She's out with friends. Dinner and a movie. She'll be home late. Quit stalling. What's going on?"

Chloe resisted the urge to unburden herself. "I can't. You'll get angry."

"Why? You haven't done anything to me. I'm your sister, I care about you. I want to help."

"I know, but you'll be hurt and—" She pressed her lips together. She had really made a mess of things. "I never thought it would get so complicated."

"Chloe, you're not making any sense. What is too complicated? I know this is about Arizona, but I don't know how. Did something bad happen? Did he hurt you?"

"No," Chloe answered, knowing what her sister was asking. Arizona had hurt her but not in a way that was anyone's fault. "I want to tell you and I will, but please don't be mad."

Cassie made an X over her heart. "I swear."

As Chloe tried to speak, fresh tears filled her eyes. She wiped them away with the back of her hand, then took a sip of the cocoa. "It's all because of that stupid nightgown," she said at last. "We had sex and it ruined everything." The knot in her stomach tightened. She'd made a complete fool out of herself and she had only herself to blame. What on earth had she been thinking? Why had she given in? He must think… Chloe realized she didn't know what Arizona thought of her, which, in a way, made things worse.

"I don't understand," Cassie said. "What does the nightgown have to do with anything? Did you take it with you and wear it?"

"No." Chloe sniffed. "I lied. The night of my birthday, when I wore the nightgown, I did have a dream. I dreamed about Arizona. It was so incredibly real and passionate. I didn't know what had happened. I couldn't really believe the family legend was anything but a joke. I was embarrassed and I thought it was stupid. That's why I didn't tell you. Then when I saw him on the television, I was so stunned, I didn't know what to say. Since then, everything has been out of control. I'm confused and scared and I'm really, really sorry."

Cassie glanced down at her mug. "I see. You didn't trust me."

Her words and her stiff posture screamed her hurt. The knot in Chloe's gut doubled in size. "I knew you'd be upset. You have every right to be mad at me, Cass. I can't explain what I was thinking except I was stunned by what had happened."

Cassie didn't look at her. She shook her head back and forth, making the gold heart earrings catch the light.

Chloe stretched her hand across the table and touched her sister's fingers. "I never meant to hurt you. You are my closest friend in life. I was very upset by what had happened and I didn't want to talk to anyone about it."

At last Cassie looked at her. "Besides, I was the one so excited about the legend. If I'd known you'd dreamed about Arizona, I wouldn't have been able to keep the information to myself." A smile tugged at her lips. "Imagine if I'd blurted it out that first night he was here for dinner."

"It would have given us something to talk about."

Cassie nodded. "I understand, Chloe. I'm a little hurt, but I'll get over it. Let's talk about you and what happened. You dreamed about him, and then you met him. Was that like the dream?"

"Not the meeting." She quickly explained about going into work that morning and finding out that Arizona was her new assignment. Everywhere she went, pictures of the man stared back at her. She described seeing the scar on his arm in her dream, then finding out he had the same scar.

"How did you know about the scar?" Cassie asked. "What was he wearing in the dream?"

Chloe cleared her throat. She could feel herself blushing. "Nothing. We made love, several times. It was amazing."

Cassie laughed. "No wonder you were stunned the next morning. There's nothing like finding out your fantasy lover is a real person to get your day started."

"Exactly. It was so spooky. You know I don't believe in the legend. I'm a reporter. I want to be able to prove my facts. I couldn't figure out what was going on and it frightened me."

"Plus you wouldn't want Arizona to know too much," Cassie said. "After all, he spends his life exploring the mystic. You couldn't be sure what he would make of the whole nightgown legend once he found out he'd been the subject of your dream."

"Exactly."

Cassie took a drink of her cocoa, then placed the mug on the table and cupped it with her hands. Her eyebrows drew together. "I still don't see the problem. You and Arizona get along well. I think you like him. I know he likes you. You made love and I'm guessing it was lovely. So why are you so upset?''

''Because it's all too strange. Yes, we get along and have fun together. The sex was amazing.'' She didn't want to think about that, about how she'd felt when he touched her. ''That's not the point. It's more complicated. I refuse to fall in love with anyone ever. I won't let myself feel that kind of pain again. Arizona might believe in myths and stories, but he doesn't believe in love, romantic or otherwise. He's the kind of man who wants to spend his life roaming the world. While I want to travel, I do also want to settle down and make a home. Eventually.''

''You already have a home.'' Cassie waved to encompass the kitchen and the entire house beyond. ''You have roots. You're from Bradley.''

Cassie's tone was light, but Chloe heard the envy in her sister's voice. She never knew what to say about that—about the fact that she'd inherited the house.

Cassie shrugged. ''Where you settle isn't important. So he wants to travel, possibly more than you do. Compromise. Couples have been doing that for generations. How do you think marriages last?''

''No one is talking about getting married. That's the last thing I want to do.''

''Are you sure?''

''Yes. I refuse to love him. I don't want to get involved with anyone. We're friends and we had a great time together.''

''Then why are you crying?''

Chloe couldn't answer the question. Nothing made sense. She wanted to explain about the helicopter and feeling tricked, but she'd had time to think and she didn't believe Arizona had deliberately set out to deceive her. She'd overreacted. Probably because she was feeling a little over-whelmed by her reaction to him.

"I don't know what to think. Maybe if we hadn't made love things would be more clear." She rested her elbows on the table and cupped her head in her hands. "I feel like I'm caught up inside a tornado. Every time it sets me down, I have to get my bearings all over again. Just when I get that all figured out, I'm caught up again, with no control over my destiny."

"Sounds to me like you're falling in love with him."

Chloe sucked in a breath. "No," she said firmly. "That's not possible."

Cassie ignored her. "Of course it is. You've cut yourself off from your heart for so long, you can't recognize the symptoms. Why else would any of this matter?"

"It's not that."

"What else could it be? You're worried about what the man does for a living and how much he travels. If this was just a fling you would be grateful that he was leaving and that you would never have to see him again. Instead it bothers you. You want to find a way to blend your lives. That's what loving someone is all about."

"No. I don't love him. I don't want to love him. I don't want to love anyone."

Now it was Cassie's turn to reach across the table and touch her hand. "Yes, you do. Chloe, it's time to let go of the past. You tend to hang on to things for too long. I miss Mom and Dad, too, but I've let it go. I have the memories. What I learned is that you never know how long you're going to have, so love fully. You learned not to trust them. You probably would have gotten over that if Billy hadn't died and you can't forgive him for being wrong. He was your first love. I remember you told me he'd promised you he would get well, and you believed him. Then he died.

It's been nearly eight years and you're still mad at Aunt Charity. It's not her fault that she wasn't in the country when her brother was killed. Was she supposed to live next door all those years, just in case?''

"Of course not." Chloe knew her voice was stiff, but she was having trouble speaking past the tightness in her throat. "I'm not a closed, unforgiving person."

Cassie's fingers squeezed her own. "That's not what I meant. You're a wonderful person and I love you very much. But sometimes, you're so stubborn I just want to shake some sense into you. Let the past go. Look forward for once. Don't lose this wonderful opportunity with Arizona. When are you going to meet someone like him again?''

"You make it sound so simple."

"It can be, if you let it."

Chloe looked at her sister. She wanted to believe her, but she couldn't. Cassie was right—after nearly eight years, she *was* still angry at Aunt Charity. The woman should have known that her brother had died. There was no excuse for staying out of contact for more than three years. If not for her, Chloe and Cassie wouldn't have been sent to foster homes. They wouldn't have been separated. She wouldn't have met Billy.

Chloe stiffened. *She wouldn't have met Billy.* Was that what she wanted? To never have known him?

She turned the thought over in her mind. She regretted his death. It had hurt to love him. But even knowing he was going to die, she wasn't sure she would have wished him out of her life. She'd learned a lot from him. She'd learned about courage and dignity. She'd learned about giving her whole heart and she'd learned about pain.

"What are you thinking?" Cassie asked.

"That this is all so complicated. I should have been more like you and gotten involved with someone like Joel."

"He could never make you happy."

Chloe wanted to ask if he made her happy, but this wasn't the time.

"What are you going to do now?" Cassie asked.

"I don't know." Chloe gave her a smile, squeezed her hand once, then rose to her feet. "I can't make any decisions until I've thought this through. I'm not going to call him or anything. I'll let him make the next move."

"You need to distract yourself." Cassie glanced at her watch. "It's not that late. Do you want to go to a movie or something?"

"Not tonight. I think I'll try to work on my article. I won't be able to get Arizona out of my mind, so I might as well take advantage of that."

She headed for the stairs, then paused and faced her sister. "Thanks for listening to me. I appreciate it."

"That's part of the job." Cassie grinned. "At least there's good news about the situation."

"What's that?"

"Now that you've slept with him, you really will be able to write an 'intimate' portrait of the man."

Arizona left the hotel bar and headed up to his room. He wasn't much of a drinker, but one beer didn't go very far to help him forget his troubles.

As he left the elevator and started toward his room, he wondered again what had gone wrong with Chloe. Okay, he should have told her about the helicopter, but he really didn't think it was that big a deal. If she hadn't been receptive, he wouldn't have tried anything. It wasn't as if he'd had to talk her into making love with him.

He hated feeling like this—knowing that she was upset

and not being able to understand why. It made him crazy that even though they could both agree on the facts and the blame, he still couldn't understand why she was so hurt by everything. It was, he decided as he used the card to unlock the door, a chick thing. Men and women were incredibly different creatures. It was amazing that the species hadn't died out several millennia ago.

The first thing he noticed when he walked into the room was the blinking message light on his phone. Chloe. She'd called! He cursed himself for not coming directly to his room. What if she wanted to see him? What if she was on her way over? She could be sitting by the phone right this minute, assuming his silence meant he was angry with her.

After tossing his backpack on the floor, he picked up the receiver and punched the numbers so that he could listen to her message.

But the voice he heard after the computer instructed him to punch "1" to hear his messages wasn't Chloe's but his father's.

"Hello, Arizona. I've been reading about the gem find and your lecture series in the paper. I wondered how you were doing. I thought I might come out to California to sit in on a couple of your talks. Please give me a call when you have a moment."

Arizona angrily hit "3" to erase the message, then sank onto the blue sofa. He swore under his breath. As if he didn't already have enough trouble in his life.

He didn't want to call back. For several minutes he thought about ignoring the message and all it implied. But he couldn't. However, he could tell the old man to get off his back.

He dialed the area code for Chicago, then the number he'd known all his life. His father answered on the first ring.

"Yes?"

"It's Arizona."

"Son, thanks for calling."

Arizona flinched. He hated being called "son" almost as much as he hated the pleasure in the older man's voice. Grant Smith had finally decided to recognize his only child's existence about thirty years too late for Arizona's taste.

"How are you?" his father asked.

"Fine."

"The series going well?"

"It starts day after tomorrow, but I'm sure it will be fine." He knew his voice sounded stiff, as if he were talking to someone he didn't really like. In a way he was. His father was a stranger. The fact that he now wanted a relationship with his son didn't change the fact that he'd abandoned his son the day he'd been born.

"I've been reading about it here. There's quite a bit of coverage. You know the sort of thing. Hometown boy does good and all that. I'm very proud of you."

Arizona made a noncommittal sound low in his throat. "How's the weather in Chicago?" he asked.

"Still chilly. Listen, son. I was thinking of flying out for a few days. I would like to listen to your series."

"That's not a great idea. I'm only in town until the lectures are finished. The next day I leave for the South Pacific."

"One of those small islands with no electricity or phones?"

"Exactly. I'll be there for three months. Besides, you know you hate to travel. Why put yourself out?"

"Because I want to see you. It's been nearly a year."

"Compared to the first twenty or thirty years I was around, we're doing much better," he said dryly.

There was a moment of silence. His father exhaled into the phone. "Is that why you're making this so difficult? I just want us to spend time together."

"Why? We don't have a whole lot to talk about."

"We're the only family we have left, Arizona. You're my son. You matter."

"You know, Grant, you waited too long to figure that out. I needed you when I was growing up."

"My father took excellent care of you," the older man said stiffly.

"He did the best he could, which is more than we can say for you. But you know what he was like. I can't tell you how many times he forgot I was along and left me behind in some village somewhere. But you never cared about that. You were too busy trying to forget I was alive. Just because you've finally remembered doesn't mean I have to give a damn."

"We're family," his father repeated. "I'm not going to give up on you."

"That's your choice. But I'm not going to change my mind."

"I can be as stubborn as you. Perhaps that's where you get it from. Have a good trip, Arizona. I'll be in touch when you get back in the fall. I love you, son."

Arizona hung up without saying goodbye.

He stared at the phone, hating both his father for wanting back into his life after all this time, and himself for being such a bastard. If only he could just turn his back and have it not matter. Unfortunately it did matter. Too much. To add insult to injury, he almost understood the old man.

Grant Smith had loved his wife with a passion that lasted more than thirty years past her death. Arizona didn't understand that kind of devotion, but he respected it. If only his father had been able to turn a little of that devotion toward his son. But he hadn't. Instead Grant had hired a series of nannies to take care of the boy. He'd left the infant and the staff in the large house by the lake and had moved into a small apartment on his own.

Once his grandfather had shown up and claimed him, he'd traveled with the old man from then on. Arizona had been twenty-five the first time he'd met his father.

He leaned back on the sofa and groaned. He couldn't do this tonight—he couldn't deal with these demons, too. He didn't want to be alone. But he was in a strange city and he didn't have many friends here. The truth was there was only one person he wanted to see right now.

He glanced at the clock. It was nearly ten. Too late to be calling her. Besides, she was still furious with him. Even so, he picked up the receiver and dialed.

She answered the phone on the first ring. "Hello?"

"It's Arizona. I—" What was he going to say? In the end, there was only the truth. "I need you. It's not what you think," he added quickly. "My father called. He wants... Hell, that doesn't matter. It's just I never know what to say to him. I was a complete idiot. I'm stuck in this hotel room, I'm alone and lonely and I didn't know who else to call. I just want to be with you. I want to see you and hear your voice. We're friends, right? Or did I mess that up, too?"

She didn't answer. If he hadn't heard her faint breathing, he might have thought she'd hung up on him.

"It's not about sex," he told her. "I swear."

"Oh, Arizona, you make it so hard to stay mad at you. Yes, we're still friends. Yes, I'll come over. I want to talk, but I'd be lying if I didn't tell you that I *want* it to be about sex, too."

Chapter Twelve

Arizona leaned back against the sofa and sighed with contentment. The remnants of their room service meal had been put out into the hallway. There was still wine in the bottle sitting in the ice bucket and two servings of chocolate mousse waiting for them. This, he thought, was how it was supposed to be. These were the moments that made up a good life.

It wasn't all about the food either, he reminded himself as he glanced to his left and saw Chloe curled up on the sofa next to him. Before coming over she'd showered and changed into a pale green sleeveless dress. The filmy fabric flowed over her body. She'd tucked her bare legs under her and left her long curls loose around her shoulders. She looked different from the sensibly dressed companion he'd had the previous day on their hike. He liked how she changed to fit the circumstances. He'd thought she was as beautiful yesterday as today and he still believed that.

But what took his breath away wasn't her attractive features or tempting body—it was the fact that she was here...in his room. He rarely invited women to his room. Because of his travel schedule, he didn't make a permanent home anywhere, so his hotel and motel rooms were his sanctuary. When he was intimate with a woman, they generally went to her place, or they were somewhere in the wilderness where rooms didn't really matter. Still it felt right to have Chloe here, with him. She was more completion than intrusion.

"You're looking pensive about something," she said, her voice low. "Want to talk about it?"

He shrugged. "It's not important. I was just thinking that I never invite women up to my room. I prefer to keep all this private."

"And the outdoors is neutral," she said.

He glanced at her, but she didn't look angry. "Exactly."

"Then I'm honored, both that you would trust me not to violate your space here, and because you called me when you needed a friend." Her gaze was steady. She took a sip of her wine, then tilted her head slightly to the left. "Tell me about your father."

Arizona knew the conversation couldn't be put off forever. No doubt he would feel better *after* talking about it; he just didn't want to talk about it now. Unfortunately he couldn't think of a good excuse to put Chloe off.

"It's not a nice story," he warned her.

"Are you afraid I'll think less of you as a person?"

"The thought did cross my mind."

She put her wine on the coffee table. "I could tease you and promise that wasn't possible, but that would be taking unfair advantage." She paused for a second. "Whatever has happened between us, however complicated it gets, I've enjoyed knowing you. You're different from anyone I've ever met, but that's just on the surface. Underneath all the travel and the unusual experiences, you're very familiar to me. I think we have a lot in common and I believe we can be friends for a long time. I'll try not to judge you."

"I guess I can't ask for more than that." Their gazes locked. "Thank you," he added. "I want us to be friends, too."

A smile tugged at her lips. "Tell you what. When you're done talking about your father, I'll think up something equally slimy in my life and share it with you. Then we'll be even."

"Sure." But he doubted she could match his story. He drew in a deep breath. "My mother died when I was born. Apparently she and my father were deeply in love. They'd put off having children for several years because they just wanted it to be the two of them. But when she found out she was pregnant, I guess they were both happy. After her death, my father withdrew. He hired a nurse and a couple of people to take care of the place, then he moved out. I never saw him. He provided a staff and paid all the bills, but he was not a part of my life."

He tried to tell the story without thinking about it. He didn't want to get buried in the details, he didn't want to think about what it had been like all those years.

"As I told you before, my grandfather showed up when I was three and took me away with him. When I was about fifteen, he answered questions I had about my family. He never used the word 'blame' but I understood the subtext of what he was saying. If it hadn't been for me, my mother would still be alive."

Chloe shifted closer and took his hand in hers. She squeezed his fingers. "That's a lot for an adult to understand. It must have been an impossible burden for a teenager."

"Agreed. When I was growing up I used to make up stories about my father—exotic tales in which he came to his senses, realized none of this was my fault and showed up begging for my forgiveness. Every night I prayed he would come for me, but he never did." He cleared his throat. "I really cared about my grandfather. He did the best he could and I had some great experiences as a kid, but there were times I longed for a normal family. I wanted to have my own room, toys, friends, and wake up in the same bed for a few weeks. Then I outgrew the dream. I stopped praying my father would come for me. At times I forgot he was alive."

"I don't believe you gave up the dream," Chloe said. "I think you still have it, but now you're an adult and it's more complicated."

"Not at all. In fact—"

She cut him off with a shake of her head. "Sell it somewhere else, Arizona. Of course you wanted your father to come rescue you. We all want to be loved. But you stopped wishing because it hurt too much to always be disappointed."

He wanted to tell her she was wrong, but he couldn't. "How the hell do you know so much?"

"Things are always clearer to those on the outside. Don't worry, your secret is safe with me."

"I never doubted that for a moment."

He wanted to pull her closer. He wanted to feel her heat next to him, to wrap his arms around her and find comfort in her nearness. He didn't. Not because he was concerned she might reject him, but because the need was so intense, it alarmed him. He wasn't supposed to need anyone. If his past had taught him anything, it was that. He'd grown up in such a way that his dependence had been burned out of him at an early age. Needing someone meant having expectations. That only gave that person the opportunity to let you down. He didn't need Chloe—he didn't need anyone.

"What happened next?" she asked.

"He contacted me when I was about twenty. I was in London. He wanted me to come to Chicago and meet with him." He tried to ignore the hurt and anger welling up inside of him.

"You refused." It wasn't a question.

"Yes. He was stubborn and kept talking away. I guess I get that trait from him."

"Did he apologize for what he'd done?"

"In a manner of speaking. He said that he'd been keeping track of me for years, that he'd wanted to get in touch sooner, bring me home, but I was doing so well with my grandfather that he decided not to upset my life twice."

"Sounds reasonable."

"It does, doesn't it." His tone was sharp.

She squeezed his fingers gently. "You didn't believe him then?"

"Of course not. He was taking the easy way out. I exploded. I told him that he was about twenty years too late to be a part of my life. I wasn't interested in him as a father or a friend. As far as I was concerned, he should never contact me again. But he kept at me." He sighed heavily before continuing. "Finally, I told him what life with my grandfather had been like. I told him about the times I'd been injured or put in dangerous situations. I detailed how my grandfather had often left me behind in strange villages or towns with minimal supervision while he ran off and explored something he considered too dangerous for a child. I told him that I'd been left in the outback with a guide who disappeared and left me, that my grandfather had forgotten where to find me and that I nearly starved to death. I told him there weren't any words to make up for that. I said I didn't want to see him or hear from him ever again. Then I hung up the phone."

He felt uncomfortable with what he'd told her, but there was no way to recall the words. "I did warn you it wasn't going to be pleasant."

She ignored that comment. "What happened when he called back?"

"How do you know he did?"

She looked at him. "What else would he do? He called and apologized for all of that. What did you say?"

"That it was too late."

She didn't say anything for a while, then she pulled her hand from his. The rejection stung. Arizona had thought she might be upset or disappointed, but he hadn't expected her to simply turn away.

He shifted to push off the sofa, but before he could, her arms came around him. She moved close and rested her head on his shoulders as she clasped him around the waist.

"You were so young to be dealing with all of that," she said, her voice muffled against his neck. "Twenty isn't really grown-up. You had more life experiences than most kids your age, but I doubt you were any more emotionally mature. He'd hurt you for so many years. You just wanted to hurt him back."

Her understanding loosened the tight band around his chest. He hugged her back. "Thank you," he murmured.

"No problem. To be honest, I'd imagined something a lot worse."

"Like what? Felony convictions in several states?"

She smiled. "Something like that." She kissed his jaw. "I appreciate you sharing this with me. I just have one question. When are you going to let it go? You can't stay angry at him forever. Yes, it hurts him and in a way you still want that, but it hurts you, too.''

Arizona straightened and pushed her away. ''Thanks for the junior psychology analysis, but it's not necessary.'' Irritation battled with disappointment. He'd thought she would understand, but she didn't.

''Why are you upset?'' she asked. She slid away a couple of feet and stared at him. Her eyebrows drew together. ''You wanted to talk about this. If you hadn't, you wouldn't have asked me to come over. You know me well enough by now to know I'm not going to keep quiet, that I'm going to express my opinion. Isn't that what you wanted?''

She made sense and that really annoyed him. ''Maybe I just wanted to get you into bed.''

He'd expected her to flinch. Instead she shook her head. ''If that was true, you would have made your move before now. I've been here two hours and you've barely touched me.'' She drew in a deep breath, then tucked her hair behind her ears. Her mouth straightened. ''Hasn't it occurred to you that the reason I can understand your situation with your father is that I'm facing something similar myself? You're not the only one caught up in the past. You're not the only one who is angry. You think I don't feel the same way? It's hard, Arizona. You want to reconcile with your father, but you don't know if he's suffered enough. I want to forgive my parents, and Billy, and even Aunt Charity, but the pain and anger are all I have. If I let that go, will I lose the last little bits of them and myself that I have?''

''You're making sense,'' he grumbled. ''I really hate that.''

''It's hard,'' she told him. ''I am so furious at my parents. I hate them for dying. I hate them for naming Aunt Charity as our guardian. Because of that Cassie and I got split up. I hate that they left me the house. I'm their daughter by birth and the house has been in the family for generations, but it was still wrong.'' Anger flashed in her eyes. ''People matter more than things and they should have recognized how their actions would hurt Cassie. She has always felt like an outsider. Her only goal in life is to belong. To find roots. That's why she desperately wants the family legend about the nightgown to be true. So she can wear it on her birthday and dream about her fantasy man.''

Arizona cupped her cheek. Chloe leaned into his touch. ''I'll never forgive Billy for dying after he promised he wouldn't,'' she continued. ''I'm enraged at Aunt Charity for being gone. I know, she had her own life. No one expected her to stay home in case her brother died without warning. I know it, but I can't make my heart believe it. I live with this pain and rage and so do you. But I'm starting to see that we have to figure out a way to let it go. We both hurt, Arizona. But if the wound stays open too long, it gets infected and then we die. I'm not talking about real death, but emotional death. Isn't that worse? Is that more tragic?''

''I don't know.''

He held his arms open and she came into them. They hugged each other. He'd felt close to her from the moment he'd met her. Their lovemaking had only cemented the strange bond he couldn't explain. But that was nothing when compared to what he was feeling now. He'd never felt this connected to another person in his life. They came from completely different backgrounds. They believed different things. Chloe was a realist and he made his living searching for the mystical. Yet underneath, they were exactly alike.

''See,'' she whispered, her breath coming in short puffs against his chest. ''I'm a horrible person.''

''No, you're a very honest one and I admire that.''

"Were you listening? I can't believe it's been eleven years and I'm still mad at my folks. I've got to learn to let that go."

"Hey, it's been more than thirty years and I still don't like talking to my father. I'm much worse."

"No, I am."

He chuckled. "Interesting argument that for reasons I can't explain I feel compelled to win. When I was ten and we were in Africa, I sneaked into the tribal elder's tent and stole a pipe. I got all the other boys to smoke it with me and we all ended up sick."

"Not bad. When *I* was ten, Cassie got a new dress for some reason, and I didn't. I was so furious, I threatened to hold my breath until I got one, too. My mother wasn't impressed. Unfortunately for her, I actually did hold it until I passed out. I really scared her. Once I learned the trick, I kept doing it for about six months. I thought she was going to kill me."

He smiled and kissed the top of her head. "I stole an elephant."

"Goodness. Where on earth would you hide it?"

"I didn't. I took it for a joyride. Well, sort of. We didn't go very fast."

She laughed. "I convinced Cassie to surprise our parents by scenting their bedroom. I had her pour perfume on the bed and the carpet. The stink would not go away. They ended up getting a new mattress and carpeting."

"I don't know if I can top that one," he told her.

Her laughter was soft and sweet. He liked this, he realized. Being with her, holding her, laughing together. He felt safe talking about his past. Even if Chloe didn't agree, she wouldn't judge him. She might speak her mind and say some things he didn't want to hear, but that was a small price to pay for acceptance. Besides, he liked that she was honest.

"It's good that we're spending time with each other," she said. "I doubt anyone else would want to put up with us."

"You know that's not true."

She tilted her head back and looked at him. "You're right, I do. But it's fun to pretend." Her humor faded. "I'm glad we talked about all of this. Our conversation has shown me that it's time to let go of the past."

"Are you ready?"

"I think so." She pulled back and gave him a rueful smile. "I don't mind forgiving my parents or Billy. It wasn't really their fault they died. But not being mad at Aunt Charity is going to be harder. I didn't get it until just a few moments ago when we started talking about all this, but I finally understand what's been going on with her. By staying angry, I didn't have to worry about her getting too close. If she died or left, I wouldn't miss her. This has all been a way to protect myself from getting hurt."

"I'm impressed," he said, and tapped the tip of her nose. "That's very insightful."

"I don't mind being insightful, but I really resent having to act on what I've discovered. Still, I'm a strong person and keeping her at arm's length out of fear is the coward's way out. I'm going to have to make peace with her and deal with the consequences."

"I'm sure she's going to live a long life and you won't have to worry about losing her anytime soon."

"I hope you're right, but it doesn't matter. I can't spend the rest of my life avoiding caring about someone because I'm afraid they're going to leave me or run away."

She raised her chin in a gesture of strength and defiance. He respected both her decision and her fearlessness. Self-examination was never easy. He knew that firsthand. But if Chloe hadn't gone easy on herself—could he do any less?

He looked at the phone. He knew what his father wanted and why. Was that enough? Could he let go of the past and forgive an old man who had been driven by pain and loss? The adult side of him was willing to give it a chance, but the hurt child inside wanted restitution. Unfortunately there was nothing his father could do to make up for hurting him.

"Only if it feels right," Chloe whispered.

It did.

He picked up the receiver and dialed the number from memory. His father answered on the first ring.

"It's Arizona."

"I didn't expect to hear from you, son." His father sounded surprised, but pleased. There was no wariness in his voice, no attempt to protect himself against possible attack.

Arizona glanced at his watch. "I didn't realize the time. It's after midnight. I'm sorry if I woke you."

"You didn't. That's one of the ironies of old age. I have less to do with my day than ever before, yet I need less sleep. I could have used this time twenty years ago but that's what happens."

"I'm sorry I was such a jerk when you called earlier."

The older man sighed heavily. "Don't apologize. You have every right to be furious with me. What I did...I won't try to excuse it. I was wrong. I've realized that over the years. I should have known that you and I could help each other out. But I was too caught up in my pain. I was so selfish."

"I understand."

"You don't have to, son. Your mother—" His voice broke. "She was my world. When I lost her, I wanted to die, too. I didn't care about anything or anyone. I'm so sorry about that. Even as I left you alone, I knew it was wrong. I knew she would be disappointed in me if she ever knew. But I couldn't stop myself.''

''It's okay.'' He cleared his throat. ''Dad, really, it is.''

Dad. He'd never said the word before. He'd always used ''Father'' or ''old man.'' Nothing friendly or personal.

Chloe moved close to him. He put his arm around her and squeezed. She was his lifeline in this unfamiliar sea of emotion.

''I should have come after you,'' his father continued. ''I didn't want you to go away, but it was also easier to try and forget with you out of the country. I didn't know about all you went through,'' he said quietly. ''With your grandfather. I thought he would take better care of you. I should have realized the truth. I'm sorry about that, too.''

Arizona suffered through a flash of guilt. ''There were some tough times,'' he said. ''But it wasn't all bad. I learned a lot. I wouldn't be doing what I do today, if I hadn't traveled all over the world.''

''I appreciate you trying to make me feel better, but I know what I did and didn't do. I was never a father to you. But if it's not too late, perhaps we could get to know each other and become friends.''

Arizona thought of all the times he'd refused the older man's invitations. Of all the times he'd sworn at him, hung up on him or ignored him. Yet his father was still trying, still asking to see him. His father was the only family he had. Why was he willing to let that bond stay broken?

His chest was tight and it was hard to speak. Even so he forced himself to say, ''I'd like that. I'm going to be busy until I leave for the island, but we could get together when I get back.''

''Could I come see you this summer? On the island?''

Despite the emotion flooding him, Arizona couldn't repress a grin. How would his banker father, a man who had only ever loved one woman in his life, who had mourned her for more than thirty years, survive in a society run for and by women? Visitors were often seduced by widows and unmarried females. Arizona had been in a couple of difficult situations himself until the shaman had taken him under her wing and offered protection.

"That might not be a bad idea," he said. "I'll get together some literature and send it along to you. If you decide you want to make the trip, you can let me know and I'll meet you in Guam."

"I'd like that, son." His father cleared his throat. "It *is* late and I should probably let you go. Thanks for giving me another chance."

"You're welcome. Thank you for not giving up on me."

"I love you, son."

Arizona sucked in a breath. "You, too, Dad. I'll talk to you soon."

He waited until his father hung up the phone before he replaced the receiver. He glanced at Chloe and saw tears on her cheeks.

"That was so great," she told him. "I'm so glad you called him and talked to him. How do you feel?"

"A little strange. Relieved and nervous, I guess. I'm not sure about him visiting me." He told her a little about the culture on the island. "My father is nearly seventy. I think he might be threatened by the ladies wanting to take his equipment for a test-drive."

Chloe wiped her face with the back of her hand and smiled. "It might be just the thing he needs to give him a new lease on life."

"I hadn't thought of that. You're right. He might enjoy the challenge." He closed his eyes and rubbed his temples. "How does everything get so complicated? These familial relationships get twisted and broken and yet we stumble on. My grandfather abandoned his own wife and child to travel the world. He was an adventurer at heart. He told me once that he never should have married, but when a girl from a good family turns up pregnant, there's not much a man can do.''

''Your father grew up without *his* father?'' Chloe asked.

Arizona nodded. ''He swore he would be different, that he would marry for love and never leave her side. Which was true, even in death. But he also abandoned me as he had been abandoned.''

''So he only learned part of the lesson.''

He shrugged, not sure what his father had learned. Maybe they were all doomed to repeat each other's mistakes.

''You break the cycle by not believing in love and I assume as a by-product of that, not marrying or having children,'' Chloe said, as if she could read his mind.

''Something like that.''

''It is one way to deal with the problem.''

''Not one you approve of?'' he asked.

''It's not my place to approve or disapprove,'' she told him. ''I'm just glad you want to work things out with your father and that you're going to see him soon.''

''Me, too.'' He wanted to say more. He wanted to tell her that she was so incredibly beautiful, sitting there in the lamplight. He wanted to tell her that he appreciated the fact that she'd agreed to talk with him tonight, to be a friend when he needed one. Her support had given him the strength to do what was right.

But he couldn't find the words. He could only look at her and want her.

Something must have shown on his face because she smiled faintly, then leaned close. ''Fine,'' she whispered, her breath soft and sweet against his face. "Change the subject if you have to. I don't mind."

Then she kissed him.

His body responded instantly. Even as Arizona moved his mouth against her, heat filled him as blood rushed to make him ready to take her. He was hard and aching in less than ten seconds.

There was little time for tenderness. They touched each other everywhere. Even as he tried to slow down, Chloe tugged at his clothing and whispered words of encouragement, telling him how much she needed him to be in her. When he touched her panties, he found her ready for him. He slipped past the elastic band and pressed a finger deep inside of her. She surged against him. As he kissed her, he cupped a breast with his free hand and toyed with the tight nipple. He moved his finger in and out of her. Within seconds he felt the rhythmic pulsing of her most feminine place surging around, drawing him in deeper. She broke the kiss enough to gasp out his name as her pleasure continued.

From then on it was a blur. One minute they were still half-dressed and on the sofa. The next they were on top of the bed, their clothes forming an untidy trail on the carpet. He plunged into her and felt her climax again. There was no way to stop either of them, he realized. The passion burned away social convention and left them only with driving need.

He dug his fingers into her hair to hold her still. She grabbed his hips and forced him in deeper. Their kisses were hot and wild and when she bucked against him in yet a third release, he exploded into her.

They clung to each other as the fire cooled. They were both slick with sweat and panting. Arizona slid out of her and settled next to her on the bed. Chloe came into his arms and they snuggled in a position that had so quickly become familiar.

Holding her felt so right, he told himself, and it was the last thought he had that night.

He felt her stir sometime well before dawn. Arizona turned onto his side and squinted as she clicked on the lamp on the nightstand.

"Good morning," she said softly, her eyes still heavy with sleep and her hair mussed. "I'm sorry to wake you, but I have to get to the house."

He nodded. "I didn't mean to fall asleep. Sorry." He motioned to his hotel room. "I know it wouldn't do for someone to see you sneaking out of my room in the middle of the morning."

"There would be talk," she agreed with a smile. "I have to go home and work on my article, but why don't you try and get some sleep? You start your lecture series tonight."

"I just might do that."

He watched as she pulled on clothes. When she was dressed, she crossed to the bed and kissed his cheek. "I'll see you tonight."

He grabbed her hand. "Dinner? After the lecture?"

"I'd like that. Thank you."

He squeezed her fingers. When she pulled away, he didn't want to let her go. He wanted to tell her something, but the words eluded him.

Don't go.

Was that it? Did he want to keep her with him? But before he could figure it out, she'd stepped into the hall and quietly closed the door behind her. He rolled onto her side of the bed. The sheets were still warm from her body and they smelled of their lovemaking. But it wasn't enough. The room had grown cold and empty without her presence. As perhaps, he thought grimly, had his life.

Chapter Thirteen

Chloe stared at the pile of notes sitting on the corner of her desk. She had too much material. It was, she supposed, the problem to have. After all, too *much* to work with meant she would only be using the very best of what she had instead of scrambling for things to fill the pages. Unfortunately, she was having trouble figuring out what to cut and what to keep. She wanted to keep it all. The article was about Arizona and she thought he was pretty wonderful.

"Not that I'm biased in the least," she said aloud, then shifted in her seat. Her insides still felt a little squishy from their lovemaking the previous night. What a way to go to sleep. If only they could do that every night.

She smiled at the thought and had a bad feeling that she was glowing with happiness. As long as the glow wasn't the least bit magnetic, she wouldn't hurt her computer. Unfortunately, she also wasn't in the mood to get any work done, either.

On a whim, she closed her word-processing program and logged onto the Internet. She found her way to Arizona's fan club. She'd noticed an icon for a bulletin board. Feeling more than a little foolish, she wrote a quick post saying that while the man was completely brilliant, he was also a hunk and wasn't that just as important as his work?

Giggling softly, she posted the message, then went to check her E-mail. After responding to her mail, she returned to the bulletin board to see if anyone had read her comments. She was stunned to see several replies. Two women agreed completely and went on to describe him in such detail that Chloe wondered if she should feel jealous. Then a third message appeared, this one berating Chloe for her shallowness. That the wonder of Arizona Smith wasn't in his physical appearance, but in the magic of his work. He was more than just a man. He was a symbol for the mystic world. He was a true hero.

She logged off the Internet. She didn't want to talk about Arizona with people who had never met him. She wanted to talk about who he really was and how he made her feel.

He *was* amazing—she could concede that with no problem. He was intelligent, gifted, motivated, kind. But like everyone else, he had his faults. He was a little self-centered and he could be stubborn. He wasn't perfect, but he was someone she could...

He was someone she could love. Someone she did love.

Chloe placed her elbows on the desk and rested her head in her hands. Love? No, that wasn't part of the plan. She wasn't supposed to love him. She was supposed to find him interesting and entertaining, nothing more. Not love. That was too dangerous. She'd learned her lesson. She didn't want to go there again. Because of her past, she'd been avoiding love for a long time. This situation with Arizona had pain written all over it.

"Why me? Why now?"

But there weren't any answers. Maybe it was the luck of the draw, or just her time. She thought she'd been so careful to hide her heart away. But she hadn't. At least not this time. She'd been so stunned when she'd first met him. Because of the dream, she reminded herself.

"So much for the magic nightgown," she said as she straightened in her chair. Didn't the family legend promise a lifetime of happiness? But that wasn't possible with Arizona. He wasn't a man who would be content to stay in one place for very long, and she was the kind of woman who needed a home. There would be no happily-ever-after for her. The only guarantee she had was that he would leave in just a few days and she would be heartbroken.

"I don't need this," she told herself. Not again. She didn't want to love him but it was too late. Love him she did.

A knock on the door interrupted her thoughts. She glanced up and saw Aunt Charity standing in the doorway. The older woman wore tailored slacks and a shirt, the conservative clothing emphasizing a figure that had stayed trim all her life. Her long dark hair was up in its customary French twist. She offered a smile.

"It's nearly lunchtime and you never even bothered with breakfast. I've brought you a snack." She placed the tray on the desk.

Chloe glanced at the pot of tea, the sandwiches and bowl of fruit. "Thank you," she said, forcing her voice to sound soft and grateful. Her natural tendency was to be belligerent with her aunt. Her conversation with Arizona about letting go of the past was still fresh in her mind. "You went to a lot of trouble and I appreciate that."

"You're welcome." As always, Charity's smile was

open. "You've been working hard on your project. How is it going?"

"Very well. My biggest problem is that I have too much material. I've made an outline of the topics I want to cover. Now I have to start eliminating the nonessentials. Unfortunately, Arizona is so interesting to write about that I want to include everything."

"That's even before you hear his lecture series."

Chloe nodded. The series started that night. "I've included a section for them, but I don't know how long it's going to be. One of the things I want to focus on is the man rather than the myths about him. I mean, the information about the fan club is fun and I enjoy teasing him about it, but he's more than just that."

Charity placed her hands in the front pockets in her slacks. "I remember the first time Arizona and I met. As I recall, he was surrounded by a group of young women. It was in India—the outskirts of—"

She paused, then sighed. "Never mind. It's not important. I should let you get back to your work. I didn't mean to interrupt." She turned to leave.

Chloe pressed her lips together. Had she really been shutting her aunt out so very much, she didn't feel comfortable telling a story about Arizona? The truth made her flush with embarrassment and shame. She rose to her feet.

"Aunt Charity, wait."

The older woman paused expectantly. Chloe tried to figure out what she wanted to say. She wasn't feeling very brave right now, but she reminded herself that Arizona had been able to make peace with his father and their history had been a lot more complicated and difficult than hers with her aunt. All she had to do was speak from her heart.

"I'm sorry," she began. "I've been a real brat and a pain. I have no excuse. I'm twenty-five, which is plenty old enough to act like an adult. I even had the fantasy that I was being subtle, but I haven't been, have I?"

Charity shrugged. "Only if you secretly think I'm a wonderful person."

"Actually, I do. I just didn't realize it until recently. You came to Cassie and me as soon as you found out what had happened. You made a home for us, and you've stayed here all these years, even though we would be fine on our own. You'd spent your whole life seeing the world, yet in the past seven and a half years, I don't think you've as much as left the state. I never realized that before. I never thought about what you'd given up to be with us."

Her aunt stepped toward her and cupped her face in her hands. Chloe allowed the physical contact, then found, much to her surprise, she didn't mind being touched.

"You don't have to apologize. I understand," Charity told her. "You had lost your parents and were separated from your sister. It was a difficult time."

"You lost your brother," Chloe pointed out. "I never thought about that, either. We'd had three years to get over the pain of missing them, but you only found out a few days before. I was so angry and hurt, and that was all I could think about. I'm sorry."

"Let's both agree to stop blaming and stop apologizing. We can start over."

"I'd like that," Chloe said, suddenly feeling shy. She motioned to the bed and when Charity sat on the mattress, she took her seat at the desk and swiveled to face her aunt. There were still things to be said between them.

"Cassie and I appreciate all you've done for us, but you've given up enough. Don't you think it's time you started living your own life?"

"Are you throwing me out?" Charity asked, a smile softening the question.

"Of course not. This is your home. At least I hope you think of it that way. But you've always traveled. Don't you miss that? Don't you want to get back out in the world?"

Charity paused to consider the question. Her dark hair was sleek and the color reminded Chloe of her father. He'd been a handsome man and his sister was equally attractive.

"That's an interesting question," Charity said. "I'll admit when I first moved to Bradley, I didn't think I could survive in this small town. While I loved you two girls and was pleased to help in any way, it was difficult knowing that I couldn't pack up and move on whenever I wanted. But gradually, I began to fit in. I'm not sure I could travel the way I did before. Of course there are a few trips I would like to make, but none of them are pressing."

Chloe leaned forward. "Then stay. When you're ready, make plans. Cassie and I are completely capable of handling things on our own."

Charity nodded. "I've known that for a long time. You're both very responsible." She shook her head. "I'm glad we had this talk, Chloe. I've wanted to get this settled for a long time, but I was never sure what to say. Which is so unlike me. I usually have a sense about these sort of things. But then I didn't know about my brother's death, so maybe I've outgrown the gift."

Chloe grinned. "I've heard these stories before. How you always just kind of *know* things. You can probably convince Arizona and Cassie, both of whom want to believe, but I remain a skeptic. I'll agree we can all have a gut instinct about things, but actual intuition…no way."

"Oh really. Is that a challenge?"

Chloe was enjoying the conversation with her aunt. Fierce regret filled her. If only she'd been willing to talk to her like this before. They could have been friends for years. "If you think you're up to it, yes."

"The stories I could tell you," Charity said. "I wouldn't want to shock you."

"So far all I'm hearing is cheap talk. Do you have at least one example?"

"Of course." The older woman crossed her legs, then gave Chloe a knowing look. "You dreamed about Arizona Smith the night you wore the family nightgown. Before you ask, no, Cassie didn't tell me after you finally confessed everything to her."

Chloe hadn't known what to expect. She'd thought her aunt might bring up some minor transgression from high school. Something that she, Chloe, had thought she'd gotten away with. She hadn't expected this—that her aunt had known the truth all along. Or had she?

"When did you figure it out?" she asked.

Charity's dark eyes were kind, her expression loving. "The next morning. It was so obvious from the look on your face that you'd dreamed about someone interesting. Then you heard the television and glanced at the screen. For a second I thought you were going to faint. Your reaction to Arizona that night merely confirmed my suspicions."

Suddenly a few pieces of the puzzle fell into place. "Did you invite him here deliberately so that I would meet him?"

Charity placed her hand flat against her chest. "Would I do that? Of course not. I had always planned to invite Arizona over during his visit. I'll admit that seeing your reaction to him sped up the timetable a little, but that's all."

"Oh, that's all." Chloe didn't know whether to laugh or bury her face in her hands. She'd been set up. No wonder she'd had the feeling that she couldn't escape the man. Fate might have conspired when she'd been given the article assignment, but it hadn't been working alone. Aunt Charity had been a willing accomplice.

"I'm impressed," she admitted. "You do know things."

"I know something else."

"I'm almost afraid to ask, but here goes. What?"

"You're in love with him, but you don't want to admit it."

Chloe slumped back in her chair. "I know. I am, at least I think I am. I've been fighting it for a while. I don't want to love anyone else. It always hurts."

"Honey, if that's the lesson you learned from your parents' death, then you learned the wrong lesson. Yes, they were taken far too soon, but they still lived. They had each other and you girls. They were happy and they were wonderful people. You should be grateful you had any time with them, not bitter because it hurt when they were gone. If it hadn't been painful, then they wouldn't have been worth loving."

Her words almost made sense. Chloe backed away from the truth. "It's not just them. I've had other heartache."

"I know about the young man you fell in love with in high school. Cassie told me."

"He died," Chloe said firmly. "He was my life. I was seventeen and I loved with my whole heart. One day he was just gone."

Charity's mouth twisted down. "Would you rather have played it safe? Knowing what you know now, if you could turn back time, would you not have loved him?"

The question stung. Chloe sucked in a breath as pain shot through her chest. Knowing what she knew now, could she walk away from Billy? She'd wrestled with this question before.

She pictured his face in her mind, remembered the feel of his hand as he held hers. She thought about the whispered promises they'd made when they thought they had forever. They had been so in love with each other, so convinced that they would never need anyone else.

Those were magical times, she admitted to herself. They'd been so young and yet it had felt right. Would it have been better to play it safe?

"No," she whispered, answering both Aunt Charity's question and her own. "I would still have loved him. I would still have wanted to be there at the end, holding his hand." She blinked back the sudden tears. "Those last months were horrible. The family tried everything, Billy fought against the cancer, but in the end, it won. He wanted to die at home, so he did. We were all there, all trying to be brave for him. I remember he kept saying it was okay to cry."

She brushed at the tears on her cheeks. "He told me I had made his life worth living."

"I'm sure you did," her aunt told her. "That has value...for both of you."

Chloe nodded. Her throat was tight. "I remember his last breath. He exhaled and then was very still. We all waited, willing him to take in another breath, but he was gone. I thought I was going to die. I prayed to go with him so that we could always be together, just like we'd promised each other."

"But your life had a different path than his."

"I know that now, but at seventeen I was devastated."

Chloe thought about all her aunt had asked, all she'd asked herself. "I can't regret loving Billy," she said slowly. "Knowing what I know now, I would do it all again. I would love him and I would sit next to him on the bed and watch him die."

"We aren't always guaranteed a happy ending," Charity said. "But that doesn't mean we are allowed to stop loving.

That is our purpose. Our great gift and sometimes the source of our sorrow. The world has much to offer, but first we must be willing to accept what is given. Love doesn't come for free, but it's always worth the effort.''

"You're telling me not to be afraid to love Arizona."

"I'm telling you that you'll regret turning your back on the gift, if that's what's offered. But there are no promises, Chloe. You know that.''

She didn't know. That was the problem. "In some ways we're so much alike, but in others…" She shook her head. "I've been thinking about what I've been doing. Here in Bradley, I mean. In my life. I keep telling everyone, including myself, that when I have the right number and types of articles, I'll go to New York and find a job with a big magazine. Isn't that the craziest thing you've ever heard?''

"No. You're very talented.''

Chloe smiled. "Thanks, Aunt Charity, but that's not what I meant. I've been sitting here wondering what I'm waiting for. Why do I need the perfect article? If I can't get a writing job, I'll bet there's something I can do at a magazine. I can intern, or be an assistant for a while. I already work for a reputable publication. I know the industry. But I've been waiting for exactly the right circumstances.''

Her aunt nodded. "You're starting to wonder if that's a symptom for something else.''

"Exactly. I'm starting to think I don't want to leave Bradley. That I love this old house and this town. My family, my job, my friends. Somewhere along the line I got the idea that to be a 'real' writer, I had to go somewhere else. Otherwise, I didn't really have a dream. But my dreams can work here just as well. I don't have to move away and I'm starting to think I don't want to.''

"Then don't. No one is making you go. I'm sure your

editor at the magazine right here would be thrilled to know you were staying.''

"But what about Arizona?'' Chloe asked softly. "I've just figured out that all I want in life is right here in my own backyard. Just like in the movies. There's no place like home. But the man I've fallen in love with doesn't have a real home. He travels the world.''

"I see your point. It's an interesting dilemma.''

Chloe rubbed her temples "He's not perfect. In fact, I'm very clear on his flaws. He can be stubborn and he does impulsive things that make me crazy. But he's a good man, with a kind heart. He's not perfect, but he's exactly right for me.'' She looked at the older woman sitting across from her. "I don't know what to do.''

"That's easy. Follow your heart.''

"But it's not saying anything. I'm torn. On the one hand I want to stay in Bradley. On the other, I love Arizona. I don't see how I can win. Even if I asked him to take me with him and he agreed, I'm afraid I wouldn't be happy.''

"There's another solution. Ask him to stay here.''

Chloe shook her head. "That's not possible. You know him. He would hate being tied down to one place. All he knows is traveling. He's not interested in putting down roots.''

"Maybe he's tired of what he's been doing and wants to try something else. What does it hurt to ask?''

"No,'' Chloe said firmly, wishing it could be otherwise. "He's not that kind of man. He doesn't even believe in love.'' She tried to make herself smile and had a feeling that it came out all wrong. "I would need him to love me and I don't think he can. So there's no point in asking him to stay. Letting him go is the right thing to do.''

Charity rose to her feet. "At the risk of destroying our newly found rapport, your logic is completely flawed.

Frankly, I think you're afraid. If you don't ask, then he won't say yes and you don't have to put anything on the line.''

''That's not true. How can you say that? By not asking, I'm guaranteeing myself that I'm going to get hurt. Do you think I want that?''

Charity stared at her. ''It's not that simple. If you don't ask him to stay or even hint that you have strong feelings for him, then Arizona is probably going to leave. While you won't be happy with that, at least you'll be safe. You already know you're going to feel pain when he's gone.'' She reached out and grasped Chloe's hand. ''You're trying to maintain control. If you confess your feelings, then you don't know what you two will decide. You don't know how much you might hope and then be disappointed. Or worse, that he might agree and then you're stuck with him. What then? You might have to actually deal with loving him. You're afraid. It's easier to let him go than to put yourself on the line and ask for what you want. The real terror isn't that he would say no…it's that he would say yes.''

Chapter Fourteen

"So there I was, up to my knees in mud in the pouring rain, staring directly at the white sapphire." Arizona paused long enough to motion to the beautiful gem displayed in a lit glass case at the front of the lecture hall.

The video camera panned to follow his gesture. Instantly the picture on the screens on both sides of the huge, filled-to-capacity lecture hall changed from a silver screen-size view of Arizona's handsome features, to a close-up of the gem.

"I knew if I could just reach a couple more inches, I would hold it in my hand." He smiled. "Talk about living a fantasy."

He paused for effect and gave Chloe a quick wink. She blushed and made sure the camera was still pointing at the gem. As she was in the front row and directly in Arizona's line of vision, he could see her easily. She didn't mind if the people around them noticed the wink, but she didn't want it on the videotape or broadcast to the large crowd. Cassie nudged her, then gave her a knowing smile.

"I would guess he's completely smitten," her sister whispered.

Chloe's only answer was a shake of her head, but she knew her blush gave her away. Whether or not Arizona was smitten, *she* was head over heels for the guy. She'd attended every one of his lectures over the past week. She could listen to him talk forever.

"I leaned forward," he continued. "Then I felt it. The steady pressure of the anaconda going past me, then turning so it was between me and my prize."

The audience gasped. Chloe found herself also caught up in his story. It had been like this each of the previous nights. Arizona wove fabulous stories from his life. They were made all the more enthralling because they were based on truth. But it was more than that. He had a way about him, about his speech patterns and word choices. While other lecture series could inform and even intrigue, his brought the audience right to the moment. He was a born storyteller in the great oral tradition. Had this been a hundred years ago, he would have plied his trade around campfires. Considering all the places he went to, he probably did.

"You can imagine what I was thinking," he said. "That this seems like a great time for a break!"

There was a moment of stunned silence, then a burst of laughter. Everyone applauded.

As the crowd began to circulate through the room, Arizona moved to the stage stairs. Chloe, Cassie and Charity stood up. Chloe glanced toward Arizona, but before she could move toward him, he was surrounded by adoring fans.

It had been like this every night since the lecture series

began. The giant ballroom filled to capacity, the mesmerized audience, Arizona the center of attention. Last night, after the lecture, when he'd led her to his bed and held her gently, he'd asked if she was angry with him.

"I don't mean to ignore you," he'd told her.

She'd explained that she understood completely. When he made the audience laugh or gasp or applaud spontaneously, he was just sharing his gift. She wasn't thrilled with the pretty young women who seemed to stand so close, but there wasn't much she could do about that. He'd responded by tickling her until she begged for mercy, all the while telling her she should know better than to think he would be interested in anyone but her. They'd ended up lost in passion.

Later, alone in her own bed, she'd thought about what he'd told her. She wanted to believe him. She wanted to think he wouldn't be interested in anyone but her. However, she had her doubts.

"I'm going to force my way into that crowd," Cassie said as she eyed the group of people around Arizona. "Tonight is the last night of the series. I want to tell him how much I've enjoyed myself. He's leaving in a couple of days and I might not get to see him again."

"I'll join you," their aunt said. "What about you, Chloe?"

"No, thanks. I think I'll head the other way and get something to drink."

She started to make her way through the crowd. As she did, bits of conversation drifted toward her.

"Oh, John, he makes it sound so exciting. Do you think *we* could go to South America?"

"Of course, Lily. Let's call the travel agent first thing in the morning."

A little farther down she heard another couple planning

a photo safari to Africa. So it went until she broke free of the crowd and found herself in the relative calm of the ballroom's foyer.

When she was in front of the bar, she reached for her small handbag.

"Can I buy you a drink, pretty lady?"

She spun toward the familiar voice and saw Arizona standing next to her. Despite all the time they'd been spending together and the fact that she'd been seeing him every day for more than two weeks, he still had the ability to make her toes curl.

"How did you escape?" she asked. "Last time I saw you, you were holding court with at least a dozen loyal fans. Including my sister and aunt."

"I spoke to them, told everyone else I needed a couple of minutes to rest, then used a side door to sneak down the back corridor away from the crowd." He nodded at the bartender. "What would you like?"

She gave her order. He took a glass of water for himself, then led her over to a couple of chairs in the corner of the foyer.

"I think it's going well," he said.

She resisted the urge to roll her eyes. "There's an understatement. You have them completely in the palm of your hand. But that's not a surprise. I've seen it happen every night." She met his gaze and smiled. "I'm impressed, as usual."

"Thank you. I've been to some interesting places and people like to hear about my adventures. I'm lucky."

It was more than luck, she thought. "You don't just tell them what happened to you, you also inspire them. I would say at least half the people in that room are talking about taking a trip somewhere they wouldn't have gone before hearing you. Maybe you should talk to the airlines about getting a finder's fee or something.''

He chuckled. "Like a travel agent. There's a thought." He shifted his chair closer to hers and slipped his arm around her. "The truth is many of them will change their minds when they find out how much it's going to cost, or when they get the list of vaccinations required for the travel. But some will go and seeing the world will change their lives.''

"Always a good thing," she said, then wondered if she was wrong to want to stay here, in Bradley. Had she discovered her true self or was she simply afraid? Aunt Charity had called her a coward. She didn't want to believe that about herself, but what other explanation was there?

"It's not just travel that changes a person," he said, then leaned toward her and kissed her cheek. "You've changed me. I'm a better man for having known you.''

His words warmed her down to her soul. "I would like to say the same thing, but I'm not a better man. In fact I'm not a man at all.''

"Brat." He grinned, then squeezed her once and stood up. "I have to get back. We're on for later, right?''

She nodded. They'd had a standing date for after the lectures ever since the talks had started.

"Good." He took a step away, then returned and kissed her on the mouth. "I hate how little time we have left. I want to spend all of it together." He kissed her again. "I wish I could talk you into coming with me. Ah, well, another time.''

And with that, he was gone.

Chloe slowly made her way back to her seat. Her head was spinning. Had he meant what he'd just said? Did he plan to ask her to go with him? No, he wouldn't. They got along well, he cared about her and he would miss her. But that's all it was. Arizona wasn't about to fall in love and she...

Chloe settled down next to her sister and aunt and tried to pay attention to the rest of the lecture, but for once, Arizona's wild tales couldn't keep her attention. Her mind raced around as she tried to figure out what was right for her...for both of them. If the truth were told, she *would* like to travel some, see parts of the world. But she wouldn't want to live somewhere else for any length of time. She wouldn't want to be a nomad. She needed roots and family around her. Arizona—what did he need? Was she wrong not to talk about this with him? Maybe Aunt Charity was right about her being a coward. Maybe she should try to figure out a way to explain the situation so they could look for a compromise.

The rest of the lecture passed in a blur. Afterward, the three women made their way to the reception. Aunt Charity and Cassie would stay an hour or so, then leave. Chloe would be there until Arizona told her he was ready to duck out, then together they would head over to his hotel.

She'd just filled her plate from the buffet line when one of the administrators from the university came up beside her.

"Ms. Wright, isn't it?" the elderly gentleman asked. "I'm Dr. Grantham, a vice president at the university."

"Nice to meet you," Chloe said, not quite sure why she was being singled out. "Yes, I'm Chloe Wright."

"Please." He motioned to a table off to the side. "If you have a moment, I would like to speak with you."

"Sure." The hair on the back of Chloe's neck prickled. She had a sudden premonition that she wasn't going to like what this man had to say. She glanced around, then spotted Cassie and motioned that she would be joining her shortly.

When she and Dr. Grantham were seated, he gave her a

disarming smile. He was older, with white hair and thick white eyebrows. He looked like an English peer.

"Yes, well, this is a bit of a delicate thing. I hope you don't think I'm intruding or prying. This is about our mutual friend, Dr. Smith."

Chloe put her plate on the table. Her stomach tightened around the knot forming there.

"What about Arizona?" she asked.

"The university has offered him a full professorship. We think a man of his experience and talent would be a great addition to our faculty. We included a generous package with plenty of time off so he could continue to explore the world." Dr. Grantham's mouth straightened. "Much to our disappointment, Dr. Smith turned us down."

Chloe told herself to keep breathing. That the tightness in her chest and throat was just shock and not an actual seizing of her body. She wasn't going to die...it just felt like it.

"You offered him a job?"

"Yes. He was very polite, but said he wasn't interested in settling in one place." Dr. Grantham gave a humorless laugh. "I can only imagine how many other institutions have offered him as much or more. I don't suppose we ever really had a chance, but we had to try."

Chloe nodded. They had to try. They'd failed. Just as she would fail if she asked him to compromise so they could maintain their relationship.

Relationship! What relationship? She was simply a convenience to him.

"I was hoping," Dr. Grantham continued, startling Chloe, who had nearly forgotten the other man was still sitting at the table, "perhaps you could have a word with him. I've noticed you two seem to be particular friends. You might be an influence."

Chloe bit back a choked gasp. Particular friends. It was a gentle phrase from another time. She was willing to admit that she and Arizona were friends. Of course they were. They had fun together. They were lovers. She was *in* love with him. But she had no influence over him. Nor did she have the courage to tackle the subject. Not now. Not when she'd just found out that he'd been offered a chance to stay in her world and that he'd refused it. He couldn't have spoken more clearly. When his time here was up, he wanted to leave her.

She didn't doubt that he cared…in some way. In *his* way. After all, he'd warned her from the beginning that he didn't believe in love. She shouldn't be surprised that nothing had changed. She'd been the one to break the rules, not him.

"I don't think I can help you," she said stiffly as she rose to her feet. "Arizona is his own man."

"I see." The elegantly dressed Dr. Grantham suddenly looked like an old man.

Chloe fought against guilt. Wasn't it enough her heart was breaking? Did she have to be responsible for the university, too? She sucked in a breath. "I'll do what I can," she said. "I'll say something to him. But don't expect a miracle."

Dr. Grantham beamed and shook her hand. "We'll appreciate anything you can do." Then he rose and left her.

Chloe stared after him. She would keep her word and mention the offer to Arizona, but she knew it wouldn't matter. Nothing mattered except the fact that in two days, Arizona would be out of her life forever.

"Dr. Smith, my wife and I have enjoyed your lecture series so much," the older man was saying. "You bring your experiences alive. We feel as if we'd been there, don't we, honey?"

His wife smiled. "Yes, indeed. William and I were just saying that we should travel more. Maybe Egypt or Africa. What do you think, Dr. Smith?"

"There are advantages to both," Arizona told them. "Go through a reputable travel agent and confirm everything in advance."

The couple nodded eagerly and started talking about pyramids versus photo safaris. Arizona felt his attention drifting as he glanced around the room. He knew what he was searching for...make that *whom*. Chloe. Always Chloe. Normally he enjoyed the "meet and greet" part of the evening, but for the past couple of nights he'd wanted to run out directly after his lecture, grab Chloe and escape to his hotel room. He wanted to be alone with her, not talking to all these people.

He tried telling himself it was just sex, but he couldn't buy it. He'd had lovers around before and he'd always been able to focus on what he was doing. In fact if Chloe told him they couldn't make love that night, he would still be as anxious to get her alone. Yes, he wanted to touch her and hold her, but he also wanted to talk with, spend time with her. Be in the same room, listen to her laugh, watch the light in her eyes.

He scanned the line for the buffet, then saw Cassie and Charity sitting at a table. Chloe wasn't with them. He frowned and continued to search, at last spotting her in the company of Dr. Grantham. The courtly older gentleman had approached him just yesterday, offering him a position at the university. The offer had been generous, and were he a different kind of man, he might have considered taking it and settling down here.

The long line moved forward a little and he greeted the next couple. They had a few questions about his lecture.

He answered them easily and again found his attention wandering.

Chloe was so damn beautiful, he thought. Tonight she wore a simple black dress. Short sleeves, scooped neck. The style didn't hug her body, but it was formfitting enough to be a distraction. She was shaking hands with Dr. Grantham, then returning to her sister and aunt.

He watched her walk across the room, her hips swaying gently, her body calling to his. What was there about her that drew him? Why did he have the feeling that leaving this time was going to be more difficult than in the past? He knew he couldn't stay. He came from a long line of men who abandoned those they were supposed to love. First, his grandfather had walked out on his wife and son to pursue a life of adventure. While they had never wanted for material things, they'd been denied a husband and a father.

The pattern had continued in his life. While his father had loved his mother to the point of obsession, he'd allowed his only son to be raised at first by strangers, then by the man who had abandoned him. Their family tree wasn't a shining example of healthy family relationships.

So where did that leave him? Wasn't he smarter to avoid that which he couldn't do well? After all, it had taken nearly thirty years for him to forgive his father. They had made tentative peace, but that wasn't the same as actually making the relationship work.

"So you really believe in all this magic nonsense?" a gruff man was asking.

"Of course," Arizona replied easily. "How can we not? There are many things on this earth that can't be explained."

The other man grunted. "I'll admit you tell a good story,

but you're not going to make a believer out of me. I believe in what I can see, touch, taste or smell.''

"Oh, Harry," his wife said, then tapped his arm. "That's ridiculous and you know it. You believe in God."

"That's different." Harry stiffened slightly. "A man's supposed to believe in God. It's in the Bible."

"My point exactly."

"Not the same thing at all," Harry told her.

"You believe in love," Arizona said. "You love your wife and your children."

"Of course." Harry narrowed his eyes. "What kind of man would I be if I didn't love them?"

"But you can't see, taste, touch or smell love," Arizona pointed out.

"Touché, Dr. Smith," Harry's wife said, then linked her arm through her husband's and led him away.

Arizona stared after them. He'd met many men like Harry in the course of his travels. Men who wouldn't believe in what they couldn't prove. But magic and the unexplainable were everywhere. One only had to be open to the idea.

How can you claim to believe in magic, when you ignore the biggest magic of all—the love people have for each other?

He tried to dismiss the voice in his head along with the question. That was different, he told himself, and knew he sounded just like Harry.

He sucked in a breath. Was that what this came down to? His belief in love? Was that what was happening with Chloe? Was the reason he couldn't forget about her and always wanted to be with her because he cared about her? Was it growing into more than caring?

The reception line finally ended. Arizona headed over to the bar and got himself a drink. As he sipped, he looked for Chloe. But instead of seeing her, he saw the people in the room and realized most of them were couples. What was it that bound two people together for a lifetime? The concept of marriage was as old as man. He'd traveled enough to know it was fairly universal. He'd seen dozens of couples who had faced great odds to be together, who were *still* together after several years.

"You're looking pensive about something," Cassie said as she, Chloe and Charity joined him.

"I'm fine."

"Good." She gave him her pretty, open smile. "The lecture tonight was even better than last night, and I didn't think that was possible. You're really gifted. Do you ever speak at schools?"

"Frequently. Kids are the best. They always have at least one question to stump me."

Cassie giggled. "I know what you mean. At the pre-school where I work, every kid's favorite question is 'why?' Sometimes I can't think of an answer. I don't know why water is wet or dogs aren't bendy when you pick them up like cats are."

"Cats are superior animals," Charity said.

Cassie shook her head. "They are not. Dogs love people, cats tolerate them."

Arizona turned toward Chloe and found her watching him. He wanted to get lost in her dark eyes and never find his way out again. He wanted to tell her all he'd been thinking and find a solution together. Which was crazy. He refused to get seriously involved, and Chloe didn't want to put herself on the line again. So there was no need to talk about anything.

Except when he thought about leaving Bradley, he thought about a beautiful woman with a giving soul and a stately Victorian house that one could easily call home.

* * *

They were the only people in the elevator. Even though Chloe had been to Arizona's room dozens of times, she found herself oddly nervous. Which was crazy.

"Come here," he said when the door closed and they started their ascent.

She stepped into his embrace and welcomed the feel of his mouth on hers. Instantly, her body was ready for him. Heat filled her as her breasts swelled and that secret place between her legs dampened in readiness.

"You're amazing," he murmured as the door opened on his floor and they broke apart. "I can't get enough of you."

If only that were true, she thought. Then he wouldn't leave. But there was no point in wishing for what could never be.

"Cassie was right," Chloe said as she stepped into his suite. "Tonight's lecture was better than last night's. I don't know how you come up with so many entertaining stories."

"It's a gift," he said as he turned on several lights. "I don't think I can take credit for it. I've always told stories. The difference is this time I'm at a podium instead of sitting around a campfire."

His description matched what she'd been thinking earlier that night. They had much in common—they even thought alike at times. In many ways, she knew him better than she'd ever known anyone before.

She opened her mouth to tell him that, but what came out instead was not what she'd had planned. "I spoke with Dr. Grantham," she told him.

"I saw you two talking," he said as he crossed to the small refrigerator and pulled out a bottle of white wine. "We had lunch yesterday. He's quite the scholar. I liked him very much."

No surprise there, she thought. They would have a lot in common. "He told me they'd offered you a job."

Arizona had reached for a wine cork. Now he placed both on the coffee table and crossed to stand in front of her. He took her small handbag and put it on the sofa, then linked his fingers with hers. He was tall and handsome. His green eyes glowed with fire and with concern.

"We should probably talk about that," he said.

"There's nothing to say, is there? After all, you turned him down." She tried to keep her voice steady, her tone light. She didn't want him to know she was starting to hurt. At first she'd been numbed by confusion, but now the pain filled her. He was really going away and there was nothing she could do to stop him.

"It's not that simple, Chloe. You know that. There are a lot of reasons I would like to stay…"

"But more reasons to go," she said, finishing his sentence.

His mouth twisted. "Yes." He raised one hand and cupped her face. "You are so beautiful. I've enjoyed all our times together. If I had ever thought about staying, it would be now. With you."

His words were a cold comfort. She had to clear her throat before she could speak. "But you can't."

"No, I can't stay." He pulled her hard against him. His arms came around her body, and she clung to him.

"Please understand," he said. "It's not about you. I come from a long line of men who leave and I don't know how to do anything else but what they've taught me. I don't make promises I can't keep. I'm not sure I believe in love."

She told herself that he'd progressed from definitely not believing to not being sure, but it wasn't enough. "I don't believe in magic," she whispered against his shoulder and closed her eyes as tears blurred her vision.

"We have tonight," he said. "And the time until I leave. Is that enough or do you want to go now?"

She wished he wasn't a gentleman. At least then when he was gone she could try to hate him. But he was. He reminded her he couldn't give her more than a temporary relationship, then offered her a chance to leave if she had to.

Chloe supposed that pride would insist that she stalk out with her back straight and a few stinging words to reduce him to dust. But she couldn't. He'd never lied to her. From that first day, she'd known their relationship was only temporary. Nothing had changed...except for her feelings. But then falling in love with him had been her own stupid fault.

So instead of leaving, she rose on tiptoe and pressed her mouth to his. If they only had a short time to be together, she would savor every second, commit it to memory and live on it for the rest of her life.

Chapter Fifteen

The last shudder of his release ripped through him. Arizona groaned out Chloe's name, then rested his head against her shoulder. Their breathing came in rapid gasps; they were both slick with sweat and tangled together. He wanted to stay like this forever.

She ran her hands up and down his back. "Thank you."

He raised himself up on his arms and gazed at her face. "Thank *you*. I have to admit, we seemed to have discovered a new level of intimacy. It's almost as if we're communicating with our bodies."

Her smile was content. "Isn't that how it's supposed to be?"

"Maybe, but I've never experienced it before." He was doing a bad job of telling her what he felt, but how was he supposed to explain the sensation of his heart and mind being opened to her? That for those few minutes, when he was inside her and she clung to him, that they really were one…just like all those old sappy songs promised.

"It's amazing," he said at last, knowing that didn't come close to what he meant.

"Well, you're the one with the expertise. All those women in your background. I'll just have to bow to your superior knowledge."

Her expression remained innocent, but the teasing in her voice gave her away. "You think you're very smart, don't you?" he asked.

"No. I don't think it. I know it."

"Oh, really. So what do you know about this?" He reached one hand down and started tickling her bare side.

"No, Arizona, don't!" Chloe wiggled and tried to get away, but she was pinned beneath him. She writhed. "Stop. You have to stop."

"Not really."

He shifted his weight all back on his legs so he could sit up and attack her with both hands. She retaliated, but he wasn't feeling especially ticklish that night. He squirmed under her wiggling fingers, but didn't have to pull away.

She laughed louder, then shrieked, "Stop! Please."

He released her. "Only if you—"

But she wasn't listening. Instead she took advantage of her freedom to lunge for his feet. Arizona scrambled to get out of her way. He knew he was definitely ticklish there.

He grabbed her around the waist and turned so he could fall backward on the bed, pulling her with him. She kicked out and tried to escape, but he held her fast. She spun in his arms so that she was on top of him, facing him.

Her long curly hair tangled around her face. They were breathing as hard as they had been a few minutes ago, but this time for an entirely different reason.

"Ready to give up and play nice?" he asked.

She blew the hair out of her face. A strand drifted up a few inches, then fell back across her nose. "I'll never give up."

He began tickling her sides. "If you insist."

She shrieked again. "No, you win. I'll be good."

"Promise?"

She nodded.

He gently rolled them both onto their side. They were facing each other. He tucked her hair behind her ears, then rested his hand on her waist.

The position was familiar. They often ended up this way after making love. They would talk for hours before she returned to her house. They only had a couple more nights together. He wished she would spend this night with him, but he understood that she didn't want to be seen leaving his hotel first thing in the morning. But tonight, more than any other time, he didn't want to fall asleep without her.

He supposed he should be used to it. After all, except for the night they'd camped out, they'd never slept very long together. He realized he wanted that. He wanted to see her first thing in the morning. He wanted to shower with her, then watch her get ready for her day. He wanted to learn what she was like in all her moods—sleepy, playful, even cranky.

Despite the airline ticket in his briefcase, he didn't want to leave her in less than seventy-two hours.

The information wasn't a surprise, he told himself. He'd been wrestling with it for the past couple of days. The question was what was he going to do about it?

She drew her index finger down his nose and his lips to his chin. There she stroked the stubbly skin. "All kidding aside," she said. "It's never been like this for me, either. I didn't know passion like this existed."

"Come with me this summer," he said without thinking.

Her eyes widened. "What?"

Arizona was a little stunned himself. But now that he'd asked, he didn't want to call the words back. "I'm serious. Come with me to the island. It's only for three months. You'll have plenty of time to write, although they don't have electricity, so you can't bring your laptop. But I'll bet you'd still get a lot done. It would be a great experience. And we'd get to be together longer."

"I could write a book about the mating customs in a matriarchal society."

"Exactly."

He tried to read her expression, but he couldn't. He didn't know what she was thinking. Would she consider it or was this too insane?

"At the end of summer...where do you go next?" she asked.

"Siberia, I think. We're still getting the details ironed out. I'll probably stop in Chicago first and visit my father. But there's always somewhere else I need to be going."

"I'm sure."

Chloe studied his familiar face. It would be easy to say yes. To pack up a couple of suitcases and go with him. It was just for the summer. Arizona was right—she could work, writing longhand. Maybe start a book of some kind. Even the one she suggested, on the matriarchal culture he was visiting. She could write down his stories and they could edit them together. Or...

Chloe kissed his mouth, then rested her head on the pillow. "I'm tempted," she confessed.

"I hear a 'but' in your voice."

"But—" The truth. It always came back to the truth. "That's not my style. I would never be happy just tagging along."

He frowned. "It wouldn't be like that."

Not at first, she thought. But eventually. Because she knew herself. The summer wouldn't be enough. If he let her, she would continue to follow him around the world. She would create work so that she could be with him. But then what? She not only needed more, she deserved more. Her own life with her own purpose. In a perfect world, their two very different lives and purposes would blend together, but life was far from perfect.

They had just made love and laughed, now they were holding each other. These are the moments, she thought. This was the perfection everyone sought. This was what it was about. The only rude intrusion was the pain in her chest that warned her it was going to be impossible to forget him.

"I can't," she said. "I need roots. I thought I was waiting until I had the right article before I went to New York. Or maybe I thought I was waiting until Cassie got married and I knew she was going to be all right. But it's not about any of that. Cassie's a grown-up and she's been capable of taking care of herself for years."

His green eyes darkened. "What were you waiting for?"

"Nothing. I thought I should go, but that was about expectations, not about what I wanted. I belong in Bradley. This is my home. I'm not saying I don't want to see parts of the world. I think most people would like to travel, but I'm not like you. I couldn't be happy with your lifestyle. At least not for any length of time."

And you couldn't be happy here, she thought. But there was no point in saying that—they both knew the truth.

She could read disappointment and hurt in his expression. "You're telling me no." It wasn't a question.

She ran her hand up and down his strong back, as if she could memorize everything about him. Later, the remembering was all she would have.

"I'm telling you that you belong out there. You're different from the rest of us, truly larger than life. Go find your magic, Arizona.''

''What will you find?''

''What I've had all along. My roots. Just like Dorothy learned in *The Wizard of Oz*. For me, there is no place like home.''

She thought about telling him that she loved him, but she was afraid. What would he do with the information? Besides, she couldn't bear to have the words hanging in the silence. Knowing that he wasn't going to say it back wouldn't be enough to keep her from hurting when he didn't respond.

''I don't like what you're saying,'' he told her. ''Unfortunately I can't seem to muster a good argument against it.'' He kissed her. ''I'll miss you.''

''I'll miss you, too. More than I should.''

He hugged her close. ''Maybe you should ask me to stay here. Then we would have each told each other no.''

The last little corner of her heart shattered. Until he'd said the words, she'd allowed herself to hope. That maybe he would offer to settle here, at least for a while. But that had never been his intention. Maybe Aunt Charity had been right and she was a coward for not asking, but at least she had the rather empty satisfaction of knowing that she'd been right.

They were silent for a long time. Finally, he reached up and clicked off the light on the nightstand. She stiffened. ''I have to be going,'' she told him.

''Don't,'' he said in the darkness. ''If you won't give me the summer, then just give me one night to sleep in your arms.''

She didn't have to think it over. It was what she wanted too. She knew she wouldn't sleep, but at least she would be able to feel him next to her. More memories to have for later.

"I'll stay," she whispered.

"Good." He shifted to get more comfortable. "I should probably warn you that I think I snore."

"I know that from last time."

"Oh. Well, I also sleep like the dead. If you have to wake me up for something, don't bother shaking me. I've slept through hurricanes, earthquakes, not to mention several alarms. I don't even bother with a wake-up call. I never hear the phone. Just turn on the light. That one always gets me. Unexpected light, and I'm instantly awake."

"I'll remember," she promised. And she would. She would think about that small detail and wonder how it would have affected their lives together...if they'd had a future.

You're getting way too weepy, she told herself. *You're with him now. Enjoy this time. Save the suffering for later. There's going to be plenty of it.*

Chloe tried to take her own advice. As Arizona drifted off to sleep, and as promised, began to snore, she relived all their time together. Everything from her stunned amazement at finding him in her kitchen, to their lovemaking just a short time earlier that night.

She must have dozed for a while because when a sharp noise woke her, she wasn't sure where she was.

The phone rang again. Chloe blinked and everything came into focus. Arizona snored on, oblivious to the sound. As she reached for the receiver, she glanced at the clock. It was a little after two. Had something happened to his father?

"Hello?"

"Good afternoon. This is—" There was a sharp gasp of air. The woman on the other end of the line made a soft moaning noise. "Oh, no. You're in California, aren't you? I'm terribly sorry. It's afternoon here in Sydney. I can't believe I woke you up."

"It's all right." Sydney? As in Sydney, Australia? "Can I help you with something?"

"What? Oh, of course. The reason for my call. I'm Jan. I'm with the travel agency Mr. Smith uses for his South Pacific travel. He'd called us a while back to have us put him on a waiting list for an earlier flight. I wanted to let him know a first-class seat just became available. He'll be leaving tomorrow." She giggled nervously. "Technically, that's later today, isn't it?"

Chloe sat up in bed. Arizona was still snoring. A couple of seconds ago she'd had trouble focusing her eyes in the dark room, but now her head was spinning. He wasn't leaving in a couple of days. He was leaving in a few hours. He'd arranged for an earlier flight. All this time she'd been thinking about how much she was going to miss him while he couldn't wait to get away.

"Give me a minute," she said. "I'll have to write the information down."

She supposed she could have tried to wake up Arizona, but the truth was, she didn't want to face him. Not now, not like this. He would be able to read everything on her face. He would know how much his leaving was going to hurt her. He would pity her. Lord help her, he might ask her to go with him again and she didn't think she could refuse him a second time.

She squinted at the two-line phone and realized there was a hold button. After pushing it, she set the receiver back in place, then made her way into the living room. Once the bedroom door was closed, she turned on a light, found paper and a pen, then released the call.

"I'm ready," she said.

"Great. He's on Singapore Airlines."

The travel agent gave her the flight information. Chloe wrote it down, then read it back to confirm that she had it right. Then she hung up and slumped back onto the sofa.

Now what? She stared at the paper in her hands and wished it could be different, but it wasn't. He was leaving and she couldn't go with him. Even if she hadn't already figured out her life was here, she could not follow a man around the world, simply to be with him. She needed more for herself.

None of which answered the question of what she should do now. The obvious answer was to get back in bed and try to sleep. In the morning, she and Arizona could talk.

"About what?" she asked in a whisper. "Gee, maybe I could ask if the service on Singapore Airlines is as fabulous as everyone claims. Or discuss ways of handling the jet lag when one crosses the international date line."

The note began to blur. Chloe brushed impatiently at the tears. "What am I crying about? I knew he was leaving. I've expected this from the beginning. Nothing has changed except for his departure date."

But that was part of it. That he was leaving early. How could he do that to her? To them? He was supposed to care, at least a little. But to be leaving *early*.

She sat there for a long time trying to make sense of it all. In the end, she knew she couldn't. She wrote a quick note explaining that the travel agent had called, then gave him the new flight information. Then she turned off the light in the living room and let her eyes adjust to the dark.

When she could see well enough to find her way back to the bedroom, she did so. Her clothes were on a chair by the dresser. She collected them, put the note on her pillow, then left the room.

Dressing took all of two minutes. Chloe stood there,

purse in hand, but she wasn't ready to leave. There was still something left to be done. She crossed to his computer and turned it on. After searching for a couple of minutes, she found the program to access the Internet and went on under her own account number. After getting into the newspaper's system, she accessed her computer there at the office and downloaded her article. She'd finished it yesterday. In a few hours she would be putting it on her editor's desk. She also wanted Arizona to have a copy.

She flipped on his printer and waited while the article came out, a page at a time. When that was finished, she logged off the computer, wrote a note on the last page of the article and returned to the bedroom.

It was after three and from Arizona's body position and loud snoring, he'd barely stirred in the past hour. She put the loose pages under the information from the travel agent, then walked around to his side of the bed.

In the darkness she couldn't make out individual features, but she knew every inch of him. She could predict his moods, recognized his voice and his laughter. He touched her as no one had before. Not just physically, but also in her heart and her soul.

It hurt so much, but knowing what she knew now, she wouldn't change anything. He'd reminded her that loving was a part of her life. That she'd been empty for a long time. She didn't think she would ever get over him, nor was she likely to give her heart to anyone else, but they had had a brief, joyous time together. They'd had a miracle and how many people could say that?

She bent over and kissed his cheek. He stirred slightly but didn't wake.

"I love you, Arizona," she murmured.

"Chloe. I dreamed about you."

She stiffened, then relaxed when she realized he was

talking in his sleep. "I dreamed about you, too," she said. "I dreamed about you the night I wore that stupid nightgown. I guess now that I know its power, I have to stop calling it names. You are my destiny, Arizona Smith. If you ever decide to settle down, come back to me."

Then she left the room without once looking back.

As he did every morning, Arizona woke with the first light of dawn. He stretched, then rolled over to snuggle against Chloe.

"What the—"

She wasn't here. He felt under the covers, but her side of the bed was cold. A quick glance confirmed that her clothes were gone, so she had probably left sometime in the night.

The disappointment cut through him. Why? All he'd wanted was one night so they could wake up in each other's arms. Was that asking too much? They only had a couple of days together until he left.

If he left.

Arizona stiffened. Where had that thought come from? Of course he was leaving. He had work to do, a life. He wasn't going to stick around in some small town. What for? Chloe? So they could be together?

He couldn't do it, he admitted to himself. He couldn't take the risk and stay. With his family history, with his poor relationship skills, there was no way he could make her happy. He was bound to blow it and then where would they be?

He cursed loudly, then flopped back on his pillow. As he did, he heard paper crinkle. When he turned he saw a handwritten note and a thick sheaf of papers. Chloe's article?

He read the note. As her words registered, a knot of pain

formed in his gut. He swore again, louder and longer this time, then crumpled the note and tossed it on the floor. The change in airline reservations. He'd completely forgotten that he'd called about three hours after he'd arrived in Bradley. At the time, he hadn't wanted to spend more time here than necessary. As soon as he'd found out the date of his last lecture, he'd gone on the waiting list to leave right after that. But since then, everything had changed. He wanted to be with Chloe right up until the last minute.

What must she be thinking? he wondered, then groaned. Probably that he was using her then abandoning her at the first opportunity. No doubt she thought he would take off later today and never give her another thought.

He rolled over and reached for the phone. But before he picked up the receiver, he glanced at the clock. It wasn't quite six in the morning. If Chloe lived alone that wouldn't be a problem, but his call was going to wake up Charity and Cassie, too.

That can't be helped, he thought. But before he could grab the phone, it rang.

"Hello?"

"Good morning. I can tell by your voice I didn't wake you."

Arizona sat up and clutched the receiver. "Chloe? It's not what you think."

"I know."

She sounded all right, but he wasn't sure he could believe that. He had to make sure she understood. "What do you know?"

"That you made the reservation before we got involved. At least that's what I'm hoping."

He breathed a sigh of relief. "Of course it is. I forgot I'd requested an earlier flight. I'm going to call them right

now and tell them I want to keep on the original schedule.''
Or maybe go later, but before he could add that, she sighed.

"Don't," she whispered.

The knot of pain returned, and with it a tightness in his chest. "Don't what?"

"Don't change the flight back. You're leaving. Whether it's today or in a couple of days, you're still going to be gone. Last night was terrific. I don't think we could top it, so why not let that be our last memory?"

Because I want to see you again. I want to hold you and hear you laugh. I want to figure out a way to make this work.

But he didn't say any of that. She sounded so calm and controlled. Maybe this hadn't mattered to her as much as he'd hoped. If she really wanted him gone, then he would go. But he made one last attempt. "Are you sure? I would like to see you again."

"Arizona, I—" Her breath caught and then he knew. She wasn't calm or unmoved by their conversation. She was clinging to composure by a thread.

"Chloe, don't make me do this. Let me stay a couple more days."

"No. It will only hurt more. I need to start getting over you and today is as good a day as any. Just promise me one thing."

"What?"

"Promise me you won't read the article until you're on the island."

His body felt strange. All tight and hurting. He wanted to beg her to come with him. He wanted... That was the problem, he realized. He didn't know what he wanted.

"You're just afraid I'm going to be critical," he said, hoping his voice sounded at least close to normal.

"That's it exactly. Promise?"

"I give you my word. I won't read it until I'm on the island. Of course I'll have to read it during the day, what with there being no electricity and all."

She made a noise that sounded more like a strangled sob than a laugh, but he let it go.

"I'm going to miss you," he said.

"Me, too. So much. You've been wonderful. All of it."

He cleared his throat. "Maybe I could come back. You know, at the end of the summer. Just to say hi and see how you are."

"I don't think that's a good idea. I won't be over you enough by then."

"Chloe?"

She exhaled sharply. "Don't ask me what that means, okay? Just accept it as the truth. I can't promise very much right now. It's j-just—" Her voice cracked. "I guess this is harder than I thought."

"Chloe, I want to see you before I leave."

"You can't. I have to go to work. Jerry's going to read the article this morning and we'll be editing it all afternoon. Your plane leaves around one, right? So there's no time."

"I'll make time. I'll keep the original flight." He wasn't sure why, but he suddenly had a sense of urgency about seeing her. That if he didn't, he would lose something very precious and important.

"Why?" she asked. "Nothing is going to change. You're still going to be leaving and I'm still going to stay here. It would hurt, too much." She paused. "Tell you what. Call me when you get back from your island. If things have settled down and you still want to see me, maybe we can work that out. Okay? But you don't have to. I mean, if you've met someone else, I'll understand."

"There's not going to be anyone else. You're the one—" He stumbled verbally. "I really care about you."

''Thank you for saying that. Look, Arizona, I have to go. Have a safe trip.''

She hung up.

He stared at the phone a long time before replacing the receiver. Something was wrong. He could feel it. This wasn't right. Usually he was itching to leave, but this time he wanted to stay. What did that mean?

He would call her back, he decided. Then the voice in his head asked, ''And say what?''

He didn't have an answer to that. What would he say? That he cared about her? He did. But that wasn't enough. He knew that now. Chloe wanted and deserved more than the temporary relationship he could offer her. She deserved a commitment.

He glanced around the hotel room, which was exactly like a hundred others he'd called home over the years. What did he know about commitment? His entire life had been devoted to wanderlust. The only thing he'd ever committed to had been getting his various degrees and those had been acquired at an assortment of universities around the world. Stay in one place? Be with one woman? Whom was he trying to kid?

Determined to put this behind him, Arizona got up, pulled his suitcase from the closet and began to pack.

Chapter Sixteen

Chloe waited nervously while Jerry finished up his phone call. He'd kept her waiting nearly ten minutes, which wasn't all that long except her nerves were shot. She'd had nearly no sleep the previous night and she didn't know how she was going to get through the day…let alone the rest of her life. She'd let Arizona go. She glanced at the clock and realized he would already be in San Francisco to catch his flight. It was too late to change her mind, too late to offer to go with him, too late to ask him to stay. Too late to realize she might have made the biggest mistake of her life.

Her editor put down the phone and looked at her. His gaze narrowed. "It's too long and too emotional," he said without even a greeting to start the conversation. "You got too close to your subject. Didn't they teach you anything at college?"

Chloe willed herself to stay calm and keep from flushing.

She'd tried so hard to be impersonal as she'd written the piece. Obviously, she'd failed.

Jerry leaned back in his seat and tucked his hands behind his head. "It's also about the best damn article I've read in years. It's powerful, both in the images you invoke and in the story itself. I'm impressed as hell."

She felt heat on her cheeks, but she no longer cared. "Really?"

"Yeah, really. You're a decent writer. Of course, I knew that all along. That's why I wanted you for this assignment."

Chloe pressed her lips together to keep from smiling. This was not the time to remind Jerry that he hadn't chosen her at all. She'd been handed the job after Nancy had turned it down because of her pregnancy.

"You know," he continued. "You could write a book on this guy. Not that I'm giving you any ideas. I don't want you to think you can parlay this article into a different career. And don't even think about leaving Bradley and heading off for New York."

"Actually, I have no intention of leaving," she told him. "My home is here."

Now it was Jerry's turn to look surprised. He straightened and slapped his hands on his desk. "Who would have thought? I figured a smart young writer like yourself would be heading off to the Big Apple at the first chance she got." He tapped the pages in front of him. "This is your ticket in. You know that don't you?"

"I know, and there was a time I was interested, but not anymore. I belong here."

"Great." He handed her the article. "I've made notes in the margins. I want the changes back to me by the end of the week. This will be the cover story, so get yourself a professional publicity photo. We'll need it for the byline.''

Chloe swallowed hard. While she'd had bylines before, the magazine had never run her photo. The cover story! "Thank you," she managed.

"Yeah, yeah." He pointed to the pages she now held. "We can talk about anything you don't agree with. I doubt you can change my mind, but you're welcome to try. Now get out of here."

She clutched the sheets to her chest and made her way to the door. Her head was spinning. So much had happened so quickly. First Arizona leaving, then Jerry telling her she was going to have the cover.

"Oh, and Chloe?"

She glanced at her boss over her shoulder. "Yes?"

"I'm promoting you to the senior writer level. You'll only be working on features now. The new title comes with a raise and an expense account." He waved his hand. "Yeah, yeah, you're so grateful, you're speechless. Now get out of here, kid. Go home, celebrate the rest of the day and in the morning get your butt in the chair and make those changes."

"Thank you," was all she could manage. She stumbled her way back to her desk and collapsed into her chair.

She'd been promoted. She was really succeeding here at the magazine. There were only two other feature writers and they had both been working here much longer than she had. She'd impressed her boss.

She laughed out loud. With a little luck, she might even get a bigger cubicle, or maybe even an office of her own. Excitement and happiness bubbled inside of her. Without thinking, she reached for the phone and punched in the number for the hotel where Arizona was staying. When the operator answered, reality hit and with it a gut-twisting pain.

"May I help you?" the woman asked again.

"I'm sorry," Chloe whispered. "I have the wrong number."

She hung up. All her excitement and happiness vaporized, leaving her feeling as if she had just swallowed poison. Her body stiffened and her chest tightened. She couldn't call Arizona and share the news with him. He was gone. She had sent him away and he wasn't the kind of man who was likely to bother coming back this way again.

Chloe walked into the kitchen and set her briefcase on the table. She'd taken Jerry's advice and had left early. But she had no plans to celebrate her promotion. She knew that in time she would be thrilled with the opportunity. She was a good writer, and she would excel at her new position. But for now none of that mattered. There was only the pain. How long would it take to forget him? Lord help her if souls really were reincarnated because she had a bad feeling it was going to take more than one lifetime to get over him.

"You let him go."

Chloe glanced up and saw her aunt standing in the doorway. Charity's hair was pulled back into its customary French twist. Her tailored slacks and fitted blouse highlighted her attractive figure. She was a familiar anchor in Chloe's suddenly storm-tossed world.

As the tears formed, she walked to her aunt. The older woman embraced her, holding her close. Chloe cried, hoping the release of tears would ease some of the pain. Sobs racked her body. She felt the physical rending as her heart tore in two.

"I h-had to," she managed between sobs as she tried to

catch her breath. "I couldn't go with him, and he doesn't belong here."

"Foolish girl. Of course he does."

Chloe sniffed and straightened. "What are you talking about?"

Charity led her to the table, then started the kettle for tea. While the water was heating, she settled in the seat opposite Chloe's and handed her niece several tissues.

"You dreamed about him, Chloe. He's your destiny. You should have asked him to stay."

Hopelessness churned with the pain. "That's just some stupid old family legend. You know that."

"Fine. Ignore the dream, but what about everything else? What about the fact that you love him and you let him go without telling him?"

Chloe blew her nose. Her body ached as it did when she had the flu. "I told him. Sort of."

"He didn't know it when he called."

Her head came up and she stared at her aunt. "Arizona called? Here?"

"About an hour ago. He was in San Francisco. His plane was about to take off, and he wanted to talk to you."

She opened her mouth, but there weren't any words. She'd missed his call? It was too devastating to consider. "I just—"

"Oh, Chloe. Why didn't you fight for him?"

"He doesn't belong here. The world is his home."

"Home isn't a place, it's a state of mind. I think he wanted to stay, but wasn't sure he would be welcome."

Chloe turned that thought over in her mind. "He never hinted that he did." She swallowed. "I've been over this a thousand times. The truth is I love him, but I couldn't ask him to stay. I don't know if that makes me a coward or not. Everything happened so fast. It's hard to have him gone, but I believe we need the time. I'm sure of my feelings, but I don't think he's sure of his. I think he's afraid of being abandoned again, so he always does the leaving. And I can't be with a man who won't trust me.''

''So what happens now?'' her aunt asked.

''Now I wait. You're wrong. I did tell Arizona how I felt. I told him if he wanted to come back to me, I would be waiting. So it's up to him. I'm giving him time to figure out what he wants. He has to come to me freely, Aunt Charity. He has to believe.''

Her aunt studied her face. ''You've become a wise, mature woman, Chloe. Your parents would be very proud of you. *I'm* very proud to have you as a part of my life.''

''I don't feel very wise. I feel broken and empty.''

''I understand.'' She squeezed her fingers, then stood up to make the tea. ''What are you going to do?''

Chloe had figured that one out on the drive home. ''I'm going to spend the rest of the day in bed feeling sorry for myself. Tomorrow, to quote my editor, I'm going to get my butt in the chair and make the changes he wants on my article.''

''He liked it?''

''Yeah.'' Chloe brushed away the tears that continued to fall. In a couple of days she would share the news of her promotion with her family, but she couldn't talk about it now.

Charity looked at her. ''Honey, go on up to bed. I'll bring you the tea.''

Chloe nodded, then did as her aunt bade. As she headed for her room, she reminded herself she was doing the right thing. She and Arizona needed time. It was the old cliché about setting something free. If he came back to her, then they would be together. If he didn't, he had never really wanted to be a part of her life. Unfortunately, the cliché didn't give any advice about getting through the waiting period or knowing when it was time to give up hope.

The air on the island was thick and humid with a sensual lushness that never failed to make Arizona feel like a non-believer entering a sacred temple. This small paradise off to one corner of the Pacific Ocean had always been one of his favorite places. Yet as he stepped off the boat onto the soft sand, he couldn't shake the feeling that everything was wrong.

For the first time in his life, he didn't want to be here. He didn't want to be anywhere but back in Bradley. What was the point of seeing the world if he couldn't also see Chloe's face, hear her laugh, touch her?

He shook off the thoughts, telling himself it was little more than jet lag. Something that was to be expected after traveling nearly forty-eight hours straight. He would get over being tired and slightly off balance, just like he would get over missing Chloe.

Several women waited for him. He waved. Nada, the high priestess and ruler of the island, came toward him. Some of his pain eased as he felt genuine gladness at seeing her.

"Welcome back, Arizona," she said in her oddly accented voice. Nada had grown up on the island, but in her late teens, she'd been sent to England. She'd stayed there nearly fifteen years, studying and learning customs of the West. Some women whispered she'd even taken an Englishman as a husband. If that were true, Arizona had never seen any sign of him. When he'd asked about that he'd been told that her husband had wanted to rule her head as well as her heart so she'd cut out *his* heart and eaten it for dinner.

"That showed him," Arizona had replied before pointing out that the people of the island weren't the least bit cannibalistic, and Nada had always frowned on violence of any kind.

True, he'd been told, but it made for a great story.

Nada walked toward him. She was tall and regal. He didn't know her age, but guessed she had to be close to seventy or eighty. She wore her hair long—to her waist—and there was little gray in the shining black strands.

He bowed to the island princess and offered her a thin gold bracelet as a sign of affection and respect.

"Thank you," she said. "But did you bring books?"

He grinned. "Two suitcases full. Romances and mysteries."

Nada smiled at him. "We do like a good bit of death to mix with our love stories," she admitted. "Come, everyone is waiting."

He left his luggage by the boat, knowing that it would be placed in his hut for him. As usual, when he walked through the village, only the women came out to greet him. The men were too busy with their chores. Besides, it wasn't correct for them to speak with strangers. On this island, men were to be seen and not heard. Which reminded him of something.

"I might have a visitor," he said.

"No, you won't." Nada spoke with the confidence of one who often viewed the future and was rarely wrong. She wore a sarong-style garment that trailed onto the ground. Her stride was long and sure.

She glanced at him. "Who did *you* think might come out to the island?"

"If you know I'm not going to have a visitor, then you should be able to figure that out on your own."

Her silence was a clear indication of her displeasure at his impertinence.

"I'm sorry," Arizona said quickly. "I didn't mean to be rude. I—" What was his excuse? He knew better. "I have a lot on my mind."

The night moved in quickly as it always did in the tropics. Torches had been lit to illuminate the path. The lush plants crowded around so that he had to push against them as he followed Nada to the ceremonial grounds.

"My father," he said at last when they stopped in the center of the open area. "We talked before I left California, and he said he would like to visit me."

"I would make your father welcome," the high priestess promised.

Arizona bit back a groan. He knew exactly what that meant. "He's pretty old and he doesn't get out much."

Nada flashed him a smile. "I would be very good for him. I would help him forget. When you go back, tell him to come without you."

Arizona knew better than to ask how she knew his father had anything to forget. Nothing about Nada surprised him. She probably would help his father to forget...if the excitement of the event didn't kill him first.

As if sensing his exhaustion, Nada kept the welcoming ceremonies brief. As she escorted him to his hut, she didn't even make the courtesy offer of one of the young women in her court. He was grateful not to have to politely turn down the gift. He had a bad feeling that tonight he couldn't have thought of anything pleasant to say.

As he stretched out on his cot, he willed himself to sleep. But instead of oblivion, he saw Chloe. Forty-eight hours and half a world later, he realized he should have stayed. Even for a few days. They still had so much to say to each other. There were many things he didn't understand. If only he'd told her...

Told her what, he asked himself? What was the mysterious message? That he would miss her? That he cared about her? But caring wasn't love and Chloe deserved more than he had to offer.

He fell asleep still wrestling with the problem and awoke at the first light of dawn, still exhausted and restless. As he rolled over on the cot, he saw Nada sitting in the only chair in the room. For all he knew, she'd been there all night.

"Good morning," she said.

"If you've come to take advantage of me, I'm going to be a disappointment," he teased.

"I am not your destiny, Arizona Smith."

There was something strange about her voice. Not just the accent, but also the tone and power. For once he had the feeling he wasn't speaking to Nada, his friend, but instead Nada, high priestess and ruler of this land. Someone privy to mysteries and secrets he would never know.

He pushed himself into a sitting position. "I'm listening," he said quietly.

"I dreamed about you, Arizona," she said. "I dreamed when you would arrive and when you would leave. I dreamed that this trip was wrong, that you were leaving behind something very precious."

Could everyone see the truth but him? he wondered. "A woman," he admitted. "Her name is Chloe."

"And?"

"And nothing. We were together for a while." He ran his hands through his hair. "It's so damn complicated. I love my life. I travel the world, I do what I want. No responsibilities, no ties. But she lives in this small town. Her family has owned her house for a hundred years. She belongs there.''

''Where do you belong?''

A simple question. The answer came instantly and with it a painful insight into the blackness of his heart. ''Nowhere,'' he said softly. He had never belonged. His father had abandoned him, his grandfather had dragged him from place to place, at times even forgetting about him. He didn't dare risk caring about people or places because he knew he would soon be ripped away from them. All he knew was being left, so he'd learned early on to do the leaving first.

''Yes,'' Nada told him. ''But you are not that little boy anymore. You're a strong and powerful man. You can choose to stay with her. You can choose to accept your destiny.''

She leaned forward and held out her hand, palm down. Without being told, he held out his hand, palm up. She placed something warm there. He tightened his fingers around the object without looking at it.

''See with me,'' she whispered.

He closed his eyes and then he knew. Images flashed through his mind. Chloe, always Chloe. He saw them laughing together, talking. He saw himself teaching. He saw their three children playing together.

How could he have walked away without telling her how he felt about her? He loved her. He'd never loved anyone before, but she was everything he'd ever wanted. With her, he could risk putting down roots. She would never abandon him. Look at how she'd always cared for the people in her life. She was his perfect other half.

He rose to his feet. ''I have to get back to her.''

"I know." Nada stood. "The boat will be here shortly." She gave a self-satisfied smile. "I arranged it last night."

He kissed her smooth cheek. "When will we be back?" he asked.

"In two summers. But your father will have visited me before then. In fact, he might decide to stay here."

Arizona laughed. "Great. Just be gentle with him. It's been a long time."

Nada's smile faded. "I will not be taking your mother's place."

Arizona wrapped his arms around her and hugged her close. "I know. But thank you for worrying about that."

She patted his face, then swept out of the hut. Then she glanced back over her shoulder. The Cheshire cat smile had returned. "Congratulations."

He waved, thinking she meant on his upcoming marriage. Good news. At least with her blessing, he was reasonably confident Chloe would say yes. Maybe he *hadn't* blown it completely.

But that wasn't what she'd meant at all. When Arizona turned to pack the few things he'd taken out of his suitcase the previous night, he remembered the small object Nada had pressed in his hand. He uncurled his fingers. Instantly his throat tightened as wonder filled him.

The small stone statue was old, weather-worn and had probably been carved a thousand years before the birth of Christ. But he could still recognize the crude rendering of a woman. He rubbed his thumb over the round mound that was her belly and knew what else Nada had seen in her vision.

Her congratulations hadn't been about his upcoming marriage, they had been because Chloe was pregnant.

* * *

The operator was very apologetic, but she couldn't seem to make the connection. Arizona thanked her, then slammed down the pay phone. He didn't know what was going on. He'd never had trouble making a call from Guam to the States before. He had the oddest feeling that fate was conspiring against him speaking to Chloe before he could actually see her in person.

He glanced at his watch and swore. His plane would be boarding in less than fifteen minutes. He didn't have time to keep trying a call that was obviously not going to go through. He closed his eyes and tried to think. Then it came to him. He sprinted across the terminal and raced up to a window.

"I need to send a telegram," he said, and began frantically writing the message.

Thirty minutes later he was in his seat on the plane, refusing the offer of something to drink before they took off. From Guam he would fly to Hawaii with a five-hour layover, then on to San Francisco. This wasn't the most direct way back, but it had been the best he could do on such short notice. At least Nada had arranged for the boat to return for him. Otherwise, he would have been stuck on the island an extra week.

Thinking of Nada made him think of Chloe, but everything did these days. He pulled out the small statue and closed his fingers around the worn stone. He doubted she knew about the tiny life growing inside of her. He hadn't decided if he should tell her or let her figure it out herself. Maybe he should just propose and then wait for her to tell him about the baby. He didn't want her thinking he was only interested in her because of the child. Even if he and Chloe could never have children, he would still want to be with her. She was the very best part of him. He ached for her the way a swimmer staying underwater too long ached for air.

He tucked the statue back in his pocket, then opened his briefcase. He might as well try to work on the long flight. He doubted he would be able to sleep.

He pulled out a folder and saw a thick stack of papers underneath. Chloe's article. He'd been too caught up in missing her when he'd been flying to the island to read what she'd written. Now he wanted to see what she had to say. Maybe reading her words would make him feel connected to her.

The article opened with a quote from him. "I'm no one's idea of a superhero. People who are heroes change the world for the better. Gandhi, Joseph Campbell, Mother Teresa…these people are heroes. I'm just a stubborn man who does his research and occasionally gets the opportunity to find something fantastic."

Chloe went on to say that there were those who would disagree with the idea that he wasn't a hero. She hadn't made up her mind, but from all that she'd seen, he was, at the very least, a good man, and how often could that be said about someone these days?

She wrote about his background, mixing humor with the sad image of a little boy often left alone in strange places. She explained how those experiences had molded him into a unique person. She detailed the myth behind the man.

Arizona didn't know whether to be thrilled or embarrassed. She made him sound like a really great guy. He liked that, but he was also aware of his limitations. Then he turned the page and froze.

"The first time I saw Arizona Smith was in a dream." She went on to tell about the family legend, the magic nightgown, and how on the night of her twenty-fifth birthday, she'd worn the nightgown and he'd appeared before her. She talked about meeting him the next day, of how he was exactly as she'd dreamed…right down to the scar on his arm.

Arizona didn't know how long he sat there, dumbfounded by the revelation. Everything fell into place. No wonder she'd acted so odd when they'd first met. She must have been terrified and confused. After all, Chloe didn't believe in magic. He closed his eyes and tried to remember all he could from the family legend. A smile curved his mouth. The fact that she'd dreamed about him meant they were—if he recalled correctly—destined for each other. It confirmed what Nada had said…and what his own heart had finally told him. They belonged together. For always.

He read through the rest of the article. Chloe's style was clear and concise. He could see her visual images clearly. As he turned to the last page he wondered if she would consider collaborating on a writing project with him. Something about his travels. Then he noticed a handwritten note at the bottom of the page.

"I couldn't let you go without telling you the truth. I love you. You don't have to do anything with that information. I don't expect you to say anything back. I know that we have very different lives and goals. At first I told myself it was enough that I'd known you and we'd had a short time together. But now I want more. I want to know if there is a way to find a compromise between our worlds. Please use your time on the island to think about this. At the end of summer, if you find you want me, I'll be waiting."

It had been there all along. Her confession. If only he'd read it that morning, or on the plane. He closed his eyes and shook his head. Or maybe it was supposed to have been this way. Maybe he had to leave to know what he'd lost.

He pulled his telegram out of his pocket and read the first two lines.

I COULDN'T LET YOU GO WITHOUT TELLING YOU THE TRUTH. STOP. I LOVE YOU. STOP.

They'd used exactly the same words.

He leaned forward anxiously, then realized that he couldn't make the plane go faster, no matter how much he willed it. So he forced himself to relax and to wait. He would call her from Hawaii. This time he would get through. He had to. He loved her.

Arizona pressed the receiver harder against his ear. The noise in the terminal was deafening. "Chloe, is that you?"

"Yes." Her voice sounded strange.

"Are you okay?"

"I'm fine. I sound funny because I'm crying."

His chest tightened. "What's wrong?"

"Nothing, silly. I'm crying because I'm happy. I got your telegram. I'm sorry you had to cut your trip short, but I'm glad you're coming home. I love you, Arizona."

"I love you, too." He practically had to shout, but it was worth it. They were actually talking to each other. "I missed you."

"I've missed you, too." She cleared her throat. "Are you sure you want to do this? I mean with your work and everything, are you sure you want to give up the travel?"

He understood that she was asking for him—wanting him to make sure that he wasn't going to regret his decision later. "I have two things to say about that," he told her.

"First, I'm going to take the job at Bradley University. Their offer gave me plenty of time to travel in the summer, along with scheduled sabbaticals. I sort of thought you'd go with me."

"Of course. I'd like that. First class all the way, right?"

"Sure. I'll get you the best camels and carts around."

She laughed. "I do love you. What else?"

"I sent the telegram before I read the article, Chloe. I sent it before I knew what you'd written on the last page."

He heard her breath catch. She was crying again.

"Chloe, don't."

"I can't help it. I'm so happy."

He looked at the crowds in the terminal. The public-address system announced the first boarding call for his flight. This was not how he'd wanted to do it, but he didn't have a choice.

"I have to go," he said. "But first I want to ask you something."

She sniffed. "What?"

"Will you marry me?"

"What?"

The terminal suddenly got very quiet. Arizona looked up and saw several dozen people staring at him. He waved, then turned his back on them. "Will you marry me? I love you and I want us to be together for the rest of our lives. We'll make it work. I know we can do that."

"I know we can, too. Yes, I'll marry you, Arizona. I'll also be waiting at the gate in San Francisco. I'll rent a room down by the waterfront and we can spend the night drinking champagne and making love."

He thought about the little statue in his pocket and knew they would have to pass on the champagne. But the rest of it sounded perfect.

"I'll see you in about five hours," he said. "I love you. I can't wait to see you."

"Fly safe. Bye."

He hung up the phone and picked up his carry-on bag. The crowd around him burst into applause. He was still grinning when he took his seat.

"Sparkling cider?" Chloe asked, as she handed him his glass.

Arizona raised himself up on one elbow to take the fruit drink and smiled. "I wasn't in the mood for alcohol. Thanks for indulging me."

She slipped into bed and snuggled close. "Right now I would do anything for you."

She would, too. It felt so right to be back together with him. Letting him go had been difficult, but in her heart Chloe knew she'd made the right decision. Maybe Arizona had needed to go away to figure out where he really wanted to be. She didn't know if it was fate, the nightgown, the stars or just luck, but they were together and they were going to stay together. She couldn't ask for anything more.

Arizona leaned over, put down his glass and grabbed a pad of paper from the nightstand.

"What's that for?" she asked.

"A list. Eventually we're going to leave this bed and head back to Bradley."

"Probably," she teased.

He kissed her, then returned his attention to the paper. "This is everything we have to do in the next few days. First, I have to call and accept the job offer at the university."

"I made an appointment for you with Dr. Grantham. It's

on Friday at ten.'' She winked. ''I know your style. You would want to see him as soon as possible.''

He grinned. ''We're going to be great together. Okay, that's done. Second, I have to call my father. Nada, the woman I was telling you about, wants him to come visit her.''

''I'm sure he'll enjoy his time there.'' Chloe glanced at the fat little statue he'd brought her. It sat on the dresser, its unblinking eyes seeming to see everything. ''There's something strange about the shape of that thing,'' she said. ''I just can't put my finger on it.''

''We need to set a date for the wedding.''

She considered that. ''I don't need anything fancy, so we can have it quickly, if you would like to.''

He kissed her again. ''I would like to very much.''

''Good, I—''

But instead of pulling back, he deepened the kiss. Chloe leaned close to him. ''What about your list?'' she asked.

He tossed the paper and pen onto the floor. ''It can wait. I think we have a little more catching up to do.''

He lowered her onto her back and slid his hand over her body. Chloe arched into his touch. His warm fingers lingered on her belly, stroking the smooth skin there. Without meaning to, she opened her eyes and saw the little stone statue. How odd, she thought. If she didn't know better, she would swear its little face was smiling. Then Arizona's fingers slipped lower and she couldn't think about anything except how wonderful it was to be back where she belonged…where they both belonged.

She closed her eyes as he entered her and for that brief second, she thought she felt straw under her back, as if they were in the cave again. Just like in the dream. As passion carried her higher and higher, she realized that nothing about life with Arizona was ever going to be completely normal, but it was always going to be wonderful and exciting. They could give each other everything and accept everything in return. They were bound by forces they couldn't see or understand, caught up in the tide of love. After all, they were each other's destiny.

* * * * *

On her twenty-fifth birthday Cassie wears the legendary nightgown, and meets her DREAM GROOM! Watch as BRIDES OF BRADLEY HOUSE *continues in Special Edition this May.*

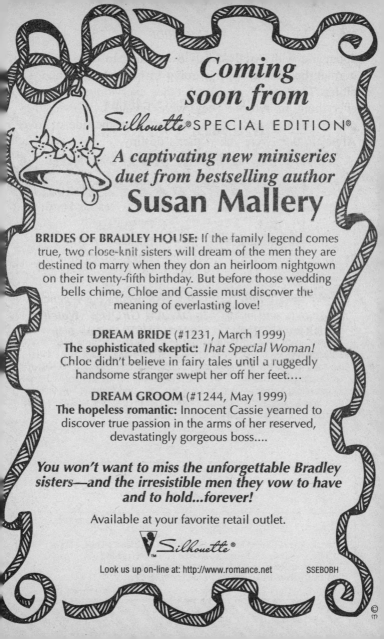

If you enjoyed what you just read,
then we've got an offer you can't resist!

Take 2 bestselling love stories FREE!

Plus get a FREE surprise gift!

Clip this page and mail it to Silhouette Reader Service™

IN U.S.A.	**IN CANADA**
3010 Walden Ave.	P.O. Box 609
P.O. Box 1867	Fort Erie, Ontario
Buffalo, N.Y. 14240-1867	L2A 5X3

YES! Please send me 2 free Silhouette Special Edition® novels and my free surprise gift. Then send me 6 brand-new novels every month, which I will receive months before they're available in stores. In the U.S.A., bill me at the bargain price of $3.57 plus 25¢ delivery per book and applicable sales tax, if any*. In Canada, bill me at the bargain price of $3.96 plus 25¢ delivery per book and applicable taxes**. That's the complete price and a savings of over 10% off the cover prices—what a great deal! I understand that accepting the 2 free books and gift places me under no obligation ever to buy any books. I can always return a shipment and cancel at any time. Even if I never buy another book from Silhouette, the 2 free books and gift are mine to keep forever. So why not take us up on our invitation. You'll be glad you did!

235 SEN CNFD
335 SEN CNFE

Name	(PLEASE PRINT)	
Address		Apt.#
City	State/Prov.	Zip/Postal Code

* Terms and prices subject to change without notice. Sales tax applicable in N.Y.
** Canadian residents will be charged applicable provincial taxes and GST.
  All orders subject to approval. Offer limited to one per household.
  ® are registered trademarks of Harlequin Enterprises Limited.

SPED99   ©1998 Harlequin Enterprises Limited

*This March Silhouette
is proud to present*

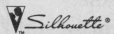 Silhouette®

SENSATIONAL

MAGGIE SHAYNE
BARBARA BOSWELL
SUSAN MALLERY
MARIE FERRARELLA

This is a special collection of four complete
novels for one low price, featuring a novel
from each line: Silhouette Intimate Moments,
Silhouette Desire, Silhouette Special Edition
and Silhouette Romance.

Available at your favorite retail outlet.

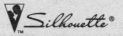 Silhouette®

And Baby Makes Three

FIRST TRIMESTER

by

SHERRYL WOODS

Three ornery Adams men are about to be roped
into fatherhood...and they don't suspect a thing!

And Baby Makes Three

APRIL 1999
The phenomenal series
from Sherryl Woods has readers
clamoring for more! And in this special collection,
we discover the stories that started it all....

Luke, Jordan and Cody are tough ranchers set in
their bachelor ways until three beautiful women
beguile them into forsaking their single lives for
instant families. Will each be a match made in
heaven...or the delivery room?

Available at your favorite retail outlet.

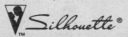

Silhouette®

Silhouette SPECIAL EDITION®

Award-winning and bestselling author
CHRISTINE FLYNN

revisits her popular miniseries

THE WHITAKER BRIDES

It took some taming, but Logan, Cal and Jett Whitaker
found true love...and their way down the aisle. Now
there's a new crop of cowboys whose wild ways are no
match for the power of love. It all starts with...

FINALLY HIS BRIDE (SE #1240, April 1999)
After nearly a decade, Trevor Whitaker still left Erin
breathless. Their bittersweet reunion brought back
memories of unfulfilled passion—and broken promises.
Could these star-crossed lovers set the past to rest?
Would Erin's fantasy of being a Whitaker bride finally
come true?

Don't miss this next installment of
THE WHITAKER BRIDES.

Only from Silhouette Special Edition!

Available at your favorite retail outlet.

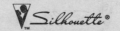

Silhouette® SPECIAL EDITION®

invites you to meet the
Men of the Double-C Ranch
a heartwarming family saga by

Allison Leigh

The Rancher and the Redhead

SF#1212, November 1998

Unmovable as granite, rancher Matthew Clay thought nothing could ruffle him...until temporary housekeeper Jaimie Greene came to the Double-C. This feisty redhead's tempting innocence and sassy rebukes drove him to sweet distraction. Was this stubborn rancher about to face the only challenge mightier than a Wyoming winter—love?

Look for other exciting love stories set
on the Double-C Ranch, coming only to
Silhouette Special Edition in 1999.

Men of the Double-C Ranch: Under the big blue Wyoming sky, five brothers discover true love.

Available at your favorite retail outlet.

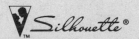

Silhouette®

SPECIAL EDITION®

COMING NEXT MONTH

#1237 A FATHER FOR HER BABY—Celeste Hamilton
That's My Baby!
When Jarrett McMullen saw Ashley Grant again, the sweet beauty he'd once loved and let go was pregnant—and alone. And though the amnesiac mother-to-be couldn't remember her past, Jarrett was determined to claim a place in her future—as the father of her child....

#1238 WRANGLER—Myrna Temte
Hearts of Wyoming
Horse wrangler Lori Jones knew she'd better steer clear of Sunshine Gap's ruggedly appealing deputy sheriff, Zack McBride, who was close to discovering her darkest secret. But then the sexy lawman took her boy under his wing—and made a lasting impression on Lori's wary heart!

#1239 BUCHANAN'S BRIDE—Pamela Toth
Buckles & Broncos
He was lost and alone...but not for long. As luck would have it, feisty cowgirl Leah Randall rescued the stranded stranger, tenderly took him in and gave him all her love. But would their blossoming romance survive the revelation that this dynamic man was a long-lost relation of her sworn enemy?

#1240 FINALLY HIS BRIDE—Christine Flynn
The Whitaker Brides
After nearly a decade, Trevor Whitaker still left Erin Gray breathless. Their bittersweet reunion brought back memories of unfulfilled passion—and broken promises. But her ardor for this devastatingly handsome man was intoxicating. Would Erin's fantasy of being a Whitaker bride finally come true?

#1241 A WEDDING FOR MAGGIE—Allison Leigh
Men of the Double-C Ranch
When Daniel Clay returned to the Double-C ranch, the tormented cowboy knew he was unworthy of his beloved Maggie. But when their night of love left Maggie pregnant, Daniel stubbornly insisted on a convenient union. But then a headstrong Maggie made a marriage demand of her own....

#1242 NOT JUST ANOTHER COWBOY—Carol Finch
Alexa Tipton had her fill of charming rodeo men. So the serious-minded single mom was beside herself when she became irresistibly attracted to the fun-loving Chance Butler. The sexy superstar cowboy began to melt her steely resistance, but could she trust their happiness would last?